3

THE GOOD SON

A Reed & Billie Novel, Book 2

DUSTIN STEVENS

The Good Son
Copyright © 2016, Dustin Stevens
Cover Art and Design:
Anita B. Carroll at Race-Point.com

My guiding principle is this:
Guilt is never to be doubted.
—Franz Kafka

Prologue

Hearing the thick Velcro straps rip free was a welcome sound to Reed's ears as he shrugged out of the Kevlar vest, letting it fall to the ground, the world instantly 10 degrees cooler. The t-shirt he had worn under the vest was soaked, the breeze hitting the damp cotton, helping to lower his body temperature.

"Man, that feels better," Reed said, closing his eyes and lifting his face to the sky. The new angle allowed sweat to stream down his face, a direct result of the situation he was just in, completely independent of the chilly October weather.

Around him, the world was nothing short of chaos, a half dozen responding units from various precincts in the city having arrived in force. Standing with his eyes closed, he could hear people moving about, radios spewing orders and coded cop talk, car doors opening and closing as fellow officers wrapped up the scene.

If he cracked open his eyes for even a second, he knew he would see the world through red-and-blue strobe lights bouncing off everything.

"Striking a pose over here?" a familiar voice asked, bringing a smile to Reed's face.

He turned at the sound, wiping the sweat from his eyes before opening them to find his partner, Riley Poole, walking his way.

Unlike him, she appeared no worse for wear, untouched by the events of the previous hour. Her Kevlar had also been stripped away, leaving her in a pair of jeans and sweater. If not for the gun and badge strapped to her hip, she would have appeared ready to see a movie or grab dinner, the same as she did every time Reed saw her.

How she managed to pull that off was anybody's guess.

"Just thanking the heavens we made it through again," Reed said.

"Yeah, well, luckily the heavens saw fit to send me down here to watch over you," Riley said, sidling up beside him. Folding her arms over her chest, she leaned back against the side of the sedan they shared, raising one foot and bracing it against the rear door.

"Oh, is that how it went?" Reed asked, allowing some mirth to creep into his voice as he assumed a matching stance beside her.

"You remember it happening another way?" Riley asked, keeping her attention aimed at the activity surrounding them. Fifteen minutes before, it had been just the two of them. Now, they were nothing more than an afterthought as they stood and watched the clean-up crews work.

Twice, Reed opened his mouth to respond, glancing over at her profile, the multi-colored lights flashing across her pale skin, before thinking better of it. "Nope. That's how it went."

"Good answer," Riley said, using her foot and hips to leverage herself up off the car. "Don't forget to tell that to your mom when you call to let her know you made it out alright."

Shaking his head from side to side, Reed let her get a few steps away before countering, "My mom doesn't even know we were involved in this mess. Better to keep it that way than have her worrying."

At that Riley stopped and turned, before finally saying, "Fine, call and tell her *I* made it out alright."

Chapter One

The Good Son left his muddied boots on the floor by the back door. He could smell the sour scent of his gym socks as he padded through the house, unavoidable given the oppressive summer humidity hanging like a wet blanket across the Midwest. It had arrived around the first of June and, as yet, showed no signs of letting up, The Good Son growing accustomed to his shirt perpetually clinging to his back.

The decision to leave the boots behind, though, had nothing to do with the summer heat, even less to do with any form of manners. Instead, it was a precautionary measure, meant to ensure that the hardened treads didn't echo through the silent house, giving away his presence before he was able to accomplish what he had come to do.

Time was beginning to run short. He could not afford to lose this opportunity over something so foolish.

Walking heel-to-toe, The Good Son eased his way from the back door through the kitchen. The smell of fried pork chops and collard greens was just beginning to dissipate from dinner a few hours before, the aroma tickling his nostrils, making him very aware of the meal he had skipped.

His heart rate increased as he silently beseeched his stomach not to vocalize any sort of request as he stepped quickly past the aging appliances and polished Formica countertops into the living room.

The floor underfoot shifted from linoleum to threadbare carpet as The Good Son stood in the doorway and surveyed his surroundings. The curtains were drawn tight over the windows, just a hint of orange hue visible behind them from the streetlight out front.

Like the kitchen, the living room was clean, though extremely dated. A well-worn sofa dominated the room, the fabric something akin to velour or velvet. A coffee table piled with tattered magazines, an old box television, and a pair of comfortable rocking chairs gave the space a lived-in look.

As he passed through the room, three framed photographs caught his eye – each of the same man and woman. The first was a wedding picture; the second showed the happy couple, older now but still smiling for the camera; and the third was the elderly pair, still arm-in-arm, but without the same spark of the other two.

Closing his eyes tight, The Good Son looked away from the photos. He balled his hands into fists and squeezed until small explosions of orange and yellow appeared behind his eyelids.

Only then did the tension leave his body, a deep breath passing over his lips.

He could not allow himself to focus on the photographs, to think of what he was doing as anything more than a means to an end. If he did, he ran the risk of losing his nerve, something he could not afford to let happen right now.

The Good Son went to the couch and grabbed the largest throw pillow.

Sweat streamed down his face and along his forearms, worse than any heat or humidity alone could ever bring about.

Feeling the shortness of breath in his chest, The Good Son stepped down the narrow hallway, ignoring even more family pictures hanging on the wall beside him.

It was not the first time The Good Son had been inside the home. He knew exactly where he was headed.

Halfway down the hallway the floor moaned slightly beneath his weight, stopping him where he stood. Gripping the pillow in both hands, The Good Son felt his body tense as he stopped and waited, listening.

The only thing more important than accomplishing his goal was not getting caught. If things went sideways, if nothing turned out as he envisioned here tonight, it would be a setback, but it would not be catastrophic. He could always try again.

If apprehended, though, that was the end of everything.

The thought brought a renewed jolt of purpose to The Good Son as he continued, reaching the end of the hallway. Stopping just short of the open door, he turned and peeked around the corner into a bedroom, moonlight filtering in through the windows illuminating the scene.

A dresser cluttered with random bric-a-brac, an old rocking chair, and a four-poster bed filled the room.

Everything exactly as it had been on his previous trip.

On the center of the bed lay a lone woman, her body motionless, deep in sleep. Positioned on her back, she drew in deep breaths, the sound finding its way to The Good Son's ears, putting his mind at ease a tiny bit.

He had made it this far. Now all he had to do was complete the task.

Again, his heart rate spiked as he took a step forward, glancing down at the pillow between his hands. His fingers squeezed tight, his knuckles flashing white as he inched his way to the side of the bed.

Not once did the woman's breathing shift, her slumber preventing her from even knowing he was there.

Just eight minutes later, he was gone.

Chapter Two

The orange sticker on the side of the wrapper said the burrito was chicken, though Reed Mattox was unable to detect even the smallest hint of it. Instead, all he could see was Mexican rice, a few black beans, and far too much green salsa. The filling was too runny, the tortilla too thin, each bite forcing the innards down his hand and onto the sidewalk.

The smell drew Reed's K-9 partner, Billie, over for a closer inspection, her ears pressed flat against the top of her head. Lowering her nose a few inches, she sniffed once, trying to decipher what it was, before showing her good judgement and turning away.

Her pink tongue shot out over her nose to let Reed know she was hungry, but even she had her standards.

"Yeah, I agree," Reed said, watching as Billie looked up at him, flicking her tongue out a second time at the sound of his voice. Retreating back a few feet, she lowered her backside to the pavement to wait for Reed to finish his lunch.

Shoving the remains of the burrito back into its wrapper, Reed wadded it into a ball and tossed it into a trash can. Reaching through the window of his unmarked sedan, he fished out the can of Mountain Dew he had purchased with it.

"Detective Mattox?" the dispatch radio on the dash bellowed, the sound piercing the quiet calm of the night. The words were punctuated with static as they passed through the open window, grabbing Reed's attention, drawing Billie to her feet beside him. "Reed, you there?"

Leaving the door closed, Reed again reached in and snatched the mic from the radio, pulling the curled cord out through the window.

"Evening, Jackie."

At his previous precinct, the protocol for handling the radio was the very definition of excessive. His captain there was perpetually worried that citizens would be listening to the police scanner and had insisted on numerical codes and professional decorum at all times. Using first names was a capital offense on par with murder or kidnapping, as far as he was concerned.

Since moving down to the 8th Precinct six months before, Reed had discovered that everyone in his new location tended to treat the radio more like a personal cell phone. First names were a common occurrence, especially after hours, and more than once he had heard guys using the band to discuss the latest on the Cincinnati Reds.

Not much of a baseball man, Reed had refrained, though it hadn't really bothered him.

All signs seemed to indicate that his new captain was of the same mind.

"How's it going this evening, Sugar?" Jackie asked, her voice containing just a trace of syrup.

Reed resumed his position against the side of his car, folded his arms across his chest and held the mic up to his mouth.

"Excellent," he said. "My partner and I were just having lunch when you called."

"Something good I hope," Jackie said. "You both look like you could stand to put on a couple pounds."

Reed smiled as he glanced down, his 6'3" frame carrying just over 200 even. Billie's head rose almost to his hip, 65 pounds of sinewy muscle compressed into a powerful package.

He was reasonably certain she was in the minority on thinking either one of them needed to gain weight.

"Fantastic," Reed lied, looking over at the trash can where the remains of the gas station burrito met its end.

After almost half a year, the check-ins were becoming a little less frequent, though still occurred more often than Reed preferred. He realized Jackie liked to fashion herself a mother hen for the precinct, but didn't particularly care for the way she had appointed herself his overseer.

He had a partner tasked with doing that.

"And how are things over at the precinct?" Reed asked, trying to make his voice suggest that he actually cared.

A moment of static passed before Jackie replied, "Well, that's why I'm calling. I just had a request come in for a detective to come and give a second opinion."

Reed's face twisted up at the words. "A request for a second opinion?"

It sounded more like something someone would say in an emergency room or a sports injury clinic, not the sort of thing he had ever heard before in the course of his job.

And after 12 years on the force, he had heard a lot.

"That's what he said," Jackie answered. "I thought it odd too, but said I would pass it on down the line."

Reed paused, trying to wrap his mind around it. In his experience, most everything requiring police intervention was cut-and-dried. Either a crime had been committed, or it hadn't.

Asking for someone else to take a look was a novelty.

"You want it, or should I phone the on-call team?" Jackie asked.

"Who called it in?" Reed asked, bypassing her question.

"Jacobs," Jackie said. "He and McMichaels are on the scene now."

"Tell them we're on our way."

Chapter Three

Using the GPS mounted above the radio, Reed pulled up in front of a single-story home just shy of 3:30 a.m. Given the early hour and the non-existent traffic on the roads, he had chosen to run without the flashers, not wanting to draw any more attention to a law enforcement car in The Bottoms than necessary.

Pulling up to see the flashing blue and red strobes of other vehicles already on the scene, though, he realized it wouldn't have mattered.

Reed felt his stomach tighten, alerting him that things weren't quite as simple as Jackie had made them seem.

Parked in the driveway was an ambulance, lights flashing on all sides. Behind it, a gleaming red fire engine from the local station reflected those lights and its own around the neighborhood.

The only vehicle not contributing to the pulsating light show was a single blue-and-white patrol car parked at the curb. Its two officers were rooted to the front steps, arms crossed, blocking the door to the home. On Reed's arrival, they glanced back and forth between him and the hostile-looking first responders nearby.

"Why do I not like the looks of this?" Reed asked over his shoulder, seeing the silhouette of Billie's ears in the backseat.

Reed cracked all four windows a couple of inches before turning off the ignition. "Stay here."

Working with Billie was still new to Reed, despite entering their sixth month together. It was a pairing that had come about only after both had lost their previous partners – Reed's, a fellow detective; Billie's, a Marine bomb squad handler.

They were starting to grow accustomed to their arrangement, though uncertainty still remained in some situations, such as approaching a new crime scene. While Billie did offer unique skills Reed was growing fonder of by the day, she still presented the concern of contaminating evidence.

A single whine escaped her as Reed looped his badge around his neck and exited, shutting the door behind him.

The half dozen stares aimed his way made him wonder just how effective his *second opinion* was going to be in fixing the trouble brewing here.

"Gentlemen," Reed said, walking across the clipped grass to a well-maintained white home. "We have to stop meeting like this."

Officer Wade McMichaels was the first to move, taking a few steps toward Reed, his hand outstretched. He was tall, lean and clean shaven, a frown hiding an otherwise handsome face.

"Sorry about calling you in," he said, pumping Reed's hand once before releasing it. "Wanted another pair of eyes on this before making any definitive conclusions."

Reed nodded once as if he understood, reaching past McMichaels to shake the hand of his partner, Tommy Jacobs. A stark contrast to McMichaels, he was a few inches shorter and several pounds heavier, a thin goatee outlining his mouth.

Both looked to be the better part of a decade younger than Reed, each in their mid-20s, paired up after completing their training years with a senior officer.

"Not a problem," Reed said, glancing between them before looking over to the clusters of EMT's and firefighters standing nearby. "What the heck is all this?"

"911 call," Jacobs said, leaving it at that.

Reed nodded. Standard procedure was for the closest medical, fire and police departments to send someone for all incoming calls. In most instances, a quick assessment was done, and whoever wasn't necessary was released.

As far as he could tell, though, nobody seemed to have any intention of moving on.

"For?" Reed asked.

"Reported a heart attack in progress and asked for immediate assistance," McMichaels said. "We were just three blocks away, so we were the first ones to arrive."

"Entered to find Esther Rosen in the back bedroom," Jacobs said. "No pulse, no breathing, body already starting to cool."

Again, Reed nodded, processing what he'd been told. He tried to picture the scene in his mind, squaring it with what stood before him.

"Okay," Reed said, "so why are they all still here? And why do they look like you just insulted their mother?"

The two officers exchanged a glance, Jacobs biting his lip as McMichaels took a deep breath.

"Like he said," McMichaels began, "she was already growing cold as we found her. She was gone, there was no bringing her back."

"And you suspected foul play?" Reed asked, filling in where they were headed. It was the only possible explanation for why everybody else was being kept back, why they continued to linger.

Once more, the two partners exchanged a quick look. The expressions on their faces revealed they had heard an earful from the other responders, were beginning to doubt their decisions.

"Sure seems that way," McMichaels said. "We'd just feel better if you took a look before we called CSU and sent everybody on their way."

"Absolutely," Reed said, his voice relaying a bit more confidence than he actually felt.

In front of him Jacobs stepped to the side, revealing the front door open, a chunk of the wooden casing on the ground from their entry some time before. The scent of sawdust still hung in the air, mixed just slightly with the aroma of fried food.

Compared to the burrito he'd just attempted to choke down, it smelled nothing short of divine, even with the sawdust.

Reed took the three short steps, pausing at the top and glancing over at the medics standing by.

"Not to make this any uglier, but can you tell them to kill the lights? Whatever this is, we don't need the media or a bunch of nosy neighbors showing up too."

The request drew a pair of smirks.

"Sure," Jacobs replied. "They already hate us. This will really make them happy."

Chapter Four

Captain Wallace Grimes was already at his desk as Reed walked up, phone pressed against his ear with his right shoulder, his left hand strumming the desk in front of him. One after another his fingers smacked against the dark wood, each louder than the previous.

"Yes, I understand," Grimes said, his voice relaying that he did anything but. "I know, I will speak to them."

Standing just outside the door, Reed waited until the conversation ended. In his right hand was the spiral-bound notebook he used for investigations. His left was wrapped around the short lead clipped to Billie's collar.

"Okay, thank you for calling," Grimes said. "I appreciate it."

The phone slammed back into its cradle without further comment, Reed looking up to see his captain scowling down at it. Beside him he could sense Billie look his way for guidance, neither one moving an inch.

"Mattox, get in here," Grimes said after a long pause.

"Good morning, huh?" Reed asked, stepping inside the office. He circled around one of the matching chairs opposite the captain's desk and lowered himself into it.

"Down," he added, his voice a bit deeper, sending Billie to her stomach beside him.

The captain watched the interaction in silence. Just minutes into the start of a new day and already dark circles underscored his eyes, his jowls beginning to sag on either side of his mouth.

"What the hell did you guys get into last night?"

Reed hadn't expected the angry phone calls to begin so early, though he wasn't entirely surprised. The assembled crews of both the EMT's and fire department had seemed plenty peeved when he arrived, their emotions rising to full-on pissed by the time he had finished his assessment of the scene.

Why the fire department was so bitter, he had not yet figured out, though he suspected that was far from the point.

An opportunity had presented itself for them to complain about the CPD, and in his experience nobody ever really let such an opening pass.

"Firefighters or medics?" Reed asked.

The scowl on Grimes's face grew a bit deeper. "Medics."

"Ah," Reed said, his head rocking back.

"I take it another complaint will be coming soon?"

"Certainly," Reed replied.

The two men had first worked together in the 19th Precinct. At the time Reed was a new recruit and Grimes a sergeant, later ascending to the post of captain. Upon receiving the promotion he had been asked to move over to the 8th, a spot that the brass claimed was a step up.

Setting squarely inside the portion of Columbus known as The Bottoms, every other person on the force knew better, the move steeped more in wanting a person of color overseeing the region than anything else.

Despite the obvious racial overtones at play, somehow they had managed to cajole Grimes into making the switch.

After the death of his partner six months earlier, Reed had shifted to the K-9 division. His first order of business after doing so was to put in a transfer to the 8th, intending to leave behind all reminders of Riley and start fresh.

For the first few months the decision had looked nothing short of foolish, though with time things had begun to improve.

"So, again," Grimes said, "what exactly did we do this time?"

Leaning back in his chair, Reed said, "911 came in this morning at 3 a.m. McMichaels and Jacobs were a couple blocks away on patrol and were the first to respond."

Reed rattled the information off without consulting his notes, having gone over it several times in the preceding hours.

"The caller claimed to be experiencing a heart attack, so they knocked once before breaching, finding Esther Rosen in the back bedroom. By the time they arrived, she was already gone. No vitals whatsoever, body already beginning to cool."

Grimes laced his fingers across his midsection as he listened, drawing his jaw back into his chest. The action seemed to give him a triple chin, folds of skin gathering along his neck.

Just weeks past his 50th birthday, the captain was slowly starting to reveal the telltale combination of his age and profession. His black hair was moving on to silver, and the midsection of his uniform shirt was showing a bit of strain.

"Officers McMichaels and Jacobs secured the scene and asked for a detective consult. Shortly thereafter, EMT and fire responders showed up."

"And all hell broke loose," Grimes finished, his tone matching the expression on his face.

"Pretty much," Reed nodded.

With his fingers still laced, Grimes tapped his thumbs together a couple of times, considering what he'd just been told.

"Why did they ask for a consult? Were there signs of foul play?"

"That's just it," Reed said, leaning forward. "No."

"No?"

"Nothing at all," Reed said. "The call had come in about a heart attack in progress, yet Esther Rosen was tucked tight in her bed."

Grimes eyes widened, though he remained silent.

"Her sheets weren't disturbed," Reed said. "There wasn't even a phone in the room with her."

The scene was so sterile as Reed entered, it had taken him a moment to realize why the officers had wanted someone else to take a look. At a glance, it appeared Esther Rosen was sleeping comfortably, or at the very least had passed away without a word.

The problem was, nobody dying from a cardiac infarction would simply lie there, especially if they had the wherewithal to call for help.

"Staged?" Grimes asked.

"Sure as hell looked like it," Reed said.

"Then why call 911?" Grimes asked.

"I don't know," Reed said, raising his eyebrows just slightly. Dozens of ideas had come and gone throughout the night, running the gamut of possibilities. "Figured I'd see if the crime scene crew could pull anything useful before rushing to any conclusions."

Grimes ran a hand over his face, thinking. Despite the heat, he insisted on wearing his uniform with the long-sleeve shirt every day, a veneer of sweat already becoming visible on his forehead.

"Christ," he muttered.

The assessment was exactly the one Reed had made hours before, though he remained silent.

"And the medics?" Grimes asked.

"Raised all kinds of hell," Reed said. "Claimed that we weren't trained to determine if someone was dead or not, that yet again, we over-stepped our jurisdiction, same old stuff."

"Did we?" Grimes asked, raising his eyebrows just slightly.

Reed thought back to the night before, playing the scene over in his mind. Prior to arriving, he could see how maybe the medics had a right to be angry, though after adding his conclusions to those of the responding officers, they should have backed off.

"No," Reed said. "Our guys were right. It was a hell of a thing to walk into, threw me when I first saw it as well."

Grimes grunted in response, though said nothing.

Both of them knew more than anything it came down to a matter of money, the medics not being able to collect for their services unless they were actually rendered.

Neither felt the need to voice it.

Grimes shifted his attention out the window to see the morning sun already above the horizon, blazing bright orange light over the parking lot. It reflected off the windshields of the cars collected there, promising another hot day ahead.

"Okay," Grimes said. "How do we want to handle this?"

"Meaning, who should I hand this off to, or what are my next steps?" Reed asked.

For their first few months, Reed and Billie's primary job had been more about containment than apprehension. They were on duty from the hours of 10:00 at night to 6:00 each morning, responding to whatever arose.

At sunrise each day, they handed the night's cases off to the daytime detectives to solve.

In the last three months their role had begun to shift. They were still primarily assigned to the nighttime hours, though on occasion, Grimes would hand them a case, providing them with the autonomy they needed to work it to completion.

The process for doing it was still a bit hazy, though the arrangement seemed to be working well for both sides. Grimes was able to provide some much needed relief to his detective teams, and Reed and Billie stayed on the shift they preferred, avoiding the occasional stares and general hubbub of the precinct during daytime hours.

"You think there's something to look into here?" Grimes asked.

Drawing in a deep breath, Reed glanced down at Billie before responding.

"What I saw last night didn't just happen. I could believe Esther Rosen calling 911 about a possible heart attack, and I could believe it happening in her sleep, but I can't believe that the two things happened from what I saw there last night."

Grimes remained silent as he considered things.

"Okay, it's yours. Same rules as usual, keep me apprised of whatever you find."

Chapter Five

The failure of the previous night weighed heavy on The Good Son. It soured his mood and brought a frown to his face that refused to waver, no matter how hard he tried to force a smile.

Everything about the situation had been perfect. Of all the people he'd considered, Esther Rosen appeared to be the ideal target. She was the right age, race and gender. She lived alone. She didn't have a dog, and her home was worn enough that the locks on the back door could be jimmied using an old Blockbuster card.

Opportunities like that didn't come along very often, especially near The Bottoms.

It was that reality that seemed to bother The Good Son more than anything. If he lived in Worthington, or Dublin, or even further south in Grove City, the failure from the night before wouldn't be such a big deal. There would be ample targets for him to choose from, chalking her up as a learning experience.

Tonight he could have another Esther Rosen lined up and ready to go.

A third one tomorrow night if need be.

The situation he was in wouldn't allow it, though. Going into any one of those areas wouldn't do, the drive too far, the variables too great to risk. Instead, he was confined to the greater Bottoms area, encompassing

Franklinton and maybe just a little piece into Hilliard, a total geographic area no more than a few miles square.

Leaning forward, The Good Son rested his arms on the back of his shopping cart. Using it for support, he shuffled through the expansive aisles of the Home Depot, the irony of his location not lost on him.

Dressed in a pair of khaki cargo shorts and a t-shirt, he was just another nameless, faceless 20-something in the suburbs, picking up a few items for some chores around the house. With the exception of the expression on his face, he could pass for nearly every other person roaming about on a weekday morning.

The Good Son gave up trying to smile, finding that it felt mechanical and odd stretched across his face.

Last night his plan had officially been put into action. He still wasn't sure he was ready for such a thing, but the ticking clock had started. From this point on he had to be aware of his actions, making sure to never draw attention to himself. Something as foolish as the way he appeared on the streets during the day could be his undoing later that night.

He couldn't allow that to happen. What he was doing was far too important, the impact too far reaching.

The Good Son reached into his pocket, extracted a scrap of paper and stared down at the list of items he had jotted down two hours before.

The debacle with Esther Rosen was good experience. It had taught him a great many things, none more important than the fact that suffocation would not work.

Now it was time to try something new.

Looking up to the signs posted on the corner of each aisle, The Good Son picked out the one announcing Garden Tools. He headed in that direction, the bitterness in him making way for a renewed sense of purpose.

Tonight.

Tonight would be different.

It had to be.

Chapter Six

The midday sun beat straight down on the top of Reed's car, turning the black sedan into a veritable sauna. With the air conditioner blasting on high, the temperature inside hovered somewhere in the vicinity of tolerable, though never came close to cool.

Billie felt the heat, too, as she sprawled on the backseat, panting. Every time Reed checked his rearview mirror he could see her tongue hanging out further and further, dripping on the plastic seat cover.

Arriving at their destination, Reed pulled the car into the far back corner of the lot and sought out one of the few parking spaces with shade from an ancient oak tree.

After parking, he reached onto the passenger floorboard for a red plastic bowl. Placing it on the ground, he pushed it away a few feet and poured in a bottle of water, saving only the last inch or so for himself.

Billie leaped from the car and headed straight for it, burying her nose and lapping away, splashing more water on the asphalt than she drank.

Once she had her fill, Reed returned the bowl to the car and finished off the bottle, the water seeming to travel straight through his body and out through his pores. He could feel his shirt sticking to him as he fastened the short lead to Billie's collar and closed the doors.

"Yeah, you get to come along this time," Reed said, as together they walked toward the Franklinton office of the Franklin County Coroner, one of the newer buildings in the CPD system. Built as one of three satellite offices meant to reduce the amount of work flowing into the main coroner's office downtown, gradual escalations in violent deaths now had all three running at or above capacity.

In the previous six months Reed had been here no less than a dozen times, the exterior of the building still never ceasing to surprise him. Instead of the brick one might expect, the place was all steel and glass with a fountain out front, looking more like a college library or modern art museum than a coroner's office.

As he passed Reed couldn't help but think of how great it would be for Billie and him to jump in the fountain out front, dismissing the idea quickly before it became too tempting. Instead, he pressed the handicap access button and watched the front doors swing open.

Cool air blasted them as they entered the wide atrium rising to a sunroof overhead. He could see a cafeteria in the distance, the last few stragglers of the day enjoying a late lunch. To the right was a bank of elevators, and dead ahead was the reception desk, a young woman seated behind it.

"Good afternoon, Detective," she said as they approached, lowering an iPad to her desk and flashing him a smile. Several years younger than Reed, she had dark hair and matching thick-framed glasses.

"Hello, Chantel," Reed said, raising his free hand in a small wave. "Dr. Solomon in?"

"She is," Chantel replied, nodding toward the elevators. "You know where she is, right?"

"Yes, ma'am," Reed said, shifting to the side, waving once more in parting. Neither said another word as he and Billie set off, the interaction a carbon copy of one that had played out several times before.

And would continue to do so over the ensuing months, Reed had no doubt.

Half a minute later Reed and Billie were in the basement, leaving all traces of the atrium and its five-star hotel elegance behind. Concrete floors and block walls were adequate here.

The smells of death were present in the air, though Reed was more than happy to put up with it in exchange for the 20 degree drop in temperature.

Billie's perked-up ears and wagging tail seemed to indicate she was of the same mind.

With the short lead gripped in his hand, Reed led Billie halfway down the hall, stopping just outside the only office door with a light on inside. Stenciled across it were the words Dr. Patricia Solomon, Medical Examiner.

Reed rapped softly against the wooden door, but it still managed to rattle loudly, echoing through the empty hallway. Beside him he felt Billie's body tense, the same reaction he had the first time he was in her position.

"Easy," he said, running his hand along the back of her neck, feeling the tension release beneath his fingers.

"Come in!" a voice called from the other side.

Together, Reed and Billie stepped inside to find an office that seemed to be getting smaller each time he visited. Gone was any semblance of free space in the room, the majority of it taken up by white cardboard boxes. On the ends of each was a series of identifying labels completed in blue marker, the stacks standing from floor to ceiling.

Seated at a battered metal desk was the person he had come to see, Patricia Solomon.

"Good afternoon, Doctor," Reed said, shifting the lead to his left hand and extending his right.

"Good afternoon, Detective," Solomon replied, standing and returning the handshake.

For his first two months in the 8th, Reed had worked with a cantankerous old man named Dr. Wilbern, someone as stodgy as anybody Reed had ever encountered. Forcing himself to stop by the coroner's office then was an exercise in self-discipline, trying to refrain from rolling his eyes and throwing a quick sucker punch each time the doctor opened his mouth.

In mid-Spring, Wilbern had retired, though, the county replacing him with Dr. Solomon. In her mid-40s, she was a woman with a few extra pounds and a head of red curls that came up to Reed's chin. When she wasn't wearing her surgical gear to perform an autopsy, she always seemed to have on a cardigan sweater and a pair of glasses hanging from a cord around her neck.

Despite her age, she always reminded Reed of his grandmother, back before she passed.

"Brought your bodyguard with you today, I see," Solomon said, settling back down into her chair and motioning for Reed to do the same.

"Down," Reed commanded, watching as Billie lowered herself flat between them before taking a seat.

"Yeah," he said, looking up to Solomon, "that heat out there just isn't for her. Hope you don't mind."

"Not at all," Solomon replied. "I will have to ask that she not enter the examination room though, for obvious reasons."

"Absolutely," Reed said, already figuring as much. It was the same reasoning he applied when keeping her out of a fresh crime scene, the chance for contamination just too high to risk.

"So..." he said, looking around the office, "I see things have really slowed down here for you this summer."

Solomon laughed in reply. "Something like that. Guess I should thank you for sending another one my way this morning, giving me something to do?"

Reed smiled in response. At this point he knew Solomon well enough to know the question was rhetorical.

If left to his own devices, Reed would prefer that he and Billie, and every other member of law enforcement, were nothing more than decorative. They would take turns driving around, being seen, their presence enough of a deterrent to ensure that the world remained at peace. There would be no need for a coroner beyond confirming the occasional heart attack, certainly no call for a building like the one he was in now.

After a dozen years in the profession, though, he knew that would never come to pass.

"Sorry about that," Reed said. "I know how busy you are already."

"Actually," Solomon said, raising her eyebrows, "this one I didn't mind in the least. Pretty straight forward, one of the easier autopsies I've done in a while."

"Yeah?" Reed asked.

Solomon nodded. "If they all went that fast, I'd be able to get ahead down here for a change."

Reed chose to remain silent, knowing Solomon would get to her findings soon enough.

Wheeling around in her chair, Solomon took up a pair of files sitting on a short stack of boxes beside her. She kept one for herself and handed the other across to Reed.

"Esther Rosen," she said, sliding her glasses onto the tip of her nose and opening the file. "58 years old, Caucasian, appeared to be in good health. No heart problems, liver and kidneys all looked good. Cholesterol was slightly elevated, though nothing to be a cause of concern."

Reed nodded as she went through the preliminary findings, checking over each thing as she highlighted it.

"Cutting straight to the chase," Solomon said, "COD was suffocation, most likely by a pillow or a similar object."

"Reason being?" Reed asked.

Glancing up at him over the rim of her glasses, Solomon said, "Petechial hemorrhaging in the eyes was the first clue to manual asphyxiation. That doesn't happen to heart attack victims."

She paused, letting Reed digest the information. "Furthermore, I removed polyester fibers from her throat. Appeared to be green and from heavy material, probably from a pillow, though I can't be certain. I had them sent over to the crime lab this morning for confirmation."

"Thank you," Reed murmured, his brow furled as he tried to recall his time in the house the night before. He couldn't remember seeing a green pillow in the bedroom, though he would circle back later in the off chance that it could be something useful.

"TOD," Solomon said, returning to the file, "sometime between 3:00 and 4:00 this morning."

Again, Reed nodded, that being consistent with what he knew.

"Any defensive wounds?" Reed asked.

"Nothing like that," Solomon said. "No marks on her hands, no skin or anything under her nails."

Something about the way she answered the question caught Reed's attention.

"Let me ask you though," she said, "were you the first on the scene?"

"No," Reed replied. "Two uniforms responded to a 911 call, found her body in bed, asked me to come take a look."

Solomon's left eyebrow arched as she stared back at him. "They didn't try to revive her?"

Reed paused, replaying the night before in his mind. "No. In fact, they were so certain she was gone when they arrived, they wouldn't even allow the EMT's in for fear of ruining the crime scene. Why do you ask?"

Solomon maintained her position, giving Reed a long look. "Because somebody sure tried to. That poor woman's sternum was cracked in two different places."

Chapter Seven

Parked at the curb in front of Esther Rosen's house, Reed repeated the drill with the water bowl for Billie. More than once during his years working with Riley she had chided him about his failure to consume enough water while working, often going entire shifts without eating or drinking a thing. It wasn't uncommon for him to return home at the end of a long day to find his body sluggish, his reflexes dulled from dehydration.

Reed knew it showed her concern, though he never much enjoyed sitting through the lectures. The part he couldn't quite get her to understand was that his actions weren't born from some misguided sense of machismo, but rather a tendency to focus all his energies on the case at hand.

Partnering with Billie, though, had brought a renewed sense of responsibility to Reed. For the first time ever, he was acutely aware of the heat and humidity, whether outside, in the car, or in the farmhouse they shared. A small cooler stayed nestled on the floorboard of the car, filled with bottles of water for their shift.

What he now understood, what Riley probably did as well but was just too nice to vocalize, was that hydration wasn't only for his own good.

It also ensured he could perform at full capacity in the event his partner needed him.

Once already, Billie had protected Reed in the face of an armed attacker. If forcing himself to slow down and make sure she always had plenty to eat and drink guaranteed she was there when he needed her in the future, he was more than happy to do so.

After the water was all gone, Reed clipped the long lead to her collar and walked her across the front yard. He tied it off around a Poplar tree, leaving her in the shade instead of the oven of the backseat.

"Three minutes," Reed said as he crossed the front lawn and hopped up the front steps with his badge swinging free against his chest, should any neighbors be watching. He ducked under the crime scene tape and pushed open the front door, the dead bolt still lying on the floor from the breach the night before.

Ten hours earlier, most of Reed's attention had been focused on the bedroom, studying Rosen's body and its immediate vicinity for any clues. Now, standing just inside the door with ample sunlight passing through the front windows, he examined the house again.

Just like the bedroom, the living room had a feel that told Reed the occupant was from a different generation. Everything in the room was clean and neat, but they were old and starting to show signs of wear. The sofa was an exact copy of the one his great aunt had when he was a child, and the television had a tube that stuck out two feet or more from the back.

Clean, functional, but extremely dated.

Reaching into his back pocket, Reed drew out a pair of latex gloves. He snapped them into place as sweat began to roll down his face, the heat indoors even more oppressive than outside.

Armed with what Solomon had told him at the morgue, Reed did a quick scan of the living room, his gaze catching on a pair of green throw pillows on the couch. Crossing over the worn carpet, he kneeled and inspected each one carefully, looking for any obvious marking or residue that would indicate it was used to suffocate Esther Rosen.

As he suspected, there was nothing visible.

Studying the pillows, an idea came to Reed, something he wouldn't have even considered six months before. He could hold each of them under Billie's nose, letting her 225,000,000 scent receptors go to work, creating an olfactory blueprint far more advanced than even the human eye. From there he would tell her to search, allowing her to ferret out whoever had entered and where they had gone.

No doubt, the trail would eventually lead to a dead end as the intruder climbed into a car and drove away, but it would go a long way in revealing how he gained access and perhaps even reveal some over-looked clue along the way.

The problem was, he didn't know which pillow was used, or if it was either one of them. He still had a few rooms to search, and there was always the possibility that the killer had taken the murder weapon with them.

Complicating matters was the fact that the pillows and the home smelled like Esther Rosen and a 1,000 other scents after years of use. Foods, lotions, candles, all sorts of things that could make picking out the single smell virtually impossible.

His new partner was good, but she was not a miracle worker.

Reed stepped away from the couch, careful to touch nothing. He backed out through the living room and onto the porch, Billie standing at the sight of him. Snapping off the gloves, he shoved them back into his pocket and extracted his cell phone from his hip.

With his right hand he dialed, while with his left he wiped away sweat.

The line rang three times before it was picked up, a gruff voice saying simply, "Yeah?"

"Earl, Reed Mattox. Can you send someone back over to the Rosen house for evidence retrieval? I think I might have found the murder weapon."

Chapter Eight

"Hellacious work on the pillows," Earl Batista said, blowing out a mouthful of cigarette smoke. It shot away from his head in a thick white plume, before slowly dispersing upward.

How anybody could stand to have fire so close to his face, especially during this weather, Reed couldn't imagine, but he knew there was no need broaching the subject.

Besides, he didn't like being lectured either.

By any definition of the word, Earl was a large man, standing several inches above 6' in height and weighing the better part of 300 pounds. A grizzled beard covered the lower half of his face and his balding head showed the first signs of gray just sneaking in.

To Reed, everything about him was a throwback in the truest sense, from the bib overalls he wore regardless of weather to the unfiltered Camels he was perpetually sucking on.

The only thing about him that didn't seem to fit was the fact that he also happened to be the best criminalist in the state.

"That one was the ME," Reed said.

Both men sat on top of a picnic table behind the building where the crime scene unit worked, the shared among several precincts on the west side, while Billie explored the nearby field.

"She was able to tweeze some green fibers out of the victim's throat," Reed said, "so I went back and took a look. Throw pillows were the only things even close to what she suspected."

Taking one last drag off the cigarette, Earl raised his foot and snubbed it out against the sole of his shoe. He set the mashed butt on the bench by his heel and took another from his pack.

"Still," Earl said, shaking his head as he fitted the cigarette to his lips and lit it, "was a good catch on both your parts. Damn guys should have thought to pull them last night."

"So it's a hit?" Reed asked.

"Doesn't get any clearer," Batista said, nodding. "First pillow we looked at matched the fibers perfectly, even had some saliva on it from the victim."

Reed thought of the old woman simply drooling after falling asleep while watching TV, before pushing that aside. It wouldn't account for the fibers actually getting into her airway.

The initial reactions of McMichaels and Jacobs were correct. Esther Rosen had been murdered, and now he had the murder weapon.

"Pull anything else from it?" Reed asked, hoping there might be something to potentially finger a killer.

"Not yet," Earl said, "but we'll keep looking at both of them. Our first task was to match it to the fibers found in her throat. Catching the saliva was pure happenstance."

"How about anything else from the scene?" Reed asked.

"Naw," Earl said, giving his head a quick shake to either side. "Whoever did this was pretty careful, had at least some idea what they were doing. Back door had a rudimentary lock on it, looks like he popped it using a card. No prints of any kind.

"Some mud on the floor inside the back door, but nothing that tells us anything. We were able to black light some footprints on the linoleum in the kitchen, but the textured surface and the fact that he was wearing socks kept us from getting too much."

Reed nodded, processing the information.

"I will tell you this much though," Earl said, "can all but guarantee it was a man who did it."

Already, Reed had been thinking that. "Why's that?" he asked, curious to hear what made Earl so certain.

"The prints," the big man replied. "We were able to get a couple of good outlines, determined that the intruder would wear a size 13 men's shoe. That's a big one, even for a man."

Earl stopped there, but Reed knew where he was going with it. A foot that large would take a 17 in women's shoes, which wasn't impossible, but not very likely either.

For the second time Earl finished a cigarette and crushed it out, picking up both butts. "Sorry we don't have more for you, but there just wasn't a lot to be found. No blood, no semen, no urine. Not enough sweat to get a clean read on."

Sensing that the conversation was over, Reed stood, sweat stains now lining the front and back of his t-shirt. He rose to full height on the seat of the table before stepping down to the ground, Billie raising her head and starting toward him as he did.

"Don't be," Reed said, "I just appreciate you taking a look for me. I hoped we'd get more from the pillows, but that was a long shot. At least we tried."

"Yes, we did," Earl agreed, both men watching Billie as she broke into trot, heading their direction.

Chapter Nine

Of the list of targets The Good Son had available, only one had both an enclosed garage and a dog.

The house was a small red brick bungalow with a matching free standing garage. A short breezeway connected the two, a rusted metal awning covering the walkway.

The dog was a shaggy, black-haired mutt with a matching bark that made The Good Son's skin crawl. Each time it yelped, he was reminded of the task he would most likely later have to perform, no matter how much he dreaded the notion.

At the same time, it was that barking that made this such a particularly attractive target to begin with.

Every 90 minutes or so, the barking would commence, followed by the rear door opening and the dog bolting into the back yard. Soon after, the owner would step out onto the concrete patio to wait for the dog to finish.

The first couple nights The Good Son cased the house, he witnessed the action play out from the safety of the alleyway. Pressed tight against a telephone pole, he had folded himself into a tight ball and sat on the hard dirt, sweat trickling down his face. There he sat, from just after dark until well past midnight, watching everything long after the last light in the house had gone out.

Tonight was the first time he had ventured any closer, waiting an extra 30 minutes to ensure full darkness before approaching. Skirting the edge of the property, he put the driveway between him and the back door, using the garage as a shield. Sweat dripped from the end of his nose as he padded silently over the concrete, his every sense tingling.

In the preceding weeks, The Good Son had read stories about people in similar situations, finding the adrenaline rush intoxicating, the one thing that kept drawing them back long after common sense told them to stop.

To him the notion seemed crazy. There was no elation in the job at hand, no joy in the anticipation. Every fiber in him hated what he was doing, what he had done the night before, having turned to it only as a necessary means to an end.

It was that inevitability that drove him as he made his way to the corner of the garage and pressed his back against it. It surged through him as he crept past the closed garage doors and inched through the breezeway, his weight raised up onto the balls of his feet.

He kept the same pace until just past the back door and pressed himself tight against the rear of the house. Completely still, he stood and waited for his heartbeat to slow down, his breathing to even out.

Only then did he spread his feet and lean against the building, content to wait as long as necessary.

It took less than 20 minutes.

The Good Son was still standing alert as the first high pitched wail of the dog found his ears, echoing out through the back of the house. The singular sound pushed a bolt of anticipation through him as he reached into the pocket of his shorts for the 3" piece of copper pipe found there.

The metal felt warm through the latex glove as he extracted it, only the tips extended from either side of his hand.

He would only have one shot. He had to make it count.

Two more barks rang out as The Good Son shifted his feet just a couple of inches. His breathing grew shallow as the telltale sounds of movement came from the house, clear indicators of someone moving closer.

The Good Son rolled his weight forward, waiting as the deadbolt was released and the door swung open. A wheeze could be heard as it pulled free from the weather stripping surrounding it and a tiny black dog launched itself into the back yard. It managed to clear the steps in just one bound, three more pushing it across the patio and out into the grass.

For one brief instant a quiver of doubt passed through The Good Son as he watched and waited, a sliver of bright light extending out across the ground. A moment passed, the dog the only sign of life, before the sound of slippers scraping against tile could be heard.

Just as fast, the hesitation melted away from The Good Son. He felt his pulse hammering through his temples as he drew his left fist up to his ear.

Last night he had failed.

It could not happen again.

Chapter Ten

Upon arrival, the exterior of the 8th Precinct looked exactly as it always did, a pair of floodlights illuminating the front of the structure.

The precinct was an old brick building rising three stories in height. With a roundabout out front, an American flag flying in the center of it, and three even rows of windows on every side, the place resembled an old schoolhouse far more than a police station.

None of those details jumped out as Reed parked in the second row of the staff lot, one of just a handful of cars around at such an hour. Instead, it was the single light burning on the first floor corner, the location of the same office he had been inside just 15 hours before.

"That's not good," Reed said, pulling his keys from the ignition, leaning in and peering over the steering wheel.

It was a well-known fact that the only people who kept normal business hours in the police department were the operational staff and the brass. Most everyone else was either a beat patrolman, meaning they spent as little time as possible inside the building, or they were like Reed, who came and went at odd times. Day in and day out, with the exception of Jackie and a few others, it was mainly Grimes and some ranking officers who could always be found between 8:00 a.m. and 5:00 p.m.

Now well past that, Reed felt a ball coil in the pit of his stomach.

Grimes was good about being around as much as his employees needed him, but even at that, Reed could count on one hand the number of times he had missed dinner.

Maybe even one finger.

"You don't suppose this has anything to do with last night, do you?" Reed asked, glancing into the rearview mirror. In response, Billie's ears went flat to her head as she watched silently.

Reed took up the keys and the case file from the passenger seat before climbing out and letting Billie free. He didn't bother affixing her to a lead as they walked to the front door, the night air only nominally cooler than the oven they had suffered through all day.

Somewhere in the distance he could hear a car alarm going off and a pair of dogs barking in response, though for the most part, the world was quiet, borderline calm.

The notion only seemed to heighten his anxiety.

The first floor of the precinct was open, large spaces with desks butted back-to-back for partners to share, no cubicles or individual offices. Metal filing cabinets were lined up against one wall, stacks of papers piled around empty chairs, employees having already gone home for the night.

A wide staircase rose in front of Reed and Billie, the wooden steps rubbed free of stain and varnish by years of foot traffic. His desk was on the second floor, along with all the other detectives in the precinct. It was there that Jackie manned the dispatch center and oversaw the occasional guests of the holding cells, with the back half of the floor housing the evidence room.

The stairs almost called to Reed as he considered them, Billie poised by his side awaiting instructions, before opting against it.

If some pissed off EMT's or firefighters were the reason Grimes was still here, it was only a matter of time before Reed was found anyway. Better to meet it head-on, with the station empty, than wait and bear the brunt of it in the morning with curious onlookers nearby.

Tapping the file against his leg, Reed led Billie through a set of double doors with frosted glass. Separated from the front of the building, the area had individual offices reserved for the captain and other senior level staff.

Billie's toenails clicked on the floor as they passed through, a puff of cool air hitting them in the face, bringing with it the stale smells of body odor and Chinese food. Yellow light poured into the hallway from Grimes's office, along with it a steady torrent of obscenities.

Reed took a half step into the open doorway, making sure he was seen without actually entering, and tapped a knuckle against the door frame.

The sound jerked Grimes's attention up from the desk, his body hunched forward. A scowl creased his features as usual, an array of papers spread before him.

"This a bad time?" Reed asked, venturing no closer.

Sensing his hesitation, Billie stayed at his side, her ribs pressed against his calf.

"Yes, but come in anyway," Grimes said. He leaned back in his chair and tossed a pencil down on the desk, rubbing both hands over his face. His tie was gone and his shirt open at the throat, the sleeves rolled almost to the elbows, easily the most dressed down Reed had ever seen him at work.

On the desk at his side was an open container of Chinese food, a pair of chopsticks rising at an odd angle from it.

"I can see you're busy, so I won't stay long," Reed opened, settling into a seat. Beside him Billie lowered herself to the floor, her head raised.

"No, actually I'm glad you popped in," Grimes said. "You can maybe clear up some of this mess for me."

Without any further detail, Reed knew what he was alluding to. "EMT's still on your ass?"

Somehow the scowl on Grimes's face grew even deeper. "And then some. They're claiming now that I owe them for their services last night, that if we don't pay, they'll sue, go to the papers with it."

Reed made no effort to hide his eye-roll. "Next time they call, tell them it's been confirmed as a murder. Our guys were right. If they had let the damn EMT's in, there's a good chance they could have contaminated the murder weapon beyond use."

Some of Grimes's anger seemed to bleed away as he stared at Reed. "Any of that true?"

"Most of it," Reed said, adding a small nod. "It was definitely a murder, and the killer used a pillow from inside the house. We found it on the couch, but they don't need to know that."

Despite the concession of the final sentence, Reed could tell it was the first good news Grimes had heard in quite a while. His mouth flickered slightly, the closest he would possibly get to a smile.

"Good," Grimes said. "Those bastards call back again I'll tell them if they don't shut the hell up, *I'll* go to the papers and crucify them for being more worried about a few dollars than the apprehension of a murderer."

Unlike his boss, Reed allowed himself a smile. "That ought to do it."

"Damn right," Grimes agreed. At that, he assumed his usual stance, drawing his hands together and lacing his fingers over his stomach. "What else have you got on it so far?"

"Right now? Whole lot of questions and not a lot of answers."

Grimes arched an eyebrow, but remained silent.

"Two big ones," Reed said, jumping right to the meat of the matter. "First, somebody called 911, and it sure as hell wasn't Esther Rosen."

"You're sure?"

"Positive," Reed confirmed. "I got a recording of the call earlier today. Male voice."

Grimes's eyes widened just slightly. "Son? Neighbor?"

"I don't know," Reed said. "That's actually why we're here now, to do some more digging and see what we can find. Intended to earlier this afternoon, but got sidetracked on the pillow, ended up making a trip over to CSU instead."

Another nod was Grimes's only response to the information. "And how is Earl?"

"Still puffing like a chimney," Reed replied.

"Yeah, he does that," Grimes agreed. "And the second thing?"

"Rosen's sternum was broken," Reed said. He laid the information out there free from inflection of any kind, knowing that Grimes would come to the same conclusions he had.

He had been prepared to wait as long as it took for the significance of the finding to be worked out by the captain, but it took less than a minute.

"So either someone found her, tried to resuscitate her, couldn't, and called 911," Grimes said.

"In which case they did so without leaving a shred of DNA," Reed added. "And it does beg the question of why he ran."

"Or this guy killed her, then tried to bring her back."

Reed only nodded, not bothering to state that he had been thinking the same thing since leaving Solomon's office earlier in the day.

Together, they sat in silence, mulling things over. Thus far, they had been successful in stymieing the petty infighting between first responders, but that still didn't get them any closer to whoever committed the murder in the first place.

Reed was just a moment away from excusing himself and heading upstairs to continue digging when the phone rang on Grimes's desk. In the quiet of the precinct the sound was exaggeratedly loud, Billie's ears springing straight up on her head.

In a flash, the scowl was back on Grimes's face as he lifted the receiver, appearing as if he might slam it back into place before fitting it to his ear. "Yeah?"

His face softened a bit as he glanced up at Reed. "Actually, he and his partner are sitting right here."

The comment pulled Reed up in his seat.

"Yeah, I'll send them over."

Without signing off, Grimes hung up the phone and again passed a hand over his face.

"That was Jackie from upstairs. Apparently, she's been trying to call you."

Chapter Eleven

The scene was a mirror image of the previous night. The house was more than a dozen blocks from the previous one, made from brick instead of siding, had a free standing garage instead of attached, but to Reed it might as well have been the same house.

A fire truck sat silent at the curb, four men in front of it. All had already stripped out of their yellow protective gear and stood in shorts and shirt sleeves, their arms folded over their chests, staring at the house.

Parked facing them was the emergency medical unit, a man and woman in uniform beside it. They leaned against the front hood, the man conveying hostility through body language. He seemed to be talking at a blistering pace, completely unaware that the woman beside him had already stopped listening, sick of the whole affair.

Parking on the opposite side of the street, Reed didn't think twice about reaching across and taking up the short lead from the passenger seat. The female medic might have given up, but it was clear at a glance that nobody else had. Seeing him approach, his badge swinging from his neck, would no doubt draw some stares and more than a couple comments.

It was moments like this that Reed especially appreciated Billie, knowing they would be far less likely to lob snide remarks with her by his side.

She wasn't as large as some of the German Shepherds on the force, though she was still quite an imposing animal, her body stretched nearly the width of the back seat. With a coat of midnight black, the only contrast was the vicious, white teeth she displayed when she needed to.

Reed had never heard of a Belgian Malinois before partnering with Billie, but it was now his favorite breed – smart, loyal and strong.

As far as he was concerned, there wasn't even a contender for second place on the list.

Attaching the short lead, Reed led Billie directly across the front yard, aware of the nearby stares without reacting in any way. Noting his tension, Billie kept her body rigid beside him, both almost daring somebody to say something.

Nobody did.

Passing through the breezeway connecting the house and the garage, Reed circled around to find McMichaels and Jacobs waiting. Both glanced up as he appeared, their bodies tensing before recognition set in, and they each visibly slackened.

"Fellas, I wasn't kidding," Reed said, keeping his voice low so as to not be overheard, "we *really* need to stop meeting like this."

Standing closest to him, Jacobs smiled. Behind him, McMichaels gave no outward sign of even hearing the comment as he said, "Yeah, sorry about calling you in again. Dispatch said you were pulled off the night shift just this morning."

"We were," Reed said, glancing down to his partner, "but I assume you asked for us by name because it was connected?"

"Maybe not," Jacobs conceded, "but close enough we thought we'd give you first crack at it. You can turf it in the morning if need be."

The officers had been correct in their initial assessment the night before, so for the time being he would give them the benefit of the doubt.

"Alright," Reed said, "walk me through it."

"Victim's name is Ira Soto," McMichaels said, consulting a small wire-bound notebook. "From what we can tell, she lives alone, and somehow managed to call 911 while committing suicide in her garage."

Reed knew from just the single statement why they had called and asked for him by name. The location was different, the MO was different, but the similarity with the calls was just too great to ignore.

Somebody wanted these women found, and fast. Why, Reed didn't know, the possible reasons still too numerous to peg. For the time being he would refrain from speculation, careful not to jump to any false conclusions.

"Alright, let's take a look," Reed said, shifting his attention to Billie. "Stay."

On cue, Billie lowered her backside to the ground. She kept her head raised, her body stiff like an onyx Sphinx.

Jacobs and McMichaels both stared at Reed's partner as she took their place guarding the crime scene.

The garage was designed to hold two cars, though only one spot was filled, a '80s model Buick that looked much newer than its age would suggest, obviously well-maintained and much-loved. The rest of the garage was filled with assorted odds and ends - gardening tools, an artificial Christmas tree, a Shop-Vac and boxes that probably hadn't been opened in years, if not decades.

Reed made a quick circle around the Buick. The windows were clean and non-tinted, making it easy to see Ira Soto seated on the front seat, her head hanging to the side, her unusually red tongue extending out of her mouth.

Two of the windows were closed tight, strips of duct tape sealing the edges. The driver's window was shattered, the tape hanging loose, from the officers breeching some time before.

The rear driver's side window was cracked less than an inch, just enough space for a length of green garden hose to pass through. Like the others, silver duct tape had been used to the seal the gap.

The opposite end of the hose snaked around the edge of the car, Reed following it to the exhaust pipe jutting from the undercarriage. A coil of duct tape had been wrapped around the end of the pipe to secure the hose, making sure all fumes were funneled straight into the car.

"Damn," Reed muttered. He stood back and assessed the scene

before him, crossing his arms over his chest. Inside the garage the heat was well above 90 degrees, his skin again damp with sweat.

"Who called it in?" he asked.

"Don't know," McMichaels said. "Another anonymous 911 caller."

"Male or female?" Reed asked.

"Not sure," Jacobs replied. "Dispatch just said we had an attempted suicide."

Reed nodded, not expecting them to have an answer, content that he could get a copy of the recording easily enough the next day.

"How long had she been here when you arrived?" Reed asked.

"Don't know that either," McMichaels said, "but she was long gone, even more so than last night."

"How much hell you catch from everybody standing outside?" Reed asked.

"Not as bad," McMichaels replied. "The one EMT was a dick, but everybody else was okay."

"I think the firefighters are just pissed their game of basketball got interrupted," Jacobs said. "Damn waste of taxpayer money that they get sent out every time somebody calls 911."

The comments drew a nod of agreement from Reed as he removed a pair of gloves from the back pocket of his jeans and opened the driver's side door. Lingering exhaust fumes greeted him, mixed with the growing smell of Ira Soto's body.

"Should have smelled it when we first cracked the thing open," Jacobs added. "I damn near vomited."

Seeing Ira Soto up close for the first time, she looked to be in her mid-to-late 40s and in reasonably good shape, much like Esther Rosen, though the similarities ended there. Her skin was the color of dark chocolate, and her feet barely reached the pedals of the car. Her hair was silver, framing her face in tight curls.

"Did you guys move her?" Reed asked.

"Just to check the vitals," McMichaels said.

Reed only response was a grunt as he knelt and stared at the body, wondering if an attempt had been made to resuscitate her as well. If the carbon monoxide had been what killed her, or if the scene was merely staged to look like a suicide.

Until Earl and his team arrived, there were only more questions adding to the growing pile, with no clear answers anywhere on the horizon.

"Hey, Reed," Jacobs said, pulling Reed from his thoughts.

"Yeah?"

"You might want to step outside here. Your, um, partner seems to be onto something."

Chapter Twelve

Reed knew the pose, having seen it dozens of times over the preceding months. Billie had alerted on something and stood tense, waiting for his command.

Remembering his own training, Reed stepped out wide and approached her from the side, making sure he was visible in her periphery. He came to her in a steady pace, bending to take up the lead from the ground.

"What happened?" Jacobs asked, uncertainty in his tone.

"She's picked up something," Reed said. "Must have been a breeze that carried a scent to her."

Neither man commented further as he got himself into position, Billie shifting slightly on her haunches, making it clear she would explode forward at the sound of his command.

"Search."

The word was barely out before Billie bolted forward, going from stationary to a full sprint in a second. The movement was so fast Reed let go of the lead, saving her neck and his shoulder both injury. He could hear McMichaels and Jacobs both gasp as he ran after her, cutting a path for the opposite corner of the yard.

The sudden burst of energy ended abruptly, no more than 25 yards from its starting point. There Billie stood in front of a short bush, her head extended, her body a flat line from the tip of her nose to her tail. She held the pose, waiting, as Reed raced forward, coming up behind her and placing a hand along her neck.

"Good," he said. "Down."

Her attention still aimed on the bush, Billie went to her haunches. There she remained as Reed removed a penlight from his belt and held it up, peeling back just enough branches to get a good look at what Billie had found.

"You good?" Jacobs called, the sound of his voice indicating neither man had come any closer.

Reed rose to full height and turned to look at them. "Apparently, Ira Soto had a dog. Looks like a dachshund mix of some sort."

Reed waited as the men approached, holding the light over the deceased animal, a few flies just beginning to buzz around its head.

"Probably a barker," Reed said, allowing each man to take a look. "Killer got rid of it before it drew too much attention."

Once each of the officers had their fill, Reed leaned in close, taking another look.

The animal was small, shaped like an oversized eggplant. It weighed no more than 10 or 12 pounds, cleared the ground by a few inches. The top part of its head looked to have been caved in with some sort of blunt object. Just a few spots of blood dotted the gravel beneath it, indicating it had probably been killed in the yard and hidden beneath the bush.

"Mark it for the crime scene guys," Reed said, allowing the branch to swing back into place.

Billie remained in position as he swung his light past the bush and inched his way forward, sweeping it along the outside of the property. His lower back ached and sweat dripped from the tip of his nose as he made the corner and started to work his way along the edge near the alley.

Halfway across the back of the property he found what he was looking for, a chunk of limestone roughly the size of a soda can. Lying along the edge of the alley, it melded seamlessly with the chunks of misshapen asphalt piled beside it, the thick smear of blood along its edge the only thing giving it away.

With his gloved hand, Reed lifted it from the ground, using only his thumb and forefinger, careful to avoid the dried blood on it.

"Can one of you bring me an evidence bag?" Reed said, raising his voice to be heard.

Behind him he could hear movement before Jacobs appeared in his periphery, peeling away an evidence bag from a thin roll in his hand. "You don't think that thing will really hold a fingerprint, do you?"

"No," Reed said, "but it will definitely hold a scent." He dropped his voice and snapped, "Come."

Forgetting her recent discovery, Billie bolted past Jacobs to Reed. Holding the rock out for her, Reed allowed her to work her way around his fingers, drawing in deep hits of the scent without actually touching it.

After several seconds she pulled back, letting him know she was prepared.

Reed dropped the rock into the evidence bag in Jacob's hand before taking up the lead from the ground again.

"Search."

Much slower than the previous time, Billie began to move across the grass of the backyard, swinging her nose in wide passes. Using a sweeping motion, she worked her way forward until finding what she was looking for, her entire demeanor shifting as she zeroed in on the scent.

A charge passed through her as she set off in a direct path, propelling Reed across the back of the property and out through the alley.

Raising his pace to a jog, Reed did his best to allow her a few inches of slack as she worked her way through the alley. At the end of it she hooked a hard left, following the sidewalk for more than two blocks.

There the trail went cold, Billie turning in several quick circles, trying to pick it up again, before dropping down to her backside and staring up at Reed, letting him know that the scent was gone.

"Good girl," Reed said, clicking on the penlight and passing it over the ground. Three feet from the curb was a small puddle of condensation on the pavement, the spot still damp despite the evening heat.

"This is where he parked," Reed muttered, turning and shining his light back the way they had come. "He pulled off here, covered the last few blocks on foot, walked right back out and drove away."

Chapter Thirteen

The Good Son felt the sack of feed slip from his shoulder, falling almost six feet to the concrete floor, two sounds emitting in unison as it hit.

A loud concussive blast from the heavy weight hitting the ground, and the skittering of dog food pellets across the polished floor.

Raising his face to the ceiling, The Good Son clenched his jaw to keep from cursing out loud. Despite feeling the stares of nearby customers, he held the pose, feeling the burning sting of sweat as it dripped down his forehead and into his eyes.

He didn't need this right now. Time was running short, and two failed attempts in a row had him on edge.

If not for the fact that his paycheck was depended on, he would walk out and never return. He would focus his attention where it was best served, making certain that the next encounter did not end in disaster.

It couldn't. There was no telling how many more chances he might have.

"Jesus, what did you do this time?"

The voice was nasal, pinched and raspy, raising The Good Son's hostility even higher. He scrunched his cheeks tight and curled his hands up into fists, despite his left hand hurting like hell. He waited until pops of light appeared behind his eyelids and his fingernails dug into his palms before releasing the tension and turning to the source of the statement.

"I asked you a question," the voice said.

Opening his eyes, The Good Son saw his supervisor standing at the end of the aisle. In true form he had stopped more than 10 feet away, far enough back that he had to raise his voice, making sure that everyone within earshot heard, making even more certain that he wouldn't have to lift a finger to help clean things up.

"Sorry, Mr. Beauregard," The Good Son murmured. "It slid off my shoulder."

Pressing his fists into his hips, Beauregard leaned in a few inches. The overhead lights shined off of the thin black hair plastered flat to his skull, and his stomach protruded well beyond his belt buckle.

"It slid?" he said, no small amount of disbelief in his voice. "Just like that?"

The Good Son allowed his abhorrence for the man to cross his face, leaving it there long enough for his point to be made. "Yes. It is hot back here, my arms were sweaty. I'll get it cleaned up right now."

Customers nearby saw the interaction, heard the flint in his voice, all pretending to browse the shelves. Every few seconds he could sense them glancing over, curious to see how Beauregard would handle the situation.

For his part, The Good Son kept his gaze leveled on the man, almost daring him to do something.

Finally, Beauregard nodded, the heavy rolls along the underside of his neck bunched together, the skin slick with sweat. "Yeah, you do that. And that bag is coming out of your paycheck, too."

There was no outward reaction from The Good Son as Beauregard disappeared back down the aisle. He remained rooted in place, staring at the spot his pudgy boss had just stood in for more than a minute before moving again.

Hate was not an emotion The Good Son was used to. His situation simply wouldn't allow it. For years he had disciplined himself to push it all aside, to turn the other cheek, to do whatever was necessary to ensure he remained a good person. Doing so was the only way he would ever make it, his only chance given the situation he was in.

Recent events, though, were making it difficult. The clock was continuing to tick, time dwindling away. Adding to it were the multiple missteps he had committed, things that were not only unthinkable but had failed to achieve their goals.

He was an idiot. He didn't deserve to be trusted with such an important task. If there was anybody else, anybody at all, who could handle things, the responsibility would have already been passed to them.

Instead, there was only him, and he wasn't getting it done.

The only thing he had managed to do successfully thus far was silence a dog.

The thoughts swirled in his head like a twisted kaleidoscope as The Good Son lifted the tail of his shirt and wiped the sweat from his face before looking down at the kibble spread on the floor around him.

He was making a mess of everything in his life right now.

It had to stop.

Chapter Fourteen

Five hours after bedding down, Reed was back up again. After spending the previous half year on night shift, sleeping during the day was not a problem. The norm was to punch out around 6:00 in the morning, swing by the precinct to drop off reports and answer a few questions, before heading home.

By 7:00, he was heading opposite the incoming traffic into the city.

A half-hour later he fed Billie and let her out a final time before both crashed for a good day's sleep.

Most days they slept until sometime in the early afternoon. Rarely did Reed have an appointment that needed tending to during business hours, his only alarm clock, Billie, alerting him she was either hungry or needed to go out, sometimes both.

It was a schedule that fit them both. Reed was a creature of habit, having retreated to nocturnal hours after the passing of Riley. At the time it had been a sort of self-imposed isolation, but once his guilt slowly ebbed away, he found himself liking the change.

Compared to the nonstop bustle of daytime hours, Reed found the relative solitude of the overnight shift liberating. The streets weren't loaded with angry drivers, and there were never any lines at the few establishments he did go to.

Now that he was lead on a case, though, his presence was required during normal working hours. Despite spending the last two nights at crime scenes, he was still forced to interact with the world, made to comply with the schedules of others to accomplish what he needed to.

The sound of the alarm clock going off on his nightstand was an audible assault on his senses, pulling him from a deep sleep. His first reaction was to lash out with his right arm, slapping the button across the top of the machine, forcing the wretched sound to stop. In the wake of it, he lay sprawled across the sheets, a sheen of sweat on his skin despite the air conditioning in the house.

It was not yet noon, easily the earliest he had been awake during the week since the last case he'd handled more than a month before.

Rolling out of bed to his feet, Reed drew himself up to full height, locking his fingers and stretching them high overhead. One after another the vertebrae of his back popped, followed in order by his shoulders and hips.

If this is what happened to his body at 35, he feared what 40, or even 50, might one day bring.

Opting only for a pair of gym shorts, he shuffled through the house, his bare feet almost silent on the hardwood floors. As he stopped just inside the doorway to the kitchen, a pair of moist half-moons stared up at him from beneath the table.

"Keep sleeping, girl," Reed said. "You've still got a little time yet."

Her eyes opened slightly at the sound of his voice, though she made no effort to raise herself from the floor. Inches to her left was the over-stuffed dog bed he had purchased for her during the winter, the option cast aside whenever the mercury rose above a comfortable temperature.

Leaving her there, Reed walked over and turned on the sink. He allowed the water to cool before cupping his hands beneath it, drinking the first two scoops and then splashing the third on his face. The feel of it against his skin pulled him from his foggy haze, another pass through the process finally bringing his senses fully alert.

Wiping himself dry with a hand towel, Reed walked over to the kitchen table and lowered himself into a hardback chair, his bottom settling onto a well-worn cushion. There he spread out the assorted files he had, everything amassed thus far for Esther Rosen and what little he had for Ira Soto.

Starting with the coroner's report, Reed flipped the top file open and rifled through it, refreshing what Solomon had outlined for him the previous day. Aside from the fractured sternum and the fibers found in her throat, nothing really seemed to jump out at him, the woman in good health for someone her age. No drugs of any sort were found in her system, whether ingested herself or forced upon her by a killer. No signs of a struggle of any kind, her body free of bruising, her nails without a single crack or trace of skin residue.

The only signs of any foul play at all were the burst blood vessels in her eyes.

It wasn't exactly going peacefully in her sleep, but as far as Reed could tell, it was about as close as a murder ever got.

Leaving the file open, the photos of Rosen lying on the examination table in plain sight, Reed slid it across the polished wooden surface. In its place he grabbed up the report from the criminalists, going through everything Earl and his crew had been able to find, which amounted to not much. They had managed to determine that the murder weapon was a throw pillow from the living room couch and that the killing had occurred in the bedroom, the body never moved.

As for forensics, they had not found a single fingerprint other than the victim's anywhere in the house. The most useful thing they had managed to pick up was the outline of a footprint on the textured linoleum of the kitchen floor, determining the killer to most likely be male, and probably, a pretty big guy.

Reed rolled his eyes as he lifted the file and piled it on top of the coroner's report. He was looking for a tall man. Not exactly the kind of thing he could take to a judge for a warrant.

First on the agenda for the day was to swing back past the coroner's office and speak to Solomon. Before turning in, Reed had asked Grimes to lean on them for an expedited autopsy, something Reed hated doing but knew the office wouldn't object to. Department policy was to pursue anything that looked like a serial killing first, and thus far the events of the previous two nights seemed to have all the earmarks of one.

At least enough similarities to justify the concern.

Rising to his feet, Reed walked to the sliding glass door overlooking a small deck. Overhead the sun was high above, beating down on a pair of lounge chairs and a charcoal grill, the grass of his yard appearing even more brittle than it had the day before.

Folding his arms across his chest, Reed ignored the promise of another sweltering summer day and focused on the scenes he'd witnessed the previous two nights. While it was true that a clear pattern had emerged and that a repeat killer appeared to be working in his jurisdiction, it didn't have any of the usual hallmarks of a serial.

Gone was any of the usual anger that was paired with multiple deaths. There was no blood at either scene, and in at least one instance it appeared an effort had been made to save the victim.

In both incidents the killer called 911, a move that usually meant someone was looking for notoriety, wanting their victims to be found, or at the very least wanting to stick around and watch the show. Thus far, though, no contact had been made by the individual, either to the police or to the media. In addition, Billie had followed his trail away from the site of Soto's killing, a spot that afforded no view of the first responders arriving.

The combination made no sense. He was missing something.

Rule one in any murder investigation was always, always, victimology. Don't just focus on the crimes themselves, dig deeper, try to determine why they were committed to these specific people.

So far, both scenes had been handled in a way that bordered on intimate.

That had to mean something.

Chapter Fifteen

Reed told Billie to stay in the hall across from Solomon's lab and left her lying flat on her stomach. The cool temperature of the basement and the tile floor beneath her ensured she would be happy for the next few minute while he went inside.

The odors of formaldehyde and decaying bodies hit him as he entered, together forming the omnipresent scent of death that Solomon seemed to barely notice, though he couldn't imagine dealing with every day.

Wouldn't want to even try.

Compared to the hallway outside, the temperature in the lab was even cooler. For the first time in weeks Reed didn't feel the slightest discomfort from the heat.

The room he now stood in was a carbon copy of the original morgue downtown, stainless steel examination tables, each with a powerful, overhead light, rolling tables with surgical instruments and larger tools for autopsy, and a row of cold lockers on the back wall, the noise of exhaust fans always struggling but failing to remove the foul smells.

Unfortunately, the lab, as always, also seemed to have a capacity crowd awaiting the skilled hands of Dr. Solomon and her staff.

The majority of the 8th Precinct's jurisdiction was known as The Bottoms because it sat below the water levels for the nearby Scioto and Olentangy Rivers, though many believed the moniker to have a much more sinister origin.

Working the night shift as a detective, Reed was firmly of the same belief.

The Bottoms was rising on the statewide lists for both crime and poverty, already worse than Cincinnati, Akron or Toledo, trailing only some of Cleveland's very worst spots.

"Good afternoon, Detective," the doctor said, snapping Reed from his thoughts. Positioned in the middle of the room, she was mid-autopsy, a halogen lamp above throwing down a harsh white light as she hunched over her newest charge, displaying the scene in far more detail than Reed would have preferred.

"Good afternoon, Doctor," Reed said, realizing his body clock was so far off that he had no idea what time it actually was. "How are you?"

Solomon paused, looking up at him through the plastic shield hanging down over her face. Spatters of bone dust and blood clung to it, the same for the blue examination gown she was draped in.

She said nothing.

She didn't have to.

She was finishing up on Ira Soto, the dark skin glowing beneath the bright light. A sheet covered the lower half of her body, the top portion bearing a wicked gash from her shoulder to her pelvic bone, the line coming at a diagonal across her breast plate and dropping straight down over her abdomen. Thick sutures held the skin together across the portion of the body Reed could see, Solomon at work on closing the other half of her chest.

Reed was glad he had arrived late enough to miss the part where her thorax was spread open wide, or even worse, where a set of pruning shears were used to snip through her ribs.

Even as a detective with a decade of experience, there were still some things he never grew accustomed to seeing, or wanted to.

"I'm early," Reed said, knowing that Solomon probably received the body no more than four or five hours before. "Should I stop by later or tomorrow?"

Again, Solomon looked up at him, an eyebrow cocked beneath her shield. "From what I hear, we both know you don't have that kind of time."

The comment surprised Reed. "Word's getting out, huh?"

He realized the inanity of the question even as he asked it, knowing full well how the departmental gossip mill worked.

In the last 36 hours alone, dispatch, first responders from police, fire, and emergency medical services, and a host of coroner's office personal had come in contact in some way with Esther Rosen. Human nature being what it was, every last person would have been curious in one way or another. From there, those people had friends, families, colleagues, all eager to hear and share the latest news.

Even without the media being involved, it didn't take long for a good story to start making the rounds.

The unusual murders of two women on consecutive nights certainly qualified as that.

Without waiting for an answer to his question, Reed asked, "Anything good coming from the talk I should be aware of?"

"Complete speculation at this point," Solomon said, pushing the curved needle through a fold of skin and drawing the heavy filament line up a few inches. "Lot of junior detective work right now. You know the drill."

Reed did, all too well, probably better than Solomon. He let it go without comment.

"If you don't mind an oral report I can give you the rundown now," Solomon said, "send a written file over later."

"Works for me," Reed said. He didn't have a pad or pen with him, but was reasonably certain he could hang on to anything major Solomon was about to share.

"Okay," Solomon said, her voice taking on a detached tone, shifting from colleague to teacher. "Victim presents as a 49-year-old African American woman in reasonably good health. No concerns for her heart, same for her kidneys and lungs. Could have stood to lose 10 pounds or so, and the hearing aid in her ear when she arrived suggested she had some auditory deficiencies, but otherwise, she was a strong, healthy woman."

Reed nodded. Just like Esther Rosen, this woman's life had ended prematurely, her reward for taking care of herself, to be cut down by someone with a twisted agenda

"TOD appears to be about 14 hours ago, official COD carbon monoxide poisoning."

"Yeah," Reed said, nodding slightly, thinking back on the elaborate scene in her garage. He raised a hand to his chest and traced a finger along his sternum, moving it up and down several inches. "Was her, um..."

"Sternum fractured?" Solomon asked, picking up his gesture and finishing the thought for him. "No, but her face was."

Reed felt his eyebrows rise, waiting for her to continue.

"Orbital bone was cracked and her jaw was completely dislocated," Solomon said, rising up to full height and gesturing to the head of the table, the needle and thread still clutched in her hand. "Single blunt force blow to the cheek."

"Damn," Reed whispered, trying to fit it with everything he already knew. "So one night he tries to revive the victim, the next he beats the hell out of her?"

"Based on what I see here, it was only one blow," Solomon said. "No signs of defensive wounds, no ligature marks to suggest she was bound in any way."

Reed worked to comprehend the new information. "We found the dog out back in the bushes, so the killer probably waited until she took it out. Lay in wait for her, hit her once to subdue her before moving the body to the garage."

Reed tried to picture the scene playing out in his head, envisioning the concrete patio behind Soto's house, imagining the killer springing from the darkness and subduing her.

"Any idea what she was hit with?"

Glancing down to Soto, Solomon said, "Wound seems to indicate a fist."

"Any shot at DNA?"

"Unclear," Solomon said. "I bagged the skin and called for a pickup from the crime scene unit, but I wouldn't hold my breath."

Chapter Sixteen

The parking lot outside the precinct wasn't as quiet as the previous night. During the week, the majority of the administrative staff shut down their computers a few minutes before 5:00, milling about with their coworkers before starting a mass exodus for the door. By 5:15, over half of the staff was nothing more than a vapor trail, most of those remaining trickling out soon after.

On days Reed needed to use his desk, he aimed for arriving after 6:00, knowing he would see the building mostly deserted. Only rarely was he stopped for awkward conversation or a case consult, the few who worked the non-peak hours having a mindset that matched his.

The clock on the dash displayed 6:06 as Reed parked in the rear of the lot. It took another six minutes for Billie to reduce a bottle of water to nothing more than thick ropes of drool hanging from her cheeks.

Together they stepped inside the precinct, both of them hot and sweating. The onset of evening had done nothing to squelch the heat, the night ahead promising no reprieve from the sweltering weather.

Inside, the building was only nominally cooler as Reed led Billie across the front foyer and up the stairs, her toenails clicking against the hardwood floor. Using the short lead, he could feel the heat passing through her thick coat against his leg, hear her panting as they climbed.

At the top of the landing Reed paused, considering going to his desk before thinking better of it and drifting to the right. More than once he had tried to slip by undetected, only managing to earn himself a severe tongue lashing that lasted twice as long as the encounter he was about to have.

As with most things, it was better just to get it over with.

It took only a moment for Jackie Randall to hear them approaching, a celebrity gossip magazine raised before her. On the desk beside her was a red and white container from Kentucky Fried Chicken, grease splotches visible on the top flaps. The scent of it hung in the air around her, Reed glancing down to see Billie's tongue flick out over her nose.

Less than an hour after dinner, and she was still hungry.

At the sight of them, Jackie's bright pink lips parted in a wide smile, her too-white teeth gleaming behind them. She dropped her magazine and stood, gaining no more than a couple of inches in height. She pressed her fists into her hips, a halo of white-blonde hair shifting above her head with each movement.

"Well, if it's not Reed Mattox coming in here to see me," she said, almost yelling the words, her voice echoing through the deserted floor.

"Hey there," Reed said, a reluctant smile crossing his face as he sidled up to the desk, Billie dropping to her haunches on the floor beside him. "How's it going?"

Despite the fact that Jackie was at most a year or two older than him, Reed couldn't shake the notion that he was addressing his grandmother each time they spoke.

"I'm good," Jackie said, the smile still set to full luminosity, "but you know me, I'm always good. Must be working here that does it."

The comment drew a sharp snort from Reed. "Yeah, that must be it."

Defying what Reed thought possible, the smile on Jackie's face grew a touch larger. "And how you doing?"

The look faded from Reed's face as he glanced down to Billie and back up again. "Oh, we're alright I guess. Getting by."

"Anything coming together with the Night Stalker?"

Biting back a wince at the fact that a name had been awarded to the killer he was chasing, and a terrible one at that, Reed forced his face to remain neutral. His earlier conversation with Solomon was still fresh in his mind, highlighting how fast gossip could travel through a police station.

In his experience, that speed was accelerated by a considerable factor when someone like Jackie became involved.

"Well, that's what we're here to work on," Reed said. "We'll be down on the opposite end for a couple of hours. Hope it doesn't bother you too much."

"Not at all," Jackie said, the mega-watt grin back in place as she lowered herself into her seat and pulled the magazine back over before her. "Apparently, another Hollywood A-lister is cheating on his wife. Should make for some good reading."

Without comment, Reed retreated back to the opposite end of the building, dropping the lead to the floor and allowing Billie to walk free beside him. Together, they cut a path through the maze of desks until coming to his in the corner.

As a matter of course, Reed tried to spend as little time in the precinct as possible. Compared to the other desks, his was virtually barren, housing only an aging desktop computer, a keyboard and a short stack of files.

Once upon a time he had a lamp as well, but it had long since disappeared, along with the high-backed chair with good lumbar support he preferred.

Both had gone missing months before, back when he was still the new guy in the building, and such antics were to be expected. Since proving himself on a major investigation nothing else had vanished, though nothing had found its way back to him either.

From what he heard, it was far worse in other precincts.

Starting with the top file, Reed rifled through to find the report from Solomon. By and large, it contained the same information she had given him that afternoon, adding only the detail that the blow to her cheek had been strong enough to dislodge two teeth, sending them down her throat where they were later retrieved.

A low whistle slid across Reed's lips as he considered the type of blow it would take to inflict that kind of damage.

Even starting to get a little older, Ira Soto was nowhere near the age where osteoporosis usually set in. Barring some sort of bone disease or defect, no single punch should have broken a bone, dislocated a jaw and removed two teeth.

No punch by itself anyway.

Making a mental note, Reed set the file aside and took up the one beneath it. Twice as thick as the previous one, it contained a full workup from Earl and his crew, covering everything from the water spot Billie found to the duct tape on the exhaust pipe of Soto's car. Along with it were dozens of photos, all from various angles and showing assorted degrees of magnification.

Attached to the top page in the file was a pale blue Post-It note, just four words scribbled across it in Earl's stilted handwriting.

Not a damn thing.

"Shit," Reed muttered, peeling the note away and pressing it onto the desktop.

Quickly, he swept through the contents of the file, the sum total yielding exactly what Earl said it would. No fingerprints. No DNA. Three spots of blood on the back patio, all confirmed to be from Ira Soto.

The duct tape yielded pine needles, grass clippings, some bits of mulch, indicating nothing of value to the investigation.

The tape and the hose were both brand new, the hose wiped clean of prints. It had been cut down to size with a sharp knife of some sort, a single slice, no serration marks in the rubber.

An analysis of the dog and the rock had also turned up nothing, the blood on the stone belonging to the animal.

Again, Reed thought the dog was too loud and needed to be silenced.

Flipping the file closed, Reed shoved it away. As far as he could tell, whoever was doing this was extremely good or extremely lucky. He knew how to avoid detection, managing to subdue two victims, and a dog, without being seen or heard.

Of course, neither of the victims lived in a high-traffic area, and both were older women living alone, making them easy targets, but still.

Leaning back in his chair, Reed laced his fingers behind his neck. While he couldn't be certain if the killer was good or lucky or a little of both, he could definitely sense that each murder had been carefully planned.

Each home had been observed, the killer learning the routines of both women enough to know the best time to strike. In the case of Ira Soto, he also determined a way to lure her out with her dog so she would come to him.

"Somebody must have seen something," Reed said, his voice low, just loud enough for Billie to finally lift her head from the floor. He mulled the statement, letting his mind process after hearing the words out loud, before dropping his hands from his head and turning his attention to the computer.

"Even in a place like The Bottoms, somebody had to have seen something."

Chapter Seventeen

The Good Son stopped outside the front door and took a deep breath, the familiar feeling of agitation that had been in his stomach all day even more pronounced as he stood with the screen door leaning against his shoulder.

He did not want to open the door and step inside.

He knew what waited there.

"I know you're out there," a voice called from inside the house. "I heard the screen door open. Get your ass in here."

Feeling the dread spike again, The Good Son stepped into the kitchen, the overhead fixture throwing down a harsh light, forcing his eyes almost shut. Behind him the screen door closed with a clatter as he placed his lunch bucket on the scratched and faded laminate countertop.

"And shut the damn door," the voice called, sounding even more agitated without the barrier of the door to soften it, "not trying to cool the neighborhood, you know."

The Good Son reached out and shoved the door shut.

Just as he did every day, he paused to collect himself before exiting the kitchen. He could not, would not, in any way let it show that the situation was starting to get to him, that anything he had done in the preceding nights was gnawing at him from within.

That her perpetual berating had worn his nerves down to a frazzled nub.

He had to remain steady for her.

This was his task. He would get it done.

"Hey," The Good Son said, his voice low as he stepped from the kitchen into the living room.

In the semi-darkness he could just make out his mother seated on the couch, her thin form spread out most of the length of it. She appeared to be in the same position as when he left 10 hours before, the only difference being the blanket that had once covered her was now in a heap on the floor.

"You're late," she said, the two words sufficient to relay her disdain for him and his tardiness simultaneously.

"I had to wait for a train to pass," The Good Son said, taking an extra step into the room. He met her gaze for just a moment, knowing full well she could see through the lie, before moving to the edge of the coffee table separating them.

The top of it was cluttered with pill bottles of every size and color, some with their tops removed, lying on their sides. Two empty water bottles and a plate with the remains of the peanut butter and jelly sandwich he had made for her that morning were waiting to be removed.

"Have you eaten yet?" he asked.

"Have you been here to make my dinner?" she replied.

The Good Son fought the urge to close his eyes, to blow out a long sigh, to let her see how much her constant state of finding fault with everything was wearing on him.

As much as he might want to, though, he couldn't do it. It wasn't her fault that things had played out the way they did, her anger a direct result of the situation they were in.

Besides, she was right. It was his job to make sure he got home in time to make dinner. His being late only confirmed the feeling that had first arisen at work that afternoon.

He had to do better.

"I'm sorry I'm late," he said, collecting the plate and empty bottles from the table. "What would you like to eat?"

It took 20 seconds and every bit of energy she could muster to turn and look back at him, her face a mix of pain and anger. A watery sheen rested over her eyes as she stared, the corners of her mouth turned down, her nostrils flaring. "At this point, I'll take any damned thing you can bring me."

The Good Son considered reaching out and resting a hand on her shoulder, reassuring her in some way, but he opted against it. Instead, he took up the TV remote from the coffee table and turned the television on, the light casting a ghostly pallor over the room.

The Good Son could now see the rest of the furniture in the room, could make out the various pictures hanging on the walls. It was all so familiar, the house he had grown up in, but in recent years had grown so unaccustomed to as well.

Without looking at the screen, The Good Son aimed the remote and keyed in the numbers for the Food Network.

"Do you love your mama?"

Above everything else that had developed in recent years, those five words were what The Good Son hated most. He knew every time it was asked what she was really trying to say. Knew just as clearly there was only one response he could reasonably give.

"More than anything," he whispered.

He kept his attention aimed at the television as he returned the remote to the table. Beside him he knew she was staring his way, searching for any crack in his façade, waiting for the slightest sign of weakness.

He would give her none.

"And you'd do anything for her, right?"

The events of the previous week, of the previous months, should have already answered that for her. The Good Son knew it wasn't actually a response she craved though.

It was something much more than that.

"Anything."

Chapter Eighteen

The day before, Reed was worried that McMichaels and Jacobs might hate him. Two straight days of canvassing duty, especially in their precinct, was a task nobody wanted. The neighborhoods they were now in were a far cry from the dilapidated and broken homes found closer to the river, but much of the general animosity that people felt toward law enforcement still lingered.

To many, especially those who had been around for a while, Franklinton was a cautionary tale of what had once been a nice area. Any decline that had occurred was because the police had failed in their duties. Instead of patrolling the streets and keeping things safe, they preferred to take their bloated government salaries and eat doughnuts all day.

Used their badges to harass honest citizens. Looked away from crime in exchange for a little money under the table.

Reed had heard the comments so many times they didn't even register with him anymore. Early in his partnership with Riley he had felt the need to lash back, to defend them whenever the conversation arose, but now he knew better. The people didn't actually care that he hadn't eaten a doughnut in years or that he rented the farmhouse he and Billie lived in, they just wanted someone to blame.

Anything to keep from thinking they had in any way contributed to their own plight.

Despite that, Reed couldn't help but feel a small bit of spite in the pit of his stomach as he wound his way through the non-existent early morning traffic. Outside, the world was still dark, only a few houses having any lights visible.

The constant jump between shifts had his body clock wrecked, feeling like he had just stepped off a direct flight from Australia and was expected to adjust perfectly upon touching down. After leaving the precinct the night before, he had toiled until well after midnight, unable to turn off his mind, wrestling with everything he knew. Every function kept perfect pace the entire time, used to being awake, finding nothing out of the norm.

It was four hours later when his alarm clock went off that his entire being seemed to rebel.

Another glance in the rearview mirror displayed the dark circles under his eyes and the layer of stubble spread across his face. His hair was still wet from his sprint through the shower, the humidity in the air so high it prevented it from drying completely.

Barely 6:00 a.m., and already the day was off to a fantastic start.

The headlights reflected off the front windows of the Washington Elementary School as Reed pulled into the parking lot. Empty for the summer, the grass around it was a little taller than usual, all of it brown. The single-story building sprawled in either direction from the small central lot, the red brick mottled with small splashes of graffiti.

The front had only two broken windows, much better than some of the other schools in the district.

Reed parked and left the engine running, cool air blasting in through the vents as a pair of headlights approached in the distance. He waited as they grew closer, the shape leaving no doubt they belonged to a police cruiser.

"Stay," Reed said, getting no reaction from Billie as he climbed out and leaned against the side of his car. The blue-and-white slid into the lot and parked parallel to him, both men exiting without turning off the engine.

"Officers," Reed said, dipping the top of his head in greeting.

"Detective," McMichaels said.

"Reed," Jacobs replied.

"Please tell me this meeting time wasn't some form of punishment for asking you guys to go on canvas duty the last two nights?" Reed asked.

A pair of smiles graced the men's features as they both matched Reed's pose against their cruiser.

"That would be funny, but not at all," Jacobs said. "Hell, truth be known, we both appreciate the overtime. You know how damn tight the place has gotten about granting it lately."

Reed nodded. It was an election year, which always managed to put the department square under the microscope for scrutiny. During those times everything got tight, from the amount of overtime pay doled out to the brand of coffee they used in the break room.

It was ludicrous, and an enormous pain, but something every last person on the force had grown used to over the years.

"Yeah," McMichaels said. "These last two days got me that much closer to a bass boat. Pretty damn easy canvas, too."

Under different circumstances Reed would have seized on the first part of the statement, asking what he was looking at or where he liked to fish. Instead, all he heard was the second sentence, a bit of dread kicking up within him.

"Easy, as in nobody saw anything?" he asked.

"Pretty much," McMichaels said.

"And they actually weren't too bad," Jacobs said. "I think with the heat they just wanted to get us on our way. Didn't even feel up to the usual barrage of jokes and comments."

Reaching into the right breast pocket of his uniform, McMichaels extracted a single piece of paper folded in half. It was no more than a few inches square, one end of it with fuzzy edges, as if it had been ripped clean from a notebook.

"Nobody heard anything or saw anybody suspicious, but a couple of folks said they saw a silver car parked around."

Reed took the piece of paper without looking at it. "A silver car?"

"That's what they said," McMichaels replied. "Sounded like a sedan, small, older. Nobody got a plate though, not even a clean make or model."

"About the only thing they could agree on was that it was a *honky car*," Jacobs said, using his fingers to make air quotes. "Whatever the hell that means."

More than once Reed had heard the expression around The Bottoms. It was the slang way of saying the car looked like something an old white person would drive.

It was a pretty safe assumption that Jacobs already knew that too and was just being dramatic.

"Two damn murders in consecutive nights," Reed said, "and all we can pull are a couple of sightings of a silver car."

Again, he came back to the same conclusion he had a night before. Somebody was either very good, or very, very lucky.

"That's it," McMichaels said, spreading his hands wide.

"I don't even think this time was a case of them jerking us around," Jacobs said. "I honestly don't think there was any more to be found."

Chapter Nineteen

Once the officers were gone, their taillights disappearing down the street, Reed opened the back seat of the car. He stood off to the side and waited several minutes, resuming the same stance with his arms folded across his chest, considering what they had told him.

Both Esther Rosen and Ira Soto lived in residential neighborhoods. There weren't but a handful of traffic cameras in the entire jurisdiction, most of those put up in The Bottoms almost immediately succumbing to vandalism. Rather than pay to keep replacing them, the city had elected to go without, arguing that their presence caused more criminal activity than they prevented.

Reed hadn't necessarily agreed with that, knowing it was more bureaucratic apathy than anything, but knew he wasn't in any position to speak out against it.

Maybe one day, if he could somehow prove their presence would have aided an investigation or even prevented a crime from taking place, but not now. Probably not ever.

Coupled with the lack of cameras was the demographic profile of the respective neighborhoods. Away from the dense urban center, both were filled with single family dwellings, most of the residents 40 years of age or older. Once the sun went down, there was precious little foot traffic, very few young people walking around with their cell-phones glued to their hands.

If a crime like this had taken place in any of a dozen different suburbs in the greater Columbus area, Reed would spend the morning sifting through Facebook and Twitter postings of personal footage filmed on the scene. Instead, he was left standing in an elementary school parking lot trying to figure out what - if anything - could be done with the tiny piece of information the officers had given him.

"You coming out?" Reed asked, glancing into the backseat.

Billie's only response was to thump the plastic of the backseat with her tail twice, making no effort to rise.

"Point taken," Reed said, pushing the door shut and climbing behind the wheel.

Dawn fast approaching, a filmy yellow light pasted a harsh glow over everything as Reed circled away from the school. He still had some time to kill before his next appointment, his body wanting nothing more than to fill the hours with sleep, his mind knowing there was no way it would ever find him again.

With nowhere in particular to be, he turned his sedan back to Ira Soto's. There was no real reason beyond hoping that perhaps seeing the scene again in daylight might somehow shake something loose. Already, Billie had told him how the killer gained entry and egress, but the spot was well beyond sight of the house.

He had to have done surveillance from somewhere closer.

Sitting up higher behind the steering wheel, Reed hooked a right and rolled down to the closest cross street. Ahead on the corner, cutting through the thin morning light, he spotted a burst of neon. Showing yellow, red, and blue, it shined down the length of the street, announcing to anybody driving by that off-brand gas was for sale.

Easing his foot back from the pedal, Reed drifted to the side of the road. As he got closer, the rest of the filling station came into view, a single small building with six pumps out front.

"You don't think?" Reed asked, his voice low, nothing more than thinking out loud as he pulled off the street and into the lot.

The concrete block building was painted blue with large windows across the front. Plastered to the walls were posters advertising various cigarettes, while neon signs announced every known brand of beer, and even a few Reed had never heard of.

Out front, the pumps were beginning to rust, but appeared to be functional.

All those details barely registered with Reed. His focus went straight to the corners of the building, where a pair of small plastic cameras were aimed out over the grounds.

From where he sat, it appeared they were positioned to keep an eye on the pumps, maybe getting a good look at the street beyond as well. It was a long shot, but it did present at least a chance that Reed could spot a silver car rolling by right after the 911 call.

The thought of getting a look at the driver, or even a license plate, brought a surge of adrenaline as he parked and glanced over his shoulder. "Be right back."

For the first time all morning Billie let out a whine as Reed climbed out. He could barely hear the sound before it was swallowed up, an ancient air conditioner protruding from the side of the building giving off a persistent rattle.

Passing through the front door, Reed could tell that despite its best efforts, the AC was already losing the battle against the encroaching morning heat.

The smell of sweat and cigarette smoke hung heavy in the air.

"Morning," the cashier behind the counter said, a heavy-set woman in a sleeveless flannel and jeans. Her red hair was tied up in a kerchief around her head, and half a Twinkie was in her hand.

"Morning," Reed said, reaching into his rear pocket and extracting his badge. "Detective Reed Mattox, CPD."

The woman gave no reaction, merely peeling back the plastic wrap and taking another bite.

"I noticed on my way in that you guys have a pair of cameras looking out over the gas pumps," he said.

The woman nodded as she chewed.

"And I was wondering how much of the intersection they're able to see."

"Not much."

As she spoke, crumbs fell from her mouth to the counter. She glanced down at them, brushing them to the floor and wiping her hand along the side of her jeans.

A trickle of sweat rolled down the small of Reed's back, a combination of the heat inside the store and his growing dislike for the cashier.

"Well, if possible, I'd still like to take a look at the tapes from the night before last," he said.

"Not possible," she replied, cramming the last bit into her mouth. She crinkled the cellophane wrapper in her hand repeatedly for effect before turning and dropping it into a wastebasket behind her.

Again, Reed's disdain grew. "Are they on a 24-hour loop? Have they already started taping over again?"

"They're not on at all," the woman said, glancing out the window. "Never have been. If you walk out there and look, you can see there aren't even cords attached to them. We just hung them up to try and ward off the vandals."

She turned her attention back to Reed, no small amount of accusation in her gaze. "Lot of damn good it did."

Instantly, Reed knew where the discussion was going. He'd heard the lecture enough times to recognize all the signs.

He left without another word.

Chapter Twenty

Two cars were in the parking lot as The Good Son pulled in. Both were parked in the spots closest to the front door, each with a single occupant.

The morning sun had burned away any dew as he parked and climbed out, sweat shining from his forehead, his cotton t-shirt already damp.

After the night he'd had, the nights he'd had, this was not how he wanted to start the morning. He was aware that his mother had been difficult and that he was running three minutes behind schedule. He also knew that nothing these people needed was important enough for them to read him the riot act, though that wouldn't stop them from doing it anyway.

It never did.

"The sign on the door says you open at 7:00," the woman closest to him said, kicking off the tirade he knew was coming. She was short, with the beginnings of middle-age pudgy forming around her midsection. Her hair was dyed too dark and teased out in a '60s style, and she wore sunglasses that hid her eyes and most of her face.

Opposite her was an older man in jeans and a short sleeve plaid shirt, buttoned at the neck, the tail tucked in. He wore a rumpled ball cap from a nearby golf course, tufts of white hair sticking out from either side.

He wouldn't be a problem, The Good Son knew. People like him never were.

"It's four minutes after," the woman said, falling in beside The Good Son as he walked to the front door. "I'm going to be late now."

"Yes, ma'am," The Good son said, his first words of the morning. "I'm very sorry. There was an accident on the way here."

The woman grunted, letting it be known she was aware the excuse was a blatant lie. She stood just inches from his shoulder as he unlocked the doors and pushed them both open wide, standing aside so the two could enter. They were already inside before he was even able to flip on the lights, the sodium bulbs offering a thin haze as they began to warm up.

Bypassing most of the usual opening chores, The Good Son went straight to the cash register. Just like the lights overhead, the machine took a moment to get going, a secondhand relic with more than 10 years on its odometer.

As it cycled up, The Good Son pulled out an apron from under the counter and looped it over his head. As the register came alive, it spit out a tape marking the time and date, The Good Son tearing it away and dropping it beneath the cash drawer to begin the day.

Opening the store was a chore shared among the half dozen low-level employees on staff. One morning a week each person was required to come in at 7:00, manning the place until help arrived an hour later. At that time, The Good Son would hand off the register to one of the cashiers, retreating to the back for a day of manual labor unloading trucks, stacking bags of dog food and seed, and stocking shelves.

At 9:00 Beauregard arrived, making life miserable for everybody.

The thought brought a grimace to The Good Son's face as he leaned against the front counter and waited, the lights above finally reaching full power. Combined with the sun streaming in through the front windows, it illuminated the dozen long aisles, the Good Son able to see everything from snack foods to landscape stones from where he stood.

The old man was the first to appear before him, a pair of white plastic elbow joints for home plumbing in hand. He dropped them onto the counter without saying a word, his mouth turned down in a frown.

The Good Son knew the look well enough to infer exactly what was being said, despite not a sound leaving the old man. He had been late, he had shown up wearing jeans and a t-shirt, the sleeves cut away. His truck was unwashed, and rooster tails of mud were splashed up the sides. Word for word he could almost recite the lecture he knew lurked inside the man, starting with some variation of *back in my day* and including words like *self-respect* and *accountability*.

The Good Son's face let it be known he was not in the mood to hear it.

If this old man, if *anybody*, knew just how accountable he had been lately, they would stare in wonder. They wouldn't dwell on a few surface imperfections, but would marvel at the lengths he was going to.

"$4.50," The Good Son said, putting an edge on his voice to drive home the point.

It worked.

The old man peeled a five dollar bill away from a small wad of cash, staying quiet as The Good Son scraped two quarters out of the bottom of the drawer and handed them back to him. "Have yourself a good day."

The words tasted caustic on his tongue as The Good Son watched the old man shuffle away.

For years - most of his life, in fact - he had fought to keep vile thoughts out of his head. He disliked the notion of hatred, absolutely despised the thought of anybody hating him.

At the same time, he found it harder every day to keep the dark energy at bay.

The things he had done were not only deplorable, they had been for nothing. They had failed to accomplish their objective, meaning they would have to continue. Realizing he would have to do something similar, or perhaps even worse, in the coming days darkened his mood immeasurably.

Knowing it was his fault they had to be done at all made it even worse.

From behind the register, The Good Son watched as the old man climbed behind the wheel of his car and drove away. He made no effort to hide his expression or look away as the car departed, for one tiny moment feeling a little better.

It was the first time in a long time he had pushed back.

Damn, did it feel good.

"Four minutes," a voice said, drawing him from his thoughts. He turned to find the woman standing before him, a plastic watering can on the counter. "I just think if a place says they open at 7:00, they should be open at 7:00."

Hostility oozed from every pore as she slid a Visa card from her pocketbook and handed it to The Good Son. Despite being inside, she had not yet removed the sunglasses, her face still hidden from view.

Just as he had with the old man, The Good Son plastered a look across his face. The thought of adding to the fabricated story passed through his mind, of telling the woman that the accident had produced a child fatality.

Instead, he pushed it aside, merely staring at her before looking down at the card.

"I'm sorry, Ms. Jurgensen, but I'm required to see some identification on all credit card purchases."

Chapter Twenty-One

The woman on the other end of the line had told Reed she was willing to meet at Esther Rosen's house, though he could tell it was nothing more than a token offer. The kind of thing a nice person does, but hopes will not be accepted.

That original inkling grew even more pronounced as he approached the corner table outside a Starbucks in Hilliard. Seated alone at it was a woman in her mid-20s, the only person brave enough to chance the metal chairs in the morning heat.

Inside the glass storefront he could see a line of people snaking throughout the building. Along the side of the place was a line of cars twice as long, everybody anxious to get their morning fix of caffeine.

"Janine Rosen?" Reed asked as he approached. He had opted to leave his badge in the car, not wanting to seem too overbearing, or even worse, for her to have to suffer the indignity of strangers gawking through the window and wondering what was going on outside.

For that reason, he had also left Billie in the car. The windows were down, and he was parked beneath a tree, but still, his timeframe was limited.

"Yes," she said, rising halfway out of the seat as she stood and extended a hand toward him. "Detective Mattox?"

"Reed," he corrected, meeting the handshake and sliding into the chair opposite her.

Based on her phone voice, she wasn't exactly what Reed had expected. She had straight dark hair that was parted in the middle and outlined an oval face, a red nose and dark circles under her eyes her most prominent features. She wore no makeup and had on a subdued summer dress, flip-flops on her feet.

On the table in front of her was an iced coffee on a small stack of napkins. Condensation had formed on the side of it, drops streaking downward before being absorbed by the napkins.

Everything about her, from her tired eyes to her slouching posture, seemed to relay she was still grieving. For a moment Reed wanted to reach out to her, to pat her on the shoulder, to offer his condolences. At the same time, he remembered the way people had done those very things when Riley died and how much he hated it.

Even more so, the look of pity on their faces.

In a way, they had made his road to acceptance that much harder, and he would be damned if he would do the same thing to this young woman.

"Thank you for meeting with me," he said. "I appreciate you making the time."

Across from him Janine nodded, saying nothing.

Twice already this the morning he had gone over the questions he wanted to ask her, knowing them verbatim without having to consult his notebook.

Badge or not, nothing screamed cop like someone reciting from a pad. Already he could see a few people watching them through the window as they waited in line.

"Our records have you listed as Esther's next of kin and emergency contact. Is that correct?"

"Yes. I'm her daughter."

Reed nodded, already knowing that but needing to ask it anyway. "And your father?"

"He passed away six years ago," Janine said, her voice sounding hollow, looking at Reed without actually focusing. "Lung cancer, never smoked a cigarette in his life."

On pure reflex, Reed felt himself wince. In half a dozen years this young woman had lost both her parents long before their time, each a victim of tragic injustices.

"Did she always live in Franklinton?" Reed asked.

"My dad worked at Midwestern paper for 30 years. It was the only house they ever owned together, bought back before The Bottoms was too bad."

It was clear there was more she wanted to add, Reed giving her time to do so. When no words came, he prompted, "But they stayed anyway?"

"Yeah," she whispered, her eyes glassing over. "Our neighborhood was a little ways out from the worst parts, and they drove me to private school every day, so I don't think they thought much of it."

"And after your father passed?"

She shifted her attention, the watery veneer still present in her eyes. "I was at Ohio State at the time. I begged and begged her to move up near me. Must have brought it up at least once a week ever since. She wouldn't dream of it though. Said it was the only way she still felt connected to my father."

The last part was the sole reason Reed had felt compelled to press on the topic. "So after his passing, there was nobody else?"

He asked it gently, without inflection of any sort, but it still brought a sharp twist of the head from Janine.

"No. Never." The words were firm, no wiggle room at all. "Why do you ask?"

Feeling the defensiveness in her, Reed sat back in his chair. "The other night a male called 911."

The anger on Janine's face bled away in an instant, a look of confusion replacing it. "A man called from my mother's house? After midnight?"

"No, the call was made from a throwaway cell-phone. Our assumption is it came from whoever did this, but we needed to be sure there wasn't somebody else who might have made it."

Pursing her lips, Janine fell silent. Reed could see her mind working, her eyes fogging over, and remained silent to give her as much time as she needed.

DUSTIN STEVENS

"No," she finally said, drawing the word out slowly. "Like I said, there was no other man, and we were close. We spoke every day, I was there often, I would have known."

Reed nodded, accepting the information without pressing it. Janine's fingerprints had been found throughout the house, proof that she was telling the truth.

"Besides, why would someone she knew call and then disappear before anybody showed up?"

"You'd be surprised," Reed said, leaning in and resting his forearms on the edge of the table. "Sometimes people find someone who needs help and call it in, but get scared they might be seen as a suspect, so they run off."

Reed paused to let her consider the statement. "Was your mother close with her neighbors? Anybody who might have stopped by and found her?"

"No, I don't think so. If you can believe it, my mother was the young one on the block. I can't imagine anybody being up at that time of night, much less coming inside and finding her in the bedroom."

Reed nodded. There now existed no doubt that the killer had been the one to make the emergency call. He still didn't know why exactly, whether it was a vanity thing or even a middle finger to the police, but he hoped to piece it together in the coming days.

He had to, because despite the reprieve last night, it wasn't likely the killer was done yet. Nobody got away with two seemingly perfect crimes on seemingly unconnected victims and just walked away.

"You mentioned The Bottoms," Reed said. "Was there anybody who would be considered an enemy? Any bad blood toward your mother, or your family in general?"

This time the veneer was too much to hold back, giving way to big tears. They hung on the undersides of Janine's eyes before streaking down either cheek.

Ignoring his better judgment, Reed reached out and slid the bottom napkin from beneath her drink, extending it toward her.

"Thank you," she whispered, accepting the napkin and running it under her nose. "No, not at all. I'm sure everyone you speak to says this,

96

but my mother was a wonderful person. She taught first grade her entire career, never failed a single student. She sang in the choir at church, bought candy bars from Little Leaguers and cookies from Girl Scouts.

"She had no enemies. I can't imagine why anybody would ever do something like this."

Chapter Twenty-Two

Three hours and a pair of false starts later, Reed pulled up to a house outside Grove City. Less than a mile from the outer belt, he could hear traffic in the distance as he parked at the curb and turned off the engine, the sound of semi-trucks carrying through the still midday air.

The home was like nearly every other one on the street, a small, squat structure with grey vinyl siding and black shutters. An aluminum awning extended out over a concrete porch, a matching carport on the side with a single car in it. The front yard was parched, the limbs on the willow tree out front hanging limp, its leaves wilted.

Reed exited the car and clipped the short lead to Billie's collar. Despite not wanting to put his next interview on the defensive in the slightest, the sun overhead was just too strong, the interior of the car too hot for him to even consider leaving her.

She, like him, was an officer of the law. Despite her appearance, people would just have to accept her.

After Riley's death, Billie had been the perfect pairing for him. She too had lost a partner when her Marine handler in Afghanistan fell victim to an IED. Together they were slowly getting to know one another as they worked out their new arrangement.

While he couldn't speak for Billie, the pairing was therapeutic for

Reed, allowing him to continue working while grieving and attempting to cope in his own way. There was no forced conversation, no having to get used to somebody else's way of doing things.

That didn't mean there wasn't the occasional challenge, moments such as this when having a big dog that resembled a solid black wolf at his side, presented problems a human partner would not. Never had he been forced to consider if Riley should stay behind or come along, not once concerned with how her presence would be taken by a key witness or a close family member.

It was the only trick his police force trainers had failed to teach him, the one thing he had to learn on his own.

Reed did his best to push the thoughts from his head as they came up the driveway together. He walked along the edge of the concrete and allowed Billie to keep pace on the lawn beside it, the dead grass much easier on her feet. Reed reached up to knock on the screen door without ascending the stairs.

The first person to appear on the other side stood no more than 3' tall, her hair a mass of short dreadlocks tied with brightly colored ribbons. She regarded Reed a moment before looking down to Billie, her eyes growing large. "Whoa, big doggie."

A smile crossed Reed's face. "Her name's Billie. What's your name?"

The girl never took her gaze from Billie as she began to twist slowly, her body moving just a few inches in either direction. "Lucy."

"Hi, Lucy. My name's Reed. I'm here to speak to your mommy."

"Okay," Lucy said, continuing to stare at Billie until she broke into giggling before turning and disappearing inside the house.

The smile grew on Reed's face as he watched her go, staring after her as a second person appeared on the other side of the screen. Standing two and a half feet taller than Lucy, she had the same dark skin and large eyes, her hair pulled back into a tight bun behind her head. She wore a pair of running shorts and a tank top, a trio of rubber bands and bracelets around her wrist.

If Reed were to guess, she was on her way out for a run. Had she just gotten back, there was no possible way she would still be dry.

"Ms. Abbott?" Reed asked, looking up at her. He switched Billie's lead to his left hand and reached into his rear pocket with his right, extracting his badge and waving at her. "Detective Reed Mattox, my partner Billie. We spoke on the phone last night."

The woman's eyes darted from Reed to Billie and back again. "You best come on inside. It's too hot to leave the door open for very long."

Her voice bore a weariness, and a wariness, that Reed recognized immediately, both very common reactions to police presence, each heightened given the situation.

"Thank you," Reed said, walking in tandem with Billie up the two front steps and entering the house. The temperature dropped as they did so, the bright light from the outside world extinguished as the door closed behind them.

Reed made no attempt to move for a moment, allowing his eyes to adjust, the space around him slowly coming into focus.

The home was much more modern than either of those he'd been in over the previous days, more so than his farmhouse as well. The open floor plan, contemporary furnishings, and trendy paint colors reminded Reed of homes he'd seen on HGTV. The plasma television hanging above a gas fireplace and an assortment of family photos lining the mantle gave it just enough of a lived-in feeling.

"Down," Reed said, watching as Billie dropped to her stomach on the square of white tile he now stood on. "Apologies, I don't usually bring her inside like this, but it's just too hot to leave her in the car."

Circling around in front of him, Abbott took a seat in one of the chairs, motioning for him to do the same across from her. "That's alright. Truth is, I don't know that I could trust a man who would leave a dog locked up on a day like this."

Reed's cheeks flushed. Perhaps his concerns earlier were nothing more than his own insecurities.

"Ms. Abbott," he began, only to stop as a hand shot up in front of him.

"Mae," she said. "Ms. Abbott is my mother-in-law."

"Okay, Mae," Reed said. "I know you must be busy, but I wanted to stop by and speak to you about..."

Again, he was cut off by a raised hand. Pulling herself up from the couch, Mae bent at the waist so she could see through the open doorway behind her and into the kitchen. "Lucy, honey, can you go play in your room for a few minutes while I talk to the nice policeman?"

There was no vocal response, just the sound of tiny feet pounding against the floor as Lucy did as she was told. A moment later a door could be heard closing somewhere in the back of the house, followed by Mae returning to her seat.

"Sorry, my husband and I still haven't told her what happened yet," she said almost as an apology, brushing both hands back over his face.

Reed nodded. The girl looked to be no older than three. Trying to explain to her that she would never see her grandmother again would not be an easy conversation.

Again, as with Janine Rosen, he wanted to offer kind words about a woman he never met, but decided to get straight to the heart of the matter, letting the family know he was committed to finding whoever had done such a vile thing.

"Mae, there is no way easy to ask this, but I have to be thorough, so I will get it out of the way right now," Reed said. "Did your mother ever give any indication whatsoever that she might be a risk to commit suicide?"

There was no outward sign of sorrow, a sour look crossing Mae Abbott's features. "None. My mother was an upright Christian woman who believed what the Bible says about suicide."

Having attended church no more than a handful of times in his life, almost all of them on Christmas or Easter, Reed wasn't exactly sure what the Bible said. He could infer from the look on her face and the tone of her voice though that it was ardently against it.

The sour look remained as she looked past him out through the front window. "These were her gravy years. That's what she always called them. After my father split when I was just a baby, she raised me on her own. Worked two jobs, never complained, I'm sure you've heard the story by now."

Reed hadn't, but he nodded along just the same.

"This was her time to take it easy. She had gotten a settlement from a car accident a while back, didn't have to worry about money anymore.

Her only job was to be a grandmother, and she loved it. Was over here all the time."

Tears came to her eyes as she snapped her focus back to Reed, the first sign of any emotion she had shown, besides the anger at the senseless crime and the loss her family would feel. "Already Lucy's starting to ask when her grandma's coming to visit. What am I supposed to tell that little girl? What am I going to say?"

The questions were clearly rhetorical, but that didn't stop Reed from wishing he had some answer to give her. Most likely anything he offered would only raise her ire, adding to the venom she felt over the loss of her mother.

If the job had taught Reed anything through the years, it was that every person grieved differently. What Mae Abbott was doing now was no better than what Janine Rosen was doing, no better than what he had gone through six months prior.

"You mentioned a settlement," Reed said. "Is there anybody who knew about it? Might stand to gain from it?"

The question further penetrated Mae's exterior, her features shifting as she pondered the question. "No. It wasn't a huge deal, an off-the-books thing with a car rental company for renting her something with bad brakes. The money wasn't that much, but her house is paid for, and she had some savings back from years of putting in double duty.

"It's not like she was living high on the hog, but she had more than enough to get by."

Reed nodded. It was the first he had heard of the settlement, though if it was handled out of court, there wouldn't be a record of it.

"Anything else? Any bad blood with someone? Anyone in the neighborhood have reason to do something like this?"

"Ha!" Mae said, spitting the word out, irony dripping from the single syllable. "My mother was loved on that street. Everybody knew if they were gone, they could ask her to keep an eye on things. If anybody was sick, she made them a pie or casserole and took it down."

She stared at Reed in silence before shaking her head and sighing deeply.

"Listen, you seem like a nice enough man, and you coming here today shows you're actually taking this seriously. I appreciate that, and I wish I could help you more.

"Fact is, though, if you're looking for some underlying reason as to why this happened, I'm sorry, but I can't help you. I've been up the last two days trying to find a reason why the hell anybody would want to harm her, and I haven't come up with one yet."

Leaning forward, her elbows resting on her knees, she stared down at the floor, the whites of her eyes again growing red, moisture apparent.

"I think that's why I'm still so damn mad about it. The whole thing just doesn't make a lick of sense."

Chapter Twenty-Three

The Good Son's first thought was to feign sickness, saying that he had a stomach bug and that he needed to head home for the afternoon. The notion had passed just as quickly as it arrived though, replaced by the realization that nobody would believe it. Every last person he worked with knew he would never dream of calling in sick. Even on days when he truly was deathly ill, when the welfare of everyone else around him would be better served by his absence, he showed up.

The worst part was that The Good Son would never be able to play it convincingly. Even with everything else going on, his guilt would be too much.

Fortunately for him, he didn't need to go that route. By being the one to open for the morning, he only had to make it to mid-afternoon before being cut loose. On most occasions he would stick around, drawing an hour or two of overtime pay, but this day he had hit the door running.

Even his mother, who believed a spare dollar should never be left behind, would not be able to argue with his reasoning.

The V8 engine on his truck rumbled slightly as The Good Son pulled away from his spot in the back row and headed out. In the nine hours since arriving, the sun had shifted overhead, pushing the shade provided by the pin oak tree away from his truck. Left to bake in the afternoon heat, the cab was stifling. Combined with the heightened sense of anxiety passing through him, his skin was bathed in a film of sweat, dripping from his chin.

The Good Son barely noticed as he drove away from the store, recalling the address from memory. He didn't know the exact location of the place, had only seen the name of the road in passing, but knew the area well enough to know where to start looking. From there it was only a matter of time, having the patience to start at one end and keep going until he found his destination.

Despite the events of the last few nights, patience was something The Good Son had in spades. His mother would never believe him, but it had been patience that allowed him to pick both Esther Rosen and Ira Soto. It was patience that allowed him to do the necessary reconnaissance to get in and out undetected.

Patience all those long nights on the internet determining the exact way to do what he needed to do.

It was that same patience that now removed any qualms he felt about leaving a few hours of overtime on the table. He had a second job, a far more important job to do, and he needed the time and freedom to do it properly.

Coming up on the street, The Good Son hooked a left and eased through the intersection. He kept his foot pressed down just enough on the gas to not arouse suspicion, leaning forward and resting both fore- arms across the steering wheel, his entire focus aimed on the residences filing by on either side.

The Good Son's lips moved imperceptibly as he whispered the number he was looking for over and over again. Blotches of shadows passed over his truck as he rolled on, the brittle leaves of sycamore and poplar trees hanging out over the street.

Once upon a time, The Good Son imagined himself living on a street like this. The kind of place where neighborhood children played ball until dark, and families got together to have barbecues. Where neighbors checked on each other, made sure everybody was taken care of.

For years The Good Son had harbored such dreams, staring in longing at the homes on the other side of the line separating Franklinton from the surrounding areas. At least once a week he had asked when they too could join the lucky ones, just a couple miles away in conventional measurements but on a different planet compared to the place he called home.

Every time the answer was much the same, a caustic remark about the costs of raising a child, until one day a sharp backhand stopped him from ever asking again.

Sliding past a cross street, The Good Son saw the numbers on the mailboxes running steadily downward and again eased his foot off the gas. His pulse began to rise as he continued inching forward, the number growing ever closer, before coming into view.

The third house from the corner was a two story Cape Cod, the outside green, the shutters dark red. Flower boxes underlined the windows and fresh lines crossed the front yard, a mower having passed over the dead grass in recent days.

The Good Son took all of this in with a few quick glances before his gaze settled on the driveway. The garage door was up as he eased past, a familiar car parked inside. Beside it was an empty space, a few scattered objects strewn about.

As many times as possible The Good Son glanced over, gathering every bit of information he could. In the coming hours he had much to do, but this would provide him with a decent place to begin.

Twice he had failed already.

Time was becoming too precious for there to be a third.

Chapter Twenty-Four

The day had turned out to be much hotter than Reed anticipated. By mid-afternoon he ran out of the water he had packed, resorting to stopping by a mini-mart to resupply. While there he had succumbed to the liter-sized bottles of Mountain Dew lining one of the coolers as well, the combined effects of sleep deprivation and encroaching dehydration causing his eyelids to droop.

Parked on the back edge of the precinct parking lot, Reed let Billie roam free of her lead. She had wandered the lawn for a few minutes, relieving herself to mark her territory, before joining him alongside the car and drinking down a bottle of water. In all that time Reed managed to make it through less than half of his own drink, hoping that 16 ounces of caffeine-infused carbonation would be enough to get him through the rest of the evening.

He only prayed his day would end there without them being called out into the night again.

More than a day had passed since his previous meeting with Grimes, though he didn't have a whole lot more to share. The thought pulled his stomach into a tight ball as he led Billie up to the front door and stepped inside, the building mercifully cool.

Unlike their previous visits, a small staff was still on hand, desk lamps on, shirt sleeves rolled up. A few glanced up as Reed and Billie passed by, their gazes lingering longer than necessary, a response Reed suspected might never change.

He was the new guy. His partner was a dog. His former partner was killed.

Whatever the reason for the looks, there appeared to be no sign of them going away anytime soon.

The door to the captain's office was closed as he arrived. The light was on inside, and he could make out several shapes through the frosted window, hear muffled voices on the opposite side. Settling himself into a chair along the opposite wall, he ordered Billie down beside him.

There they remained, both motionless, for the better part of five minutes before the door burst open. Reed looked up at the sound of it to see a pair of detectives emerge, neither one looking especially pleased.

The first one through the door was Pete Iaconelli, a senior detective in the precinct. Weighing north of 250 pounds, it was obvious the heat was getting to him, heavy sweat marking the underarms of his polyester button-down. His khaki slacks were wrinkled and dotted with stains of various origin.

One of the very first things he had ever said to Reed was that he was less than nine months away from retirement, and at the moment Reed got the impression that day couldn't come too soon.

Behind him stood his partner Martin Bishop, a harsh contrast in every way. Regardless what the calendar said, his skin was albino-white and his hair was buzzed short. Weighing far less than Iaconelli, he managed to stretch it over an additional six inches of height, the results giving him a gaunt and hollow appearance.

As self-appointed ringleaders of the old guard in the precinct, the pair had given Reed an especially hard time when he first came over. They had seized on the passing of Riley and his pairing with Billie to poke fun at his ability as a cop, even dubbing him Ace Ventura for the first few months.

The abuse had been enough to leave both sides with a certain amount of wariness, even after a case had required them to work together. No longer was there any overt hostility, thought the atmosphere still settled somewhere close to begrudging collegiality.

"Gentlemen," Reed said, reading their body language to mean they weren't especially pleased with whatever just happened.

"Mattox," Iaconelli replied. He paused less than a second before moving on, passing through the double doors and into the front part of the station.

"Detectives," Bishop said, glancing down to Billie before looking to Reed. "Heard you're working the Night Stalker case."

Reed wasn't aware the moniker had become official, hating everything about the archaic term, but he let it go. It was well known around the precinct who was the good cop and who was the bad cop in the Iaconelli-Bishop pairing. If the taller man was willing to take a moment and attempt professional decorum, he would certainly do the same.

Especially standing outside the captain's door.

"We are," Reed said, nodding. "So far a lot more questions than answers, but we're working the process. Just have to hope another one doesn't turn up before we get there."

Bishop nodded, remaining silent.

"How about you guys?" Reed asked. "The Bottoms keeping you busy?"

"Oh yeah," Bishop said, drawing it out. "Just got handed another one in there. Damn drop off."

At the end of the hall the double doors cracked open, Iaconelli on the other side. He said nothing, simply glaring at his partner, before allowing the doors to swing shut again.

Not one word had been said. It didn't have to be.

"Well, good luck with the Night Stalker," Bishop said. "Let us know if you need anything."

He was already drifting away as he said it, passing through the doors before Reed had a chance to respond. Staring in his wake, Reed smirked before rising from the chair.

"Come," he said, drawing Billie up beside him as he knocked against the outside of the doorframe.

"Yeah," Grimes said, seated behind his desk with his fingers laced.

He looked directly at Reed, as if he'd been listening to every word of the exchange, waiting only for his next appointment to enter.

"Captain," Reed said, sliding into a chair. "Down."

Billie resumed her position at his feet as Reed looked across the desk at Grimes. He appeared to be no happier than Iaconelli had been a moment before, his resting face a heavy frown.

"That bad, huh?" Reed asked. He kept any trace of inflection from his voice.

Grimes turned his chair and stared out through his office window into the parking lot, watching as Iaconelli and Bishop left, Iaconelli's arms flapping about as they went.

"What do you think he's out there saying right now?" Grimes asked, his voice making it clear who he was referring to and how much he didn't appreciate it.

Glancing to the side, Reed considered making a crack about how he was probably praising the captain and his decision to give them the case.

Instead, prudence won out.

"How bad?" Reed asked.

"Bad," Grimes said. "Less than an hour ago a woman was dropped off at the Franklinton Memorial Hospital. No ID, no nothing. Somebody had taken a bat or a pipe or some such object to her head and dropped her off outside."

"Damn," Reed whispered, his face crinkling. "She going to make it?"

"Sure," Grimes said, turning back to look at him, "just as long as the family is willing to keep her on life support."

Reed winced, "Damn."

The reason Iaconelli was so hostile was now clear. Less than an hour from the end of his shift, just months from the end of his career, he was being handed a case that prior experience would prove is almost unsolvable.

Nobody liked being handed a losing ticket, especially with so little time left.

"It's not like I wanted to hand this one their way," Grimes said. "That man bitches enough that I would rather give it to just about anybody else. Fact is, you're my floater, and you're a little tied up at the moment. That means it goes to the next in the rotation, which is them.

"Either I hand it their way and listen to him bitch, or I break protocol and have the union reps down on my ass."

It was obvious the captain was venting, but Reed let him go ahead anyway. He nodded, fully aware of the inner-precinct politics that colored every law enforcement house in the country.

Handling situations like these was why Grimes was the captain, and a pretty astute one at that.

The look of hostility ebbed just slightly as Grimes swallowed down whatever else he was thinking, pushing his attention back to Reed. "So tell me you've got some good news."

"I had McMichaels and Jacobs canvas the neighborhoods for both victims. All they managed to pull was a few people noticed a silver car, though no definitive make and model or, better yet, a license plate."

He skipped over the part about giving them both a good chunk of overtime, hoping the captain wouldn't have any objections to it.

"I stopped by the Buckeye Gas-and-Go a few blocks from Soto's place this morning. It's the only business in the area and I was hoping maybe their cameras could have gotten a glimpse of a silver car in the right time frame, but they aren't even hooked up."

Reed watched an additional fold of skin appear at the underside of Grimes's neck as he drew it back into his chest a little further.

"I spoke to Janine Rosen and Mae Abbott, the daughters of our respective victims, today. Neither one could think of any person who would want to harm their mothers or any reason why someone would even dream of it."

"Does reality match, or are they looking through rose tinted glasses?"

Reed knew what the captain was alluding to, the kind of thing every cop had seen 100 times before. No family member ever wanted to believe a victim might have a shady underbelly, scrubbing away even the most obvious shortcomings to jibe with some inner image they had of the person.

In The Bottoms, such things were commonplace, despite obvious indicators. More than once Reed had seen someone with known gang affiliation, carrying drugs on their person, killed, only to have a grieving mother later swear they were salt of the earth.

"Seems legit," Reed said. "Both lived on the outskirts of Franklinton, out where the neighborhoods are lower class but still a long way from the worst of The Bottoms. Esther Rosen was a school teacher, faithful to one man her whole life. Ira Soto was a single mother who worked two jobs, now lived as a full-time grandmother."

There was no outward reaction of any kind from Grimes, which usually meant he wasn't pleased.

"Any whiff of the media yet?" Reed asked, hating to ask the question but knowing he had to anyway. It was better for him to know how much pressure he might soon be facing and where it was coming from than to pretend it didn't exist.

"Not yet, but I have a feeling the case I just handed off will catch a few people's attention. Once their attention is aimed our way..."

He let his voice trail off, not needing to finish the thought. "What's your next step?"

"Mae Abbott mentioned a father who split when she was a baby. I'll follow up on that, make sure he's still gone, then circle back on what I have. The crime scenes, the bodies, start digging through the files and see if anything similar has happened in the area before."

It was one of the first things every officer learned at the academy, step two in any investigation, following only the crime scene itself, whether the offense was a murder, a robbery, or anything in between.

"Work the victims," Grimes said.

"Work the victims," Reed agreed.

Chapter Twenty-Five

Two opposing emotions fought for top billing in The Good Son's mind. The first was concern, worry that despite his best efforts, despite taking every precaution he could imagine, somewhere along the line he had messed up. Left a fingerprint behind, allowed a camera to get a look at his face, done something that would trip him up.

Thus far, he had been careful, but he had also been lucky. Neither of the previous victims had fought back in the slightest or presented any unforeseen obstacles. Both had been extremely low-visibility, limiting his chances of being spotted.

Even the phone calls, carefully planned and carried out, brought with them virtually no chance at detection.

This time was different. The target lived in a better area, on a street where people were out and about. As best he could tell, nobody had spotted anything, but that didn't mean someone wasn't sitting on their front porch watching the whole thing through the screen of their cell phone, seeing his every movement.

The concern was real, very much present, but for the first time in days it wasn't the predominant thing he felt deep within. In its place was something foreign.

Something vaguely resembling hope.

He had pulled it off. The first two incidents were failures because he had tried to do too much. His scrupulous internet research had provided ideas and measures that were beyond his capabilities. This time he had reigned himself in. He had stuck to what he was good at, using a quick strike and a surefire method.

It had worked.

This was the break they needed.

The elation had him walking high on the balls of his feet, each step feeling like he was floating. It carried him from the garage to the house, pushing him through the back door without even pausing to remove his shoes. A smile crossed his face as he stepped into the living room, a renewed sense of purpose pulsating through him.

His mother would be pleased. She had to be. He had done what was asked of him. They could move on. It was all soon to be over.

Every bad thing he did would be nothing more than a distant memory.

"What are you so damn happy about?" she snapped as he entered, her body still twisted up on the sofa. Despite her obvious discomfort, she appeared to have moved no more than a few inches from that morning, no more than a few feet over the previous week combined.

The Good Son stared at her, feeling the smile recede from his features. "You don't know?"

"Know what?" she said. "Know that this is the second night in a row my son's been home late to make dinner?"

Venturing a step into the room, his stomach clenched tight. All elation bled away, replaced instead by dread.

It had worked. There was no doubt it had worked. He had checked her before making the drop. She was less than 100 yards away when he left her. Nobody, not even the idiots at Franklinton Memorial, could have messed it up.

"They haven't called yet?" he asked, his voice receding to a whisper.

At the sound of it, the usual venom faded from his mother's face, her gaze shifting before realization seemed to set in.

"You do love your mama," she whispered.

"Of course," he replied. "So very much."

Her lips parted a fraction of an inch, her face growing a touch more pale. "And you did it?"

"I did. Again."

All feeling seemed to recede from his lower half as he walked on numb legs and fell into his chair. Without consulting her, he took up the remote and changed the channel, in search of the local news.

It would be there. It had to be. It would prove to her that he was successful, that he had done as she asked, that soon everything would be okay.

"They'll call, right?" he asked, trying to control his nervous energy.

Rolling onto a shoulder, his mother looked up at him. "You're sure you did it? You blew the first two."

"No, Mama, I swear. Just like I promised you."

After his second pass through the channels, The Good Son gave up on the television. He glanced at the old-fashioned clock hanging on the wall, telling him it was still just after 8:00. The next round of news wouldn't be on for another couple of hours, leaving them both in suspense.

It had to be on there. A person being beaten and dropped off outside a hospital was too big to be ignored. That's part of why he had chosen to do so during the day this time, so it wouldn't get swept away like the previous nights, and he could monitor things.

"They will call, right?" he asked again.

He needed this to happen. He needed to prove to her that he could be trusted. That he had done everything she asked and then some.

"I'm sure they will," she whispered, extending her hand over the side of the couch, The Good Son grasping it in both of his.

"They have to," he said, feeling her clammy skin against his palm. "I did everything right. They have to."

Chapter Twenty-Six

The Good Son woke with a start. One moment he was immersed in a dream, more of a memory really, of a better time. He was just a child, no more than 10, running around the park in a pair of cut-off jeans and bare feet. His parents, both of them young and happy, were sitting on a blanket nearby.

The next moment he was awake in the chair, his body contorted to the side, his hip and lower back both aching from being cramped in an unnatural position. A line of dried saliva extended down from the corner of his mouth.

The light of day had receded, nothing visible against the blinds hanging down over the windows.

The television was off, his mother sitting up for the first time in days. She watched him wake without a response of any kind, impassive as he rubbed his eyes and passed the back of his hand over his cheek.

"Morning," she said, her voice completely monotone.

"Morning," The Good Son managed. He shifted to sit flat on the chair and laced his fingers together, extending his upper body out in front of him. The bunched up muscles of his body tugged in protest, a series of pops coming from various locations. "What time is it?"

"Morning," she repeated, her empty gaze still on him.

Releasing his stretch, The Good Son looked at her, startled by how different she now appeared from the image he'd had in his dream. Just 15 years or so had gone by according to the calendar, but to see her in person, it would appear that more than twice that had passed. All color was gone from her skin, her body pale. Any extra few pounds she might have once carried had been sucked away, leaving her looking almost skeletal.

"Morning," The Good Son whispered. His eyes slid closed and his head hung, realization setting in. "They never called."

"Oh, they called alright," his mother responded. This time there was a trace of something more in her tone. It wasn't humor or optimism, but something that concerned The Good Son even more.

Sarcasm.

"They called?" he asked, his eyes opening to look at her.

"Yup," she said. "They called Nancy Underwood. She was taken in last night. Far as I know, everything was a success."

The Good Son had no words. His stomach bunched tight, his pulse quickened, his throat went dry. He opened his mouth once, twice, to speak, but couldn't muster anything.

This was not how it was supposed to have gone. He was the one who had taken the risks, had put in the planning, had been meticulous in making sure everything went off without a hitch.

He was the one bearing the weight of the heinous acts he had committed.

The fruits of all that should not have gone to Nancy Underwood. Or any of the others. He did the work. It should be his family who benefited from it.

"Freddie called this morning to tell me *the good news*," she said, putting heavy emphasis on the last three words. "Apparently the whole gang - everybody who's able to anyway - is going over once she gets out to congratulate her. You believe that shit?"

The Good Son said nothing. He couldn't believe a word he was hearing, could feel the room beginning to tilt on its side. His chest struggled to pull in air.

He and his mother had discussed it. They had thought of every angle, looked into every eventuality. They both knew he didn't want to do it, but if he did, things would be better. All his effort, his struggles, the horrible images he saw as he tried to fall asleep, was supposed to mean something.

And that something damned sure wasn't supposed to be this.

"How?" he whispered, his voice sounding timid and far away, like it was coming from someone else.

His mother shrugged, her thin lips resembling a snarl on her face. "I guess she took a turn. Just yesterday they bumped her up."

Dropping his gaze, The Good Son stared at the floor. The last three days had drained him. Not only physically, the heat and lack of sleep beginning to take their toll, but mentally and emotionally as well.

He was not one for hate. He did not believe in random acts of violence, no matter what growing up near The Bottoms might have tried to instill in him. The things he had been forced to do went far beyond anything he would have ever thought possible, but he did them with a noble purpose in mind.

He wasn't taking life, he was saving it.

"Do you love your mama?"

The question ripped him from his thoughts. His gaze jerked up to her, accompanied by the familiar sense of dread the question always called up inside of him.

"You know I do."

"And you'd do anything for her?"

Blood flushed The Good Son's cheeks. For the first time in ages he felt the urge to cry, pulling in a long breath, forcing himself not to show such vulnerability.

It would only make what she was about to say worse.

"You know I would," he whispered.

A smile stretched across her face. "Good, because there's a way we can fix this."

Chapter Twenty-Seven

Just 13 hours had passed since the meeting with Grimes, but already Reed felt like a new man.

After speaking with the captain the night before, he had made one more trip through the files before calling it a night. On the way home he had stopped by Old Smoque Barbecue and gotten two pulled pork sandwiches and a half dozen sausage links, bringing it all straight to the couch where he and Billie both indulged themselves. Once they had eaten, it didn't take but a few minutes of a preseason game on ESPN for their respective body clocks to finally catch up with them, exhaustion pulling them under.

At 8:30 it was still light outside, but Reed didn't care. He allowed himself to drift past REM sleep and into a deep slumber, not to move for nearly nine hours.

The food and rest rejuvenated him immeasurably, waking well before the dawn. He padded into the kitchen to find Billie awake as well, staring at him from beneath the table.

"You up for some exercise before it gets too hot?"

It took only a split second for the question to register with Billie before she was up across the hardwood floor, her toenails clacking as she fought for purchase. Once her feet were under her, she bounded across the kitchen and out through the back door, disappearing into the darkened morning, nothing more than a bolt of black fur.

Miles from the closest neighbor, Reed didn't bother to dress as he stepped out onto the deck, the aging pine boards rough against the soles of his bare feet. Morning dew clung to the surface of everything, the air having a clean, damp scent to it that he hadn't noticed in weeks.

In less than two hours it would all be gone, burned off with the start of another steamy day, but for a time all was right with the world.

Every few minutes an inky blur flashed across the back yard, darting between pine trees, their heavily laden limbs dragging the ground. Whatever Billie was after, she kept up the chase for more than a quarter hour before giving in and making her way back to the deck, her pink tongue the only splash of color as she trotted forward.

"You good?" Reed asked, turning to watch her move right past him and into the kitchen. A wry smile formed as he followed her in, both of them standing under a cool shower together before eating and heading into the precinct.

More than two hours later the memory of the rare break from the job, a brief interlude into normality, still buoyed Reed's spirits. It gave him a glimmer of optimism as he went at the case, intent to pull on the few loose threads he still had before creating new ones if he must.

The first thing he had to follow up on was the disappearance of Mae Abbott's father. She had alluded to his leaving when she was only a baby, and at best guess Reed pegged her somewhere in her late 20s.

The search started with a check through the area hospital records for the name Mae Soto. When that yielded nothing, he made the assumption that at the time she was probably born under her father's name.

Having no idea what that was, he ran a search for Ira Soto, finding an admission receipt for her from 1988. Doing the math in his head, Reed figured that would put Mae at 27-years-old.

Maybe a year or so younger than he suspected, but overall pretty much in line with the person he had met the previous day.

Drawing up the admission receipt to full screen, Reed scanned through it quickly, finding that Ira Soto had been admitted on May 17th at 9:35 in the evening. She had not given birth until the morning of the 18th and was discharged first thing on the 19th. There had been no health insurance for the service and the hospital had ended up writing off a large portion of the bill to uncompensated care.

Reed nodded, everything about the receipt, from the inability to pay to the origin of Mae's name, all fitting with what she had told him. Armed with a first name and a date, he went back into the search and was able to pull a record for Mae Lynn Bester, daughter of Ira Soto and Darian Bester.

"Darian Bester," Reed whispered. He flipped open the crime scene file from Soto's home and scribbled the name across the bottom of Earl's Post-It note, underlining it twice before dropping his pen and going back to work.

The first place he began was the national databases, both run by the FBI. In order he entered Bester's name into ViCAP – the Violent Criminal Apprehension Program – and NCIC, the National Crime Information Center. Each served as national repositories for the names of perpetrators of all violent or heinous crimes, a definition which encompassed everything from serial killers to white collar embezzlers.

When neither one turned up anything, Reed shifted his attention to the local files, finding only a citation for truancy and a speeding ticket, both from the mid-80's. In each instance the fine had been paid, albeit late.

The information added to the preliminary picture Reed was already beginning to have of the man. He wasn't a criminal, wasn't prone to violent acts, he was merely lazy, and most likely had a hard time holding onto a job. It would explain the delinquencies in paying the fines and offer the most viable explanation for why he had cut out on Mae and her mother.

As much as Reed hated typecasting, knowing it could be a very dangerous practice for a detective, there was also a reason stereotypes existed.

Reed had been fortunate enough to have two active, loving parents, but he only had to look as far as Riley to know that was very often not the case.

Knowing what the odds were that Bester suddenly found the straight and narrow after walking out on Mae and her mother, Reed opened up a broader search. Using property records, he wasn't able to identify a single Darian Bester in the country.

The same was true for income tax reporting.

Either he had become a ghost, or the original supposition was growing stronger by the moment, the man staying well below the grid, holding odd jobs or none at all, reporting none of the income to the government or the mother of his child who might want some support.

Exiting all official databases, Reed pulled up a basic internet search engine and went to work. He started with just Bester's name, adding in bits and pieces of information he found as various websites came up.

In total there were only four Darian Bester's in the country. Two of them were Caucasian, something that Mae Abbott was definitely not, not even by a factor of 50%.

Of the other two, one was a 22-year-old student at South Florida University.

The last was killed in a car accident in Albuquerque in 2004.

The article describing the incident was very specific, citing that Darian Bester's vehicle was hit by an oncoming train when he ignored warning lights and bells and tried to jump the track. The train clipped the back half of his truck, cleaving the bed free from it, and sending the front end hurtling. The cab flipped three times before coming to a stop, the lone occupant dead before authorities arrived on the scene.

Blood alcohol analysis showed him to be operating at more than double the legal limit.

He was 40-years-old at the time of death.

"That sounds like our guy," Reed said with a heavy sigh. He leaned back in his chair and glanced down to Billie, her head tilted to stare up at him.

Looking into Bester had been a long shot, but it was still something Reed was hoping would pan out. At the moment it was the last concrete lead he had.

More than once he had solved a case working with less, but he knew it would get infinitely more difficult.

Reed and Billie were still locked in the gaze as Reed's phone began to vibrate on his hip. Reclining in his chair, he raised his backside and dug the phone out, staring at the name displayed on the screen.

DISPATCH.

His brows pulled together as he kept the phone in his hand, choosing to rise from his seat instead of taking the call. "Come," he said, both moving through the maze of desks as the phone fell silent in his hand.

They passed through the foyer at the top of the stairs and into the open space on the opposite side, Reed wagging the phone in his hand at the dispatcher seated there.

Unlike Jackie, the operator working the desk during the day was a man just past 50. Only a few wisps of blond hair remained on his head, all of them pushed to the side, his thin form nearly swallowed by the uniform he wore. In the last six months Reed had yet to have a conversation with him that lasted more than a minute, the man's social skills on par with the chair he sat in.

"Hey, Lou," Reed said, drawing the man's attention his way. He waved the phone once more for Lou to see before pocketing it. "What's up?"

Just hours into his day, Lou bore the look of a man who had already had a few drinks, or was in dire need of one. His skin shined beneath the overhead lights, his shoulders slumping into his work station.

"Oh, thank God," he said. "After you, my next call was going to Iaconelli and Bishop."

Reed let the statement go, remembering the show the detectives had put on in front of Grimes the day before.

"What's up?" Reed repeated.

"A body was found over at the Overland Dog Park on Upton," Lou said. "Responding officers just arrived, called it in."

Reed nodded. He knew that summer was vacation season and that the detective staff was stretched thin. He also knew that he was the cover guy, and that meant taking on more than a single case at a time, no matter how important that one case may be.

Besides, the fact was, he could use a change of pace for a few hours to clear his head. He was out of things to do on the strangling case for the time being, the one thing that would help him most being something he absolutely did not want.

"Who made the call?" Reed asked.

"Greene and Gilchrist."

"Tell them I'm on my way."

Chapter Twenty-Eight

Reed knew there was no real difference about who called in a crime. As a detective, he showed up regardless of who made the request. He was also human though, and that meant there were some people he preferred working with more than others.

McMichaels and Jacobs he liked because they were both young and good natured, knowing how to intersperse the tense moments with occasional bursts of levity. Those things mattered when working a crime scene into the wee morning hours.

It also mattered that neither one of them had ever said a foul word about his partner.

Joining them at the top of the list for preferred workmates were Derek Greene and Adam Glichrist.

Pulling up along the curb outside the dog park, Reed slid to a stop behind their blue-and-white cruiser. In front of them a van was already on the scene, Earl and his team no doubt somewhere nearby. The bright morning sun glinted off the front of both vehicles, drawing the full attention of every passerby on the street.

Slumped behind the wheel, Reed sat without turning off the ignition or attempting to climb out. Compared to the scenes he was usually called to, everything felt just a bit off. Operating under full daylight bathed everything in a harsh glow, highlighting all the inconsistencies, doing nothing for the blemishes the darkness was usually kind enough to hide.

On the opposite side of the street, he could see people walking by, some with the social grace to be pretending to walk a dog, most not bothering with the charade. They shuffled along or came to a complete stop and outright stared, no regard for anything beyond their own curiosity.

In Reed's experience, for all the good it did in keeping people out, there was nothing like yellow crime scene tape to bring out the public in mass. While just two inches in width, capable of stopping absolutely nothing, it drew curious stares by the thousands. Within an hour the curb would be lined with onlookers, many with their hands extended at arm's length, cell phone cameras recording everything.

Thankfully for him, both the Rosen and Soto murder scenes had been wrapped by the time the sun came up, otherwise he would have been staring at himself on the morning news.

"You ready?" Reed asked, casting a glance over his shoulder to Billie in the backseat.

The adrenaline of the morning run was long gone, her body poised and ready to be moving again. She remained standing upright as he clipped the short lead to her collar and let her down, both ducking under the yellow tape stretched across the entrance.

The park, as it were, consisted of nothing more than a grassy expanse roughly the size of a football field. On one end was a series of metal objects fitted into the ground, at one point the makings of an obedience training course. Time and vandalism had stripped away anything that wasn't cast iron, a layer of graffiti covering most of what was left.

A chain link fence encircled the grounds, the metal just beginning to oxidize and turn brown. Tufts of grass stuck up at odd intervals along the bottom.

Along the back half of the park was a small cluster of people, Greene and Gilchrist along with a trio of criminalists. The two groups stood in sharp contrast to one another as they moved about, the officers in black uniforms with short sleeves, the techs in white paper suits covering most of their body.

The attention of all five was aimed at the ground, a bright red smudge standing out against the scorched lawn. Several thoughts and observations sprang to Reed's mind as he approached, gently pushing each one aside, waiting until he was briefed before making any conclusions.

Halfway across the lawn one of the techs noticed Reed and Billie approaching, prompting the others to look up as well. Just as fast the criminalists dismissed him, the two officers stepping back and drifting his way.

Derek Greene was the first to arrive, his hand extended. Reed met the shake, nodding in greeting. "Officer Greene."

"Detective," Greene replied. The same height as Reed, he carried a few extra pounds and half an extra decade, grey hairs starting to show on his head. They stood in contrast to his mocha colored skin, a series of scars around his nose and cheeks most likely from childhood battles with acne or chicken pox.

Reed turned and extended his hand to Gilchrist. "Officer."

"Hey, Reed," the younger man replied. Still in his 20s, he was fresh from the academy, a trainee assigned to a senior officer. He stood a couple of inches taller than Reed and Greene both, still bearing the boyish features and thick hair of someone not nearly as seasoned as his cohorts.

"When did you move to the day shift?" Greene asked, all three watching the techs work.

Reed folded his arms across his chest, the leash in his hand still giving Billie a couple inches of freedom. "We're not. Grimes gave us two other murder cases. We just happened to be on the desk this morning when the call came in."

"Ahh," Greene said. "You drew the short straw."

"More like I saved Lou from having to call Ike and Bishop and tell them they did."

Gilchrist snorted. For the time being only one of the techs was doing much, photographing the body from every feasible angle. Beside him the other two were unpacking hard plastic cases, their tools glistening under the morning sun.

Chancing a couple of steps forward, Reed rose onto his toes and peered down at the victim. It was a male with brown hair, his body painfully thin, veins and bones obvious beneath his skin. Based on clothing and haircut, Reed would put him somewhere in his late 20s to early 30s, though that was purely a guess.

"What have we got here?" Reed asked. Just a few minutes out and already he could feel sweat beginning to form on his scalp, causing it to itch. A trickle of moisture ran down the small of his back.

"Jogger was passing by this morning, saw someone lying out here," Greene said. He delivered the information flat and even, as if reading it from a printout, although he held nothing in his hands. "Thought it was just somebody who had too much to drink and was passed out, but called it in anyway. Said she knew kids liked to play here sometimes."

Reed grunted in acknowledgement. It wasn't the kind of call that came in often in Franklinton, almost never in The Bottoms, but more than once he and Riley had been sent on similar errands.

"We got here about an hour ago," Greene said. "Found the victim lying face down. We tried to roust him, but when he showed no signs of responsiveness we rolled him over."

"Cause?"

"ME hasn't shown up yet, but my guess would be a broken neck," Greene said. "No outward sign of injury, but when we rolled him over, I thought his head was going to slide right off his shoulders."

Again, Reed nodded. It was the kind of statement that fellow officers could say to one another, but would deny if anybody ever claimed to have heard.

Had the situation been reversed, it was the same way he would have described it to them.

"Done here or body dump?" Reed asked. He knew there was no way to know for sure just based on the body, but hoped they had seen something to give an indication.

"Not sure," Greene said, shaking his head just slightly. "With a broken neck..." He let his voice trail off, Reed filling in the gap. "I will say his body was cold when we arrived though. Not yet stiff, but he's been dead a while."

Reed sighed and ran a thumb along his eyebrows, moisture running down into his palm. With a flick of the wrist he cast the drops aside, the feeling of rejuvenation he'd felt that morning falling to the wayside.

Unless he was seriously mistaken, he'd just been handed his second killer in less than a week.

"I don't suppose they were kind enough to leave us with an ID were they?" Reed asked.

At that, Gilchrist took a half step forward, notebook in hand.

"Victim was found with his wallet in the back pocket of his jeans. No ID, but $12 in cash and two hefty gift cards were left untouched."

The information settled into Reed's mind, before it began to fester. The inconsistency of it grew larger, the off-feeling Reed had felt upon pulling up strengthening, before his face contorted itself into a mask of confusion.

"Wait...*what?*"

Chapter Twenty-Nine

The sun was well past its high point by the time Reed finished at the dog park, the majority of the morning spent alternating between making sure Billie was hydrated and watching the criminalists work. For several hours they had pored over the area, searching in vain for any scraps or fibers that might give some clue to the killer's identity.

The closest they were able to find were a few partial footprints from the area around the body. Given the fact that dead grass held a shape long after it should, their best guess was that the killer wore a large shoe, somewhere in the 12-14 range.

Reed was less than optimistic that the finding would hold up in court, if it ever got that far.

Once they were done, the ME had the body taken to the morgue for further examination and autopsy. Maybe in the controlled environment and with aid of scientific tests, something would turn up.

A dog park was not the kind of place where violent crimes occurred. Reed's initial thought that the location looked more like a dump site than anything seemed to be confirmed, the lack of evidence too noticeable to ignore.

Standing out in the heat any longer was a waste of his time. Offering a handshake to both Greene and Gilchrist, Reed left them to scrub the scene. A body had been found there, but nothing else. Keeping the park closed any longer than necessary would only anger the local residents.

Reed led Billie back under the crime scene tape, opened both driver side doors and turned on the engine, blasting the air for a few minutes, allowing the interior to cool before both climbed inside.

The seat still burned the backs of his thighs as he sat. Billie chose to remain standing on the hot plastic seat cover, not even considering lying down just yet.

Keeping the air on high, Reed dropped the windows on either side as he pushed hard back toward the precinct, the movement swirling some of the hot air out, his mind in several different places as he drove.

Somehow in the last four days, a series of random, senseless, seemingly perfect crimes had popped up in their jurisdiction. It was well known that the hottest days of summer tended to bring the worst out in a community, but this was an unprecedented run even for a place like The Bottoms.

Making matters worse was the fact that none of the occurrences had really happened in The Bottoms. They had occurred further out in the surrounding neighborhoods, the portion of the precinct's coverage area where they rarely ever had serious crimes.

Running a hand over his face, Reed wiped away moisture and brushed it onto the passenger seat beside him. Sweat stung his eyes as he pointed the car back toward the station house.

Already he had two unexplainable murders on his plate, the urge to offload this third one tempting. Making another trip to the precinct wasn't high on his priority list for the afternoon, especially after burning more than half a day at the dog park, but he needed to pass along the information he had.

And the allure of soaking in the precinct air conditioning for a few minutes seemed appealing for both him and his partner.

Reed parked in a visitor stall and went straight for the front door. He kept Billie on the short lead as he went, her panting a means of coping with the heat.

For a moment, Reed felt the urge to just stand in the front foyer, close his eyes and raise his face to the ceiling. The air inside was stale, smelled of bad coffee, but it was a full 20 degrees cooler than the sizzling temperature outside.

Right now, that was all that mattered.

The feel of Billie's weight leaning against his leg confirmed that she felt the same way.

Smiling at his partner's reaction, Reed led her to the frosted doors before them, the cool air picking at the perspiration on his skin. For the first time in months goose pimples appeared on his arms, his smile growing a little larger as he stopped outside of Grime's office and knocked twice.

The smile faded in an instant as Grimes looked up from his desk, his scowl in place. His tie was loosened and a pencil was jammed behind his ear, a blizzard of printouts spread before him. "Great," he said as a way of greeting, surmising the reason for the unannounced visit and leaning back in his chair.

He dropped the highlighter in his hand onto the desk, withdrew the pencil from behind his ear and tossed that down as well.

Only once he was reclined in his seat, both hands folded behind his head, did he tell them to enter.

Walking into the room, Reed could tell that the captain had been hard at work on something, strain and frustration plain on his features.

At the same time, he could only imagine what he and Billie must look like. Both were showing the effects of the heat, matted with sweat, dust, and dead grass.

No place on earth abided by the adage *misery loves company* like a police station. If the captain was busting his hump, his detectives better damned sure be as well, or things would get ugly.

Unfortunately for Reed, his appearance was about the only thing he had going for him on this trip.

Knowing better than to even acknowledge whatever the captain was working on, if not to avoid any unintended wrath, then to prevent himself from being assigned something tangential to assist with, Reed said, "Just coming in to give the report on the John Doe found this morning at the Overland Dog Park."

Grimes's mouth twitched slightly, the warning shot for a frown about to arrive. "John Doe?"

"The crime scene guys have his prints," Reed said. "They should be running them any minute now and hopefully have a name for us soon."

"No ID?"

"Damnedest thing I ever saw. They took his ID, but left the cash and a couple of gift cards behind."

"Meaning this was a specific target, not a crime of opportunity."

"Sure looked that way," Reed agreed, nodding. "COD was a broken neck. That seems personal."

"Very," Grimes agreed.

Crimes of opportunity, as the captain alluded to, were often messy. They included grabbing whatever was on hand, usually a club or pipe or some other blunt object. Such crimes involved very little forethought, arising on the fly once a situation presented itself that could be taken advantage of. As a result, both the crime scene and the body itself were generally messy.

Bruises, wounds, and blood were a standard part of the MO.

"And the place was clean," Reed said. "Looked like a pretty clear drop point, but even beyond that, the body was immaculate."

"Damn. Scrubbed?"

"Didn't appear to be. No smell of ammonia or bleach, and the techs didn't mention finding any."

Reed left the statement there. Grimes had been doing this much longer than he had, would know exactly where Reed was going without having to be told.

The look on his face already said he didn't need to hear any more bad news for the day.

Keeping his hands in place, Grimes rotated his chair to look out the window. If he objected to Reed's sedan parked in the front stall, or even noticed it, he said nothing, his gaze fixed on the line of trees in the distance.

"I know this isn't exactly Dublin," he said, "or New Albany, or even Bexley, but damn. In what, four days, we've had four murders?"

Reed was not aware that the assault victim Iaconelli and Bishop were given had passed away, though he remained silent.

"Only two of them seem related and none of the four left behind a damn thing, or even have a suspect at the moment."

Reed knew the captain was only venting, espousing the same exact thoughts he had. This was far beyond anything that could be written off as the heat causing people to do crazy things. The heat made people steal things, get into fights, it escalated crimes of convenience.

It did not suddenly turn suburbanites into vicious killers.

Holding the thought a moment, Reed allowed his mind to work around the edges of it. Deep in the recesses of his brain an idea formed, something so outlandish he couldn't believe he was even thinking it. He glanced up at Grimes, almost afraid to say anything for fear of what the response might be.

"Captain, maybe it's time to bring the media in on this."

Chapter Thirty

There was never a good time to bring in the media. Their presence was such a distraction from the day-to-day operations of the precinct that not once before had Reed considered it until sitting in Grimes's office listening to his boss vent.

Even then, his natural inclination was to dismiss it almost just as fast.

The vast majority of the time, the media was a nuisance. They thrived on the sensational and salacious, twisting facts and misinterpreting cases, using quotes out of context, all for the sole purpose of building ratings, and careers. It was a fact that Reed had learned the hard way years before, content from then on to let Riley handle all such matters.

His strict policy of not speaking to the media had been eased somewhat by a general disinterest in The Bottoms. Everyone knew crimes occurred there, and no one cared. Only once in the preceding six months had he been lead on something that piqued media interest, but in that instance Grimes had handled things personally.

The first reaction Grimes gave to the suggestion was exactly what Reed expected, the same thing he would have done if sitting on the opposite side of the desk.

"You're kidding, right?" Grimes said, snapping his attention back over to him. "That was some piss poor attempt at a joke?"

The look on his face was so intense that for a moment Reed considered trying to play it off as such. "Look, Captain, you just said it yourself. This is a rash of incidents unlike anything we've ever seen before, and we don't have a lot of leads. We'll keep looking, because that's what we do, but right now we're giving it the two-hands-and-a-flashlight treatment."

The interworking of Grimes's thought process played out clearly on his face. For a moment he flashed anger, wanting to snap at Reed for even suggesting such a thing. After that he retreated a tiny bit, registering the merit of the suggestion for the first time. Next came a consideration of the notion, the sour expression relaying that the very idea tasted bitter in his mouth.

Finally, after almost a full minute, came step four, the part where logic won out.

Or at least motivated the man to ask a couple of follow-up questions.

"Why?" His tone, already laced with venom from a long afternoon at his desk, came out more accusatory than Reed knew he intended.

Still, Grimes did nothing to correct it.

Reed's damp t-shirt had been begun to cool off, but he could feel it growing warmer, his body threatening to start sweating again. "It's the last thing you said that keeps rubbing me the wrong way. With both of my cases, and now this one today, we have *nothing* to go on. No evidence, no eyewitnesses, no nothing. You know how rare that is nowadays?"

Aware that he too was beginning to tread dangerously close to venting, Reed backed off. He stopped there, letting the captain fill in blanks, hoping to make this more of a two-way conversation than a request on his part.

To do so would imply that he was sold on the idea, which he decidedly wasn't. He was merely open to the thought of employing a necessary evil to jumpstart their investigations and hopefully stop whatever was going on in Franklinton.

"Damn near impossible," Grimes agreed, begrudgingly, the words coming out slow and pained. He fell silent again, appearing to process what he'd just said, none too happy about it. "What did you have in mind?"

From that point on the topic of bringing in the media went from theoretical to a work in progress, the two batting around ideas for the better part of a half hour. Their initial reaction was to call a press conference, but they agreed that would require too much lead time and include too many competing stations with their own agendas. They needed something small they could control, while at the same time giving the impression they were being clear and forthright.

The idea was to open the gates to useful information, not to get jammed up fielding requests from reporters craving information.

It took over two hours to put everything together. The mutual decision was to bring in Channel 4, the local NBC affiliate with the largest share of the local news viewers. It would not follow the standard protocol, instead having Grimes seated with a single reporter, nothing more than a conversation.

The hope was that the piece would relay sincerity in asking for any information from the public. The goal was not to create a Crimestoppers scenario and have the phones ringing nonstop for the next week, but to solicit genuine feedback.

At least, that was the impression they were looking to create.

In truth, the hope was that pasting the story across the television in such a way would have one of two effects. It would either slow the culprits down, letting them know that more eyes and ears would be on the lookout for them, or it would encourage them to do something foolish.

Either way, the report would put people in Franklinton on alert, making them more aware of their surroundings. Women like Esther Rosen and Ira Soto would not be so easy to gain access to, men like whoever Reed had found that morning would no longer be stumbled upon by a morning jogger.

The more the two kicked around the notion, the more it grew on Reed. His next strategy was to go back to the previous crime scenes and let Billie have a look around, to start really scouring through the backstories of Rosen and Soto. Even at that, the likelihood of finding something new or paradigm shifting was slim.

Speaking with Channel 4 presented the chance for new information to become available without the need for another victim to provide it.

That feeling still held firm as Reed stood outside the interrogation room on the second floor and stared through the one-way glass. On the other side of it was a standard square room, the walls made of concrete block painted slate grey. In the center of the room was a metal table of the same color, a steel ring rising from the center of it in case a prisoner needed to be handcuffed.

Seated in the chair closest to Reed, the back of his uniform coat a solid black, was Grimes. He leaned forward with his elbows resting on the table, his fingers laced in front of him.

Less than three feet away sat Yasmin Leveritt, a well-known local reporter in her mid-30s. She had glossy black hair parted down the middle and a heart shaped face with green eyes. She wore a somber expression as she settled herself into her seat, her attire matching her demeanor. Despite the heat she wore a blue wool suit, pearls visible in either ear and around her neck.

The only other person in the room was the camera operator who worked with Leveritt, a tall, skinny guy who looked like he still belonged in the local high school's A/V department. Standing several inches over 6', he had red hair pulled back into a pony tail and wore a brown fishing vest over a plain white t-shirt. He was crouched down behind the camera as he worked out the perfect angle to capture both people, eventually getting things where he wanted them and offering a thumbs up.

Reed turned on the speakers in the observation room, the sound of Leveritt and Grimes's voices became audible, the volume a bit louder than expected, the sudden blast of sound bringing Billie to her feet in a flash.

"Easy," Reed whispered as he turned the sound down.

"Captain Grimes," Leveritt began, her voice neutral, bordering on solemn, "I understand that there has been a recent outbreak of violence here in the Franklinton area. Is that correct?"

Reed could sense Grimes's shoulders tense, the question deliberately framed to force him to correct her.

"This week there have been incidents that resulted in the loss of four lives," Grimes said, sticking to the script he and Reed had discussed. "Right now our department is working every possible angle, but we would appreciate help from anybody who may have seen anything that would aid our investigation."

Leveritt offered a sympathetic nod. "And is that to say that your department is at a loss right now regarding these incidents?"

Once again Reed could see tension draw Grimes's shoulders together, could almost imagine him trying to keep a dour look from his face. "Not at all. We just felt that with so many crimes occurring in one week, this was the right time to put residents on alert, and to ask for anything that might help us accelerate our investigation."

Chapter Thirty-One

Hot water ran down from the faucet and across the top of The Good's Son hands, washing away a thick mound of suds. In a sequence of practiced moves, he held the dishpan in one hand and the scrub pad in the other, working to extricate every last trace of scum from the bottom of the pan.

His mother would check later, after he'd gone to sleep, just as she always did.

The woman barely had the energy to take herself to the bathroom, but without fail she would drag her body to the kitchen to inspect his handiwork.

The thought was only one more in a series of mixed emotions passing through The Good Son as he stood over the sink. With his shoulders hunched and his gaze aimed down, gravity won out, allowing the tears to fall from his eyes. The thought of his mother inspecting his work, of the things she had asked him to do this week, caused resentment to course through him. His face flushed with blood, made him angry that again she was reducing him to crying.

More than that, though, he couldn't shake the events of that morning. Try as he might to push aside the memory, to chalk it up as nothing more than what he had done to the previous women, it was different.

That man did not need to die. He had done nothing wrong, and more important, he presented no obvious gain. Their situation was exactly the same as it had been 12 hours before, whether his mother wanted to admit it or not.

Left to his own devices, The Good Son would have let the man go. He might have scared him, perhaps even told him to disappear for a while, but he would not have gone through with it.

That would never do, though. The man was too close, was too visible, to ever let him go. The tongue lashing he got over an unclean pan would pale in comparison to what he would hear if he let the man live. No matter what he tried to do to cover it, she would find out, and she would come after him for it, just as she always did.

The encounter had not been like the previous ones. The man was not a stranger, someone who was crept up on in the dark, dispatched before a word could be uttered or a tear shed. Instead, he was sitting at the kitchen table when The Good Son arrived, staring through the screen door as if he had been expecting the visit.

There was no look of surprise as The Good Son entered, no pleas for his life. The man acted almost thankful, the feeling of relief noticeable as The Good Son did what he had to before carrying him to the car and dropping him off at the park.

His original intention was never to leave him lying in the grass, especially so close to the jogging trail, but he just couldn't do it any longer. The remorse, the guilt, the sorrow, that flowed through him each time he glanced into the passenger seat was too much to bear, the man propped up, his body stationary as he reclined against the window.

A week before, The Good Son had never committed a crime in his life. Not once had he swiped a candy bar from the corner gas station, never had he jaywalked or gotten a parking ticket.

Now he was a killer. The others were a means to an end. This man was different. He was a preemptive strike, a move spurned by greed, the look in his mother's eye as she explained it bordering on gleeful.

"That water's not free you know," she called from the living room, the same level of scorn she often employed present in her voice.

The Good Son passed the pan under the faucet a final time, washing the white porcelain clean before turning off the water. His hands were bright pink and stung from the prolonged exposure to heat, sweat continuing to drip from his face as he placed the pan on the drying rack and took up the towel from the counter beside him. He used it to wipe his cheeks before starting in on the dishes beside him, drawing in deep breaths, careful not to let his mother hear a sound.

He knew what it would cause, just as it always did.

"Hey!" she called again. "Get in here, you need to see this."

The Good Son felt his eyelids slide shut as he raised a hand to wipe his nose. He rubbed it along the leg of his jeans as he walked into the living room and pressed a shoulder against the edge of the open doorway.

On the couch, his mother paid him no mind. She was seated upright in the back corner, her attention aimed at the television, her body bathed in the pale glow from the picture tube. Following her gaze, The Good Son focused on the screen, the back of a woman's head in the foreground, a large, black man in a police dress uniform sitting across from her. Looking to be in his late 40s to early 50s, his hair was graying and heavy bags hung under his eyes.

A banner was stretched along the bottom of the screen - Police Seek Information on Franklinton Murders - spelled out in bold letters.

The Good Son felt his jaw drop open as he stared at the screen, the dish towel sliding between his fingers. It fell onto his bare feet, his body not even registering it as he stared in abject horror at the screen.

"Can you turn it up?" he asked, not bothering to look over at his mother. When she ignored his request, he walked across the floor and snatched the remote from the table beside her, using it to raise the volume several notches.

"*In recent years,*" the man on screen said, "*we have made tremendous strides in cleaning up the crime rate here in Franklinton. Until this past week, our numbers were some of the best in the metro area.*"

Pulling in short, choppy breaths, The Good Son shifted his body a few inches to the right. He dropped himself heavily into his chair, his legs too wobbly to support his weight, his back slapping against the faded material as he sat and watched.

The interview lasted no more than four minutes, a telephone number flashing across the screen at the conclusion inviting viewers to call with any information they might have. From there it cut to a commercial, The Good Son lowering the volume again and tossing the remote onto the coffee table. It landed with a clatter, sliding a few inches before stopping.

This was bad. Worse than bad.

The Good Son had been incredibly lucky so far. He had been careful, and he had done his research, but this was becoming too much. The stakes were as high now as they had ever been, but any element of surprise was gone. Now every cop and every citizen in the area would have an eye out for him.

It was over. Everything he had done, everything he had put himself through, all the pain he had inflicted, the certain damnation he had subjected himself to, was all for nothing.

More feelings bubbled to the surface with that realization, threatening to unleash more tears. His lower lip quivered as he considered the situation.

"This is a good thing. You know that, right?" his mother said.

Pressing his eyes closed, The Good Son made no effort to hide the tears that slid out from the corners of his eyes.

"What this tells me," she continued, "is that nobody knows a damn thing yet. They're desperate."

Still, The Good Son remained silent, fearful of what might come out if he were to speak.

"And it means we've still got some time left."

Chapter Thirty-Two

Reed didn't bother to wait around until the end of the interview. Grimes was doing a pretty good job of sticking to the points they had outlined in his office that afternoon, only getting tripped up once by a question that was posed in a purposely provocative manner. Despite that, he could still tell by his boss's body language that he was not enjoying himself one bit, thinking it better to be somewhere else when it ended and everybody came filing out.

Exiting the observation room, Reed stopped just long enough to throw a wave to Jackie before heading to his desk. Given the hour, she was too preoccupied with her dinner to protest, fluttering her fingers at him, the ends of them shiny with some form of grease, before returning her attention to the paper sack in front of her.

Not a single person was at work as he made his way through the desks, a fact that wasn't all that surprising. The sun outside had faded to nothing more than an orange ember, the day having somehow slipped away. He could see the faint glow above the horizon in the west, knowing that its absence would do nothing to alleviate the extreme heat outside.

The late hour, coupled with the ongoing shortage of detectives, had cleared the place even earlier than usual, most of his colleagues either working a case or hiding somewhere to make sure they weren't handed another.

Having fallen victim to that very thing not 12 hours earlier, Reed felt reasonably certain he wouldn't be the next one on the list.

"Ten minutes," Reed said, Billie looking up at the sound of his voice as he led them to the corner desk and took a seat. "I know you're hungry, but there's one thing I want to check before we go."

Billie's tongue shot out over her nose as she settled into her position beside the desk. She remained up on her front paws, her body turned to face him, her posture reminding him that he was on the clock.

"Yeah, yeah, I get it," Reed replied, reaching down and running his fingers through the thick hair between her ears. Four thick furrows appeared in the fur as he pulled his hand back and turned to face the desk.

The hope was to find out if Earl and his crew had finished their report on the morning's crime scene. He knew from watching the criminalists work that there was precious little they found on site, but he was hoping for an ID to have come back on the fingerprints. It wasn't much - to be honest it was painfully little - but any tiny victory was enough for the night, allowing him to go home and look through his previous files a little longer before beginning again with fresh eyes in the morning.

He just needed a name.

Piled in the center of his desk was a pair of folders, much like the two from the Soto case the day before. Both were thinner than the previous ones, neither holding more than a few sheets of paper.

Starting with the top one, Reed pulled it toward him and flipped it open. At a glance he could tell it was from Earl's lab, the top sheet a printout from AFIS – The American Fingerprint Information System. On it was a scan of every fingerprint from the John Doe found in the park that morning, his name coming back as Henry Ruggles.

The sheet listed him at 38-years-old, 5'11" in height, weighing 175 pounds.

The reason for his fingerprints being taken was listed as the acceptance of a position with a financial planning firm.

Pausing for a moment, Reed raised his gaze. Focusing on nothing, he chewed on the information, superimposing it on what he'd seen that morning.

The man who had been found was nowhere near 175 pounds, though everything else seemed to fit. Given his attire and the shaggy cut of his hair, Reed would not have pegged him as a Henry, but perhaps he went by Hank among his friends. He let the notion play out in his mind another moment before shoving it aside, clearing his head with a quick shake.

The remainder of the file was quick and blunt, highlighting what had been discovered at the crime scene, which was to say nothing of use.

Giving his head another shake, Reed closed the file and set it aside. He glanced down to Billie still standing silent vigil beside him and said, "I know. Five minutes."

Once more her tongue passed over her muzzle, her dark brown eyes watching as he pulled the second file over and opened it. Affixed in the middle of the page was a yellow Post-It note. On it were several hand-written lines, Reed recognizing it instantly as belonging to Dr. Solomon.

Detective Mattox,

Apologies if this arrives at the wrong desk, but you were listed as the assigned detective on the case. If you're still on it, please come see me in the morning to discuss.

I will be arriving at 7:30 a.m.

Best,
Patricia Solomon

The formality of the note surprised Reed, his eyebrows rising as he peeled it away and pressed it against the inside of the front cover. Numerous questions came to mind, each one trying to force its way forward, as he bypassed the pictures and went straight for the write-up, finding it halfway through the file.

The official cause of death was a fractured spinal column occurring between the C1 and C2 vertebrae, just as Greene and Gilchrist had surmised at the scene. The time of death was around 6:00 that morning, also in line with everything that had been gleaned prior.

His confusion mounted as Reed examined the page, nothing jumping out at him to explain the note from Solomon. Folding it back against the silver fasteners, he moved on to the next page, the paper lined with black lines for notes. More than half of the space was filled, all of it done in blue ink in Solomon's neat script.

With each word Reed read, he felt his confusion grow. Before speaking to Solomon he couldn't quite be sure what he'd been handed, but his every instinct told him it could be a game changer.

Uncertainty gave way to a tiny spark of optimism as he read the page once more before slamming the file shut and snatched them both up from his desk. The quick movement made Billie jump.

"Come on girl, let's go get a shower and something to eat. We've got an early appointment in the morning."

Chapter Thirty-Three

There were two cars in the parking lot as Reed pulled up. The first was an aging Honda Civic with condensation covering the windows, obviously having been there overnight and possibly longer. In a less chaotic time Reed might have thought to check on it, but given the situation, it failed to even register with him.

The second was an older model Dodge Dakota, a few dents showing in the side, but otherwise in good repair. The owner shuffled by as Reed pulled to a stop along the front row, a middle-aged man in matching blue canvas pants and shirt. In his hand was a key ring the size of a softball, which he used to gain entry through the front door of the building.

Another five degrees warmer and Reed would have followed him in, suffering through any necessary small talk to wait in the lobby. As it were, he and Billie were both okay, each no more than 15 minutes from a shower, having not yet started to sweat for the day.

The previous 10 hours had been almost torturous, Reed's mind refusing to slow down, keeping sleep at bay. New information had been so hard to come by that the list of questions he had for Solomon had grown exponentially. His only hope was that she would be able to unlock something he needed, to finally begin narrowing things down.

Three more cars appeared in the lot, all parking close to an area that would eventually be shaded over. Reed watched them with mild detachment, examining them only long enough to see that they weren't the person he was looking for before dismissing them and moving on.

Two minutes before 7:30, a silver Cadillac SUV rolled into the parking lot. It bypassed any pretense of finding shade and drove directly to the front stall in the lot, Patricia Solomon emerging a moment later. Despite the heat, she wore a pink cardigan over a white blouse and slacks, her glasses already hanging from the chain around her neck.

Watching her approach, Reed couldn't help but wonder if the woman had arrived out of the womb like that, the outfit a close copy of the one she wore every time he saw her. He considered the thought for a moment before shrugging it off, realizing she probably thought the same of him and the jeans-and-t-shirt attire he sported each time he stopped by.

Reed allowed her to make it halfway across the parking lot before climbing out. He opened the back door for Billie, the metal moaning once in protest, before clipping the short lead to her collar. Together they stood waiting as Solomon approached, slowing her pace as she grew closer.

"Good morning, Doctor," Reed opened.

"Good morning, Detective," Solomon replied. Her face betrayed the slightest hint of weariness, though her voice carried none of the same inflection. "I take it you are staying on the John Doe case?"

As she asked the question, all three began moving toward the door, Reed and Solomon on either side, Billie in the middle.

"Henry Ruggles," Reed corrected. "Earl sent over a hit from AFIS last night."

In the periphery of his vision he could see Solomon's head tilt upward in understanding, though she said nothing.

"And yes," Reed said, reaching the front door and holding it open for her, "for the time being I'm staying on. Hoping your note means you have something that might help it along."

Solomon cast him a glance as she passed through, leading them to the bank of elevators along the side. For the first time ever Reed noticed both the front desk and the cafeteria behind it were empty, the building bearing a stillness that seemed strange.

"Just you wait," Solomon said, pushing the button for the basement, adding nothing more to her statement.

More questions came to Reed's mind as they rode down in silence, stepping into the hallway and going straight for her office. Overhead the lights buzzed just slightly, the only sound in the corridor, everything cast in a filmy yellow light.

"Since you've already had a chance to read the file, I won't walk you through all of it," Solomon said, using a key to unlock her door. She flipped a pair of light switches on the wall beside it, the fluorescent tubes above clicking on one at a time. "But there was something I wanted to point out to you in the event you might need it."

Dropping her purse onto the floor beside her desk, Solomon lowered herself into her chair. On the desk beside her was a trio of folders, the top one bearing the name John Doe, though she didn't bother to consult it. She motioned for Reed to take the only other chair in the room, waiting as he did so and Billie lowered herself to her haunches beside him.

"The official COD was a broken neck," Solomon said, "but another week and it wouldn't have mattered."

A pang of excitement traveled the length of Reed's back, pulling him forward to the edge of the chair. He pressed his palms into his thighs and leaned in a few inches, trying to force out everything he'd read before and all the thoughts it had elicited since. He needed to make sure he heard exactly what Solomon was about to tell him, uncolored by anything preexisting in his mind.

"Simply put, the man's liver was shot," Solomon said. "So much so that it's a wonder he was even alive."

It was the exact same thing, down to the word even, of what Solomon had written in her notes. Still, hearing it out loud, seeing the look on her face as she said it, brought a renewed seriousness to Reed. He had no idea how or why, but couldn't shake the notion this was about to completely redirect every thought he's had about the case in the previous 24 hours.

Not sure how to best articulate the cluster of new questions forming in his mind, Reed made a circular gesture with his hand, motioning for Solomon to continue.

She opened her mouth before pausing, extending one finger straight up in the air. "Actually, this might be easier if I show you."

Without waiting for a response, she stood and exited the room, leaving Reed seated in her wake. He sat there for a moment, his brow pinched in confusion, before glancing down to Billie. "Stay."

The dog dropped herself flat to the floor as Reed rose and exited, jogging a few steps to catch up with Solomon just outside of her lab. Together they entered the chilly room, the space almost completely dark as Solomon crossed the floor, her shape receding to just a shadow, her shoes the only sound, before flipping on a bank of light switches.

Unlike the bulbs in the hallway and her office, these were of a much lower wattage. A pale haze settled over the space as Solomon crossed to the cold lockers along the back wall, raising a finger, signaling for Reed to follow.

"The liver is the largest internal organ in the body," Solomon said, "second only to the skin overall in terms of actual size."

She reached for the far right drawer in the middle row and unclasped the steel handle, a rush of refrigerated air escaping as the door swung back. Reaching in, she grabbed the end of the tray table inside and pulled it back.

A pair of pale white feet was the first thing to exit, a small tag wrapped around the big toe. Halfway up the calves a white sheet appeared, covering the majority of the body, stopping just shy of the armpits. On either side the arms lay atop the sheet, Solomon continuing to pull until Henry Ruggles was on full display.

Stripped naked and lying prone, the man looked even smaller than Reed remembered. His features were well past gaunt, his body appearing nothing short of skeletal.

"The main functions of the liver," Solomon said, her teaching voice now in full effect, "are to prevent infections and remove toxins from the blood. An extension of that is, of course, controlling immune responses, processing nutrients and medications, things like that."

She paused and looked up to Reed, who only nodded in response. The information sounded vaguely familiar, the kind of thing he had read long ago and not given much thought to since.

The kind of thing most people prayed they never had to give a lot of attention to.

Stepping back a few feet, Solomon extracted a pair of blue surgical gloves from a box on the steel countertop behind her. One at a time she pulled them on before returning, using her right index finger as a pointer.

"All the telltale signs are present," she began, motioning first to his exposed arms and shoulders. "See all this loose skin here? How thin his arms are?"

Rising onto his toes, Reed peered down. When he'd first encountered Ruggles, he'd thought the man was extremely skinny, but hadn't given it a second thought. "Yeah."

"Common symptoms are decrease of appetite, loss of muscle mass, weight loss, weakness," Solomon said, rattling off the list in quick sequence. Stepping to her left a few inches, she pulled back the sheet, exposing Ruggles's pale bare legs to mid-thigh. Green and blue blotches mottled both extremities like spots on a leopard, the ratio of bruised-to-unbruised flesh extremely high.

"Damn," Reed whispered.

"When a person's liver is damaged," Solomon said, "their blood doesn't clot. That's why all the bruising." She put the sheet back into place and said, "I'll save you the visual, but suffice it to say his digestive system and bowels were full of blood as well."

Reed watched the sheet slide back into place, his face wincing, a sharp breath passing over his lips.

"This is the big one, though," Solomon said, moving to Ruggles's head and peeling back an eyelid. Keeping himself several inches back from the body, his hands folded behind him, Reed leaned in to look, another sharp breath entering him.

Henry Ruggles had brown eyes, that part coming as no surprise. What caught Reed's attention was the tissue surrounding it, all the color of straw, not a trace of the usual white visible.

"Jaundice," Solomon said, holding the eyelid one extra moment before letting it fall back into place. "If he wasn't so pale, or so bruised, you'd see his skin probably has a yellow tint to it as well."

Taking a step back, Reed left his hands behind him, his fingers laced tight. "Yesterday, the sun was so bright I didn't even think to notice."

"Nor should you," Solomon said, returning to the foot of the tray and sliding it back into place. The apparatus worked in near silence, Henry Ruggles disappearing from view, locked away once again.

"Find a body like this in a park, you're not looking for signs of liver failure."

"No," Reed agreed, shaking his head once before moving his eyes over to the drawer containing Ruggles.

Of everything he had expected to find when he arrived, this was not near the top of the list. He couldn't quite shake the feeling he'd been given an important piece of information, even if he had no idea what to do with it yet.

"Drugs?" he asked. "It would certainly be a motive."

"It would," Solomon said, "but unfortunately in this instance, there's no evidence of that at all. Alcohol either. Aside from the failing liver, the guy was a pretty healthy 30-something."

"So...?" Reed asked, leaving things open ended.

"Hemochromatosis," Solomon said, "excessive iron in his blood. Completely genetic, it builds up in the liver, eventually becomes too much for it to handle."

Reed nodded. Like most of what he'd been given this morning, he had no idea what to do with the information. His hope had been that Solomon had left out some small detail in her report that would present him with a proper motive, giving him a heading that would allow him to develop a suspect list.

This seemed to be doing quite the opposite.

"So what are you telling me?" Reed asked.

Solomon considered this a moment, her lips pursed. "I know this doesn't give you the answers you were looking for, but it does strip away a lot of possibilities. Body found dead in the park, guy beat all to hell, looks strung out, not hard to assume the worst."

To that Reed had no counter, her thinking exactly in line with his own.

"I just figured you should know that wasn't the case here."

Chapter Thirty-Four

For someone who had made it a point to be invisible the previous six months, Reed lately found himself spending a lot of time in Grimes's office. Despite the fact that he was in his mid-30s and had done nothing wrong, he couldn't shake the feeling of being a kid sitting in the principal's office as he stared across at the man almost 20 years his senior. Try as he might, he couldn't quite pin down why the sensation nagged at him, though he suspected it pertained to the glower on his boss's face, the steaming demeanor that hinted he could explode at any moment.

"I take it the idea to go to the media wasn't well received?" Reed opened.

An eyebrow was arched in return, Grimes saying, "Not quite. Last night I got home to a pair of nasty voice messages from Brandt downtown, followed by another from her lackey Dade."

Reed nodded, resisting the urge to offer his condolences. Eleanor Brandt was the chief of the Columbus Police Department, a small, severe woman he had gone toe-to-toe with just a few months before. It was no secret around the precinct that the only reason he still had a job was because he was right in the matter, though the fact that he had saved the lives of her and her nephew in the process didn't hurt.

Working under her was a man named Oliver Dade, someone Reed

had seen a few different times but had barely heard speak. His official title was Senior Media Consultant, though as a civilian employee, Reed suspected his official capacity was closer to Spin Doctor.

"They say anything useful?" Reed asked, bypassing any side commentary.

The captain waved a hand in his direction. "Same old stuff. Asked what we were thinking going to the press, did we have any idea this could create a public outcry, why weren't they consulted first..."

"That all coming from Brandt," Reed said, having heard a similar tirade himself once before.

"Right," Grimes said. "Dade was his typical even-handed self, tried to make it seem like he was my friend, just wanted to help, offered some suggestions for any media engagements in the future."

For a moment Reed envisioned Grimes just arriving home at the end of a long day, already tense and angry after his interview with Leveritt, only to have Dade lecture him on how to handle an interview.

The image was equal parts humor and horror.

"Please tell me you called back and let him have it," Reed said, wanting to siphon off some tiny bit of satisfaction from the encounter, the first he'd had in days.

The scowl on Grimes's face deepened. "I thought about it, even dialed his number, but eventually hung up before I got the chance to do something really stupid."

"Ah," Reed said, keeping his voice low. He'd worked with the captain long enough to recognize when an outburst might be lurking, opting against pressing the matter any further. He waited another moment, allowing the residual tension to bleed away, before starting on a different track. "Has the phone line yielded anything worthwhile yet?"

"Not that I know of," Grimes said. "The call center is handling everything and sending me updates every so often, fast tracking anything that seems important."

He paused there, inserting an eye-roll for effect. "So far most of the stuff coming in has been from angry citizens, people either wanting to bitch about what's going on or bitch about us not doing our jobs."

"Hmm," Reed said, having heard every tired line too many times before. "Pigs. Bacon. Waste of taxpayer money."

"Isn't there a donut somewhere needs saving?" Grimes continued. "Barney Fife. Dudley Do-Right."

"Keystone Kops."

"And apparently something called Super Troopers," Grimes finished, "whatever the hell that means?"

For a split second Reed considered updating his captain on the pop culture reference before deciding against it. The question was only rhetorical, more venting from a tired and frustrated civil servant.

"Did either one acknowledge we made the right decision?" Reed asked. "That even if we risk reinforcing what everybody already thinks of us, it was worth it to make the public-at-large aware of what was going on?"

Scrunching the left side of his face, Grimes raised a hand, wagging it on edge at Reed. "In a backhanded sort of way. They did say it needed to be done, but were quick to point out we botched the handling of it."

It was the fourth or fifth time in the conversation Grimes had used the first person plural pronoun *we*, denoting that he and Reed were lumped together. Whether that was by design or in response to what the higher-ups were saying he couldn't be certain.

"How about your end?" Grimes asked. "Anything shake loose?"

That very question had been ping-ponging through Reed's mind all morning, from the moment Solomon slid Ruggles's body away until Reed entered Grimes's office. He still didn't have a complete handle on what he'd been given, unable to shake the thought that the doctor had been correct in pointing it out, but not sure what to do with it.

"Had an interesting discussion with Dr. Solomon over at the coroner's this morning," Reed said. "Henry Ruggles, our John Doe from the park, was in the late stages of liver failure. As she put it, if somebody had just waited a week he would have been dead anyway."

The news brought the same reaction from Grimes that it had from Reed, his eyebrows tracking higher up his forehead. "Meaning what? Drug addict?"

"Nope. That was my first guess too," Reed said. "Guy was completely clean, suffering from some genetic disease."

"You think it means something?" Grimes asked.

"I can't decide yet, but I'm going to go speak to Ruggles's ex-wife right after this, see if maybe something more kicks loose. That work?"

"Do what you need to," Grimes said, "just do it fast. I don't think I need to point out what Brandt had to say about making this disappear as soon as possible."

Chapter Thirty-Five

There wasn't a phone number listed for Bethanee Cleary, so Reed had no choice but to show up unannounced. It wasn't his preferred manner of arriving, especially in search of the kind of information he was after. He was also reasonably certain that nobody had notified her about the death yet, making the prospect of what he faced even more difficult.

Not only did he have to deliver such horrific news, he had to be the jerk that stuck around and tried to pull any meaningful information he could from her.

The prospect brought a dour expression to his face as he worked his way north up the outer belt, well beyond the reach of the 8th Precinct. He pushed past the geographic parameters of his old jurisdiction to the north as well, passing through Hilliard before turning into the southern outskirts of Worthington. Every few minutes he glanced over to the GPS mounted to his dash, preferring to read for himself rather than hear the annoying automated voice tell him every time he missed a turn or needed to merge lanes.

Thirty minutes after exiting Grimes's office, Reed pulled up in front of a small, single family home.

The front of it was white, with red brick trim across the bottom half. Most of Reed's view of it was blocked by a neatly trimmed hedge, a smattering of maple trees dotting the yard between him and the front door. Their wilted leaves provided just enough shade to cover the front lawn, the occasional patch of sunlight just barely making it through.

As he sat out front, Reed couldn't help but notice that not one other car was parked along the street. For a moment he considered pulling into the driveway before thinking better of it.

Given everything that was about to occur, he figured the last of Cleary's concerns would be whatever the neighbors thought.

"You ready?" Reed asked, climbing from the front seat. Before opening the rear door, he touched his back pocket to make sure his badge was still stowed before letting Billie out and clipping her to the short lead.

The other upside to having a number to call ahead of time would be to ensure somebody was home, the thought crossing Reed's mind as he stared at the closed aluminum garage door. There were no windows along the top of it, no way of seeing inside.

The trip north had been a bit of a detour, the thought of doing so again not something Reed was particularly fond of.

The grimace on his face grew more pronounced as he walked to the front door and rang the bell, Billie pressed tight against his leg. Taking her cue from him, she tensed just slightly as steps could be heard, her senses picking up on his slightest physiological shift. She stayed that way as the sound grew ever closer before stopping, the light behind the peep hole disappearing.

Again Reed felt his pulse rise, Billie reacting similarly beside him, before the door was jerked backwards, a gust of cool air flowing out.

Standing before them was a woman in her late-30s with dark eyes and sharp features, her ears, nose, and chin all pointed in hard angles. Her hair was pulled up behind her head, a thick gray headband around the front to hold down any strays. Of average height and weight, she wore jeans and a plain black tank top, her feet bare.

If there was any surprise at seeing Reed, or even any question as to who he was, she didn't let it show.

"He finally did it, didn't he?"

The voice, deep and abrasive, was just as much a shock to Reed as the question it asked.

"Excuse me?"

"Well, aren't you here to tell me Henry finally offed himself?" she asked.

The words, void of any compassion, caustic in every way, set Reed back a moment. His mouth opened once, then twice, as he tried to formulate a response before giving up and starting again. "I'm sorry, are you Bethanee Cleary?"

She gave him a look that managed to simultaneously relay that he was an idiot and she was bored. "Yeah, that's me."

"Ex-wife of Henry Ruggles?"

"Yes," she said, forcing the word out in a huff. "Isn't that why you're here? To tell me he's finally gone?"

Confusion roiled within Reed. Of everything he did as a detective, delivering bad news was one of the very worst tasks. It was something he had gladly handed off to Riley whenever the situation arose in the past, resigning himself to playing the strong silent type in the background.

Now it was Billie's turn to assume that role, leaving him to decipher the reaction before him.

"Ms. Cleary, why do you believe your husband, um, took his own life?" Reed asked, almost being tripped up into using her own words, despite the inappropriateness of the expression.

"*Ex*-husband," she corrected. "And have you seen him? Damn man has wasted away to nothing. Kept saying for years he was just going to end it one day. Guess he finally got the guts to go ahead and do it."

Unlike every other similar situation before, Reed didn't have to remind himself not to apologize or offer condolences. He certainly didn't need to remember the most important thing, which was to never make any promises he couldn't keep. Instead, he had to force himself not to lash out at her, to tell her that her ex-husband was dead in the most vicious way he could, if for no other reason than just so she would feel bad about the callous way she was acting.

He didn't, though. All that would do was fill him with shame after the fact, something he could not afford at the moment.

"No," Reed replied. "He was killed sometime night before last. His body was found yesterday at the Overland Dog Park in Franklinton."

Most people react in some variation of the same way to hearing that someone has been killed, whether they knew the victim or not. Their eyes grew large, their body became rigid, and after a few moments of fumbling, they asked what happened.

Bethanee Cleary did none of those things. She simply leaned her shoulder against the edge of the door and stared out at him, her body language letting it be known the conversation could end at any moment. "Well, I was here all that night. My boyfriend and his two kids can vouch for me. They'll be back any time now."

The urge to lash out grew even stronger, finally overtaking the confusion Reed felt about the entire thing.

"That's actually not why I'm here," Reed said. "You were listed in his records as a next of kin, so I came to tell you what happened and to ask if there is any reason you might know why it occurred."

Cleary's lips moved just slightly as she stared off at some point above Reed's head before shifting her gaze back down to him. "Next of kin, huh? I don't suppose there's been a reading of the will yet, has there?"

The combination of heat and his growing disdain for Bethanee Cleary pushed a rush of blood through Reed's body. For the first time all day he began to sweat, starting with his brow, followed shortly by his forearms and lower back. "I really wouldn't know, ma'am. That's pretty far outside my area of interest."

A smirk drew her head back, an obvious retort on her lips, though she refrained from sharing it. "Yeah, well, there can't be much left at this point anyway. He spent every last dime he had for treatment or on that damn support group of his."

Pushing past the comment, Reed asked, "Ms. Cleary, how long have you and Mr. Ruggles been..."

"Divorced?" she asked, cutting him off mid-sentence. "Since the day he found out he needed a transplant. He told me it was going to be a long hard road, and I told him he'd better get walking then."

There were no words for Reed to respond with. He stood slack jawed on the concrete sidewalk, sweat streaming down his face, staring at arguably one of the most vile creatures he had ever encountered.

A tall order considering everything he'd seen in the last 12 years.

"Point being, I can't help you. I don't know any more about that man's life than I know about yours."

Chapter Thirty-Six

"You alright?"

The question was asked softly, in a tone that was almost timid. It was barely audible, The Good Son barely noticing it, the words pulling him from his haze.

The entire day had been a blur, the night before it as well, and the previous several days too if he really wanted to get down to it. He had done things, things he never would have thought himself capable of doing, things he still didn't quite believe were possible.

The only proof he had that any of it had been real were the images, forever seared into his mind, waiting for him every time he closed his eyes. They began with Esther Rosen, culminated with Henry Ruggles, contained every last wretched act in between.

"Hmm?" The Good Son asked, his eyes puffy, just barely slits, the result of more time spent crying than sleeping over the last two days.

"Are you okay?" Cindy Neely asked, taking a step closer, her hands clasped in front of her.

At 43-years-old, Cindy was the oldest employee in the store. Twice she had been offered the manager's position, and twice she had turned it down, telling them each time that she preferred the flexibility and people interaction of remaining a cashier.

More than once The Good Son had wanted to point out to her that had she only accepted the position they would be free of Beauregard, though he had never actually voiced that opinion out loud. Most everybody in the store already knew what he thought of the man. It was the same opinion held by them all.

There was no need to make Cindy feel bad about it.

"Oh, yeah, I'm good," The Good Son replied, looking up from the box of weed killer he was loading onto a shelf. He glanced down and forced a half smile, the muscles feeling awkward in his face. "I think one of these bottles is leaking and got fumes in my eyes."

Matching the half smile, Cindy inched a bit closer. "Yeah, it looks pretty bad. Maybe you should go wash them out?"

The Good Son appreciated her concern. Of everyone in the store, she was the only one he'd believe was asking him out of sympathy and not a deep rooted desire to be the first one to determine some bit of gossip and go running back to share it with the others.

"Oh, that's alright," The Good Son said. "Thanks for asking though."

He watched as she nodded in acknowledgement, venturing a few inches closer. Despite the fact that she was standing, she rose no more than a few inches above him, her tiny body weighing 100 pounds if she was lucky. The red apron she wore around her neck hung almost to the floor, the hem resting just above her shoelaces.

"Listen," she said, lowering her voice a bit more. She closed the gap between them to less than a foot, glancing in either direction before saying, "Can you do me a quick favor?"

Her voice betrayed a slight crack as she asked it, drawing The Good Son's gaze up to hers. A spider web pattern of red veins were spread across her eyes, her upper lip trembling just slightly.

"Sure, Cindy," The Good Son said, leaning back and resting his bottom on his heels. "What's up?"

"Can you man the front register for me for a few minutes? I have kind of, an, uh, emergency..." Her voice receded with each passing word, her face, her body, somehow managing to do the same.

By the time she was done, her shoulders were pinched so far inward she measured less than a foot from side to side.

The Good Son felt his mouth drop for a moment before the realization of what she was saying settled in. His eyebrows rose, his puffy eyes unable to do the same.

"Oh," he said, a hint of surprise in his voice.

As much as he liked Cindy, under normal circumstances would have no problem helping her, at the moment there was nothing in the world he wanted to do less. His stomach churned and his chest tightened, his breaths becoming slower and more pained as he thought about what his mother had said the night before.

He didn't want to do it. He had told her that, and no matter how much berating she lobbed his way, he couldn't bring himself to change his stance.

Being resolute was easy though when he was tucked away in the back of the store. There was no temptation before him, trying to garner his attention, teasing him to take one step back across the line. As long as he was out of the way he could do the right thing. He was free from hearing his mother's words in his ears, didn't have to think about her repeated challenges causing him to prove his love for her.

"Please," Cindy said, tears beginning to pool on the underside of her eyes. "Ten minutes, tops."

The clenching in The Good Son's stomach ceased as he watched the tears hang from her bottom eyelashes. The resentment he felt toward his mother, his innate desire to be left alone, both bled away, seeing only a person in need before him.

There was no way he could ever rectify the things he had done. His only hope, now and forever, was to return to the person he was before, to live well, and hope that others viewed what he did through the necessary lens.

As much as he hated the thought, that had to begin with moments like this.

"Sure, Cindy," The Good Son said, nodding once before pushing himself to his feet. "Take all the time you need."

For a moment it looked like Cindy might rush in and hug him.

"Go," he whispered, jutting his chin toward the employee restroom in the back of the building, "before Beauregard sees you."

Without a word, Cindy pivoted and took off down the aisle, her short legs almost sprinting as she made the corner and disappeared from sight. The Good Son waited until she was gone before letting out a sigh and beginning his slow trudge toward the front.

Things were getting out of control. What had begun as a very clear plan with a finite directive had spiraled badly. He was ready to let things go, but it wasn't that simple. It never was. And now it threatened to get even worse.

The thought hung over The Good Son like a personal rain cloud, following him the length of the store as he took his place behind the register, a man on the cusp of 50 waiting patiently in line.

"Sorry about that," The Good Son said, calling the register to life. "Lunchtime, lot of shuffling going on."

He offered a small smile, hoping the lie would stick, but the man just waved it off.

"No worries," he said. "I just got up here myself."

One at a time, the man unloaded some garden decorations and work gloves onto the conveyor, The Good Son ringing each up in turn. "That'll be $27.48 with tax, sir."

Starting with his shirt and moving to the front of his jeans, he patted every pocket he had. His face fell flat for an instant as he turned toward the parking lot, the slightest hint of color flushing his cheeks. "Oh my, I seem to have misplaced the money my wife gave me."

Again he ran a hand over each pocket before reaching to his backside and extracting a battered leather wallet, the letters PNT punched into it with an old fashioned branding tool.

"Do you take MasterCard?

Chapter Thirty-Seven

The meeting with Cleary left Reed with a bitter aftertaste. The complete disinterest she had shown about the passing of her ex-husband was appalling. The manner in which she had referred to his ailment, the fact that she had the temerity to ask about a will, was on a different level entirely.

Seated behind the steering wheel, Reed drove with his left hand, his right clenched into a tight fist. He raised it once and swung it downward like an oversized hammer, the ball of it aimed at the middle console, stopping just millimeters from making contact. With his teeth gritted, he repeated the motion twice more, each one coming even closer to connecting with the console, until on the third he tapped the side of his hand against the smooth plastic, a crescent of sweat left behind.

People like the killers he was currently investigating were easily the worst part of his job. They leveled pure and indiscriminate hatred, taking people like Esther Rosen long before their normal expiration date. They committed the worst of sins and seemed to do them for no more concrete reason than the fact that they could.

Coming in a close second were people like Bethanee Cleary. Void of any compassion, they saw the world entirely through a set of very narrow, very self-serving lenses. Not only did they make his job of apprehending others harder, they made him seriously question why he did it in the first place.

That feeling, wondering if it all was worth it, was something he could not abide. He could not allow himself to harbor such thoughts, and he damn sure wouldn't allow someone like Bethanee Cleary to put them there.

"Okay, so that was a dead end," he said out loud, his voice pulling Billie up into the rearview mirror behind him.

It was obvious Cleary had nothing to do with Ruggles's murder. She was too cavalier to be hiding anything, offering up an alibi without provocation. If Reed really felt vindictive he could press the matter and check it for corroboration, but the exercise would accomplish little beyond making him feel better by lashing out at her.

Right now he just didn't have the time for it.

Drifting over a lane on the freeway, Reed exited toward Franklinton. His gaze fixed on the sign along the roadway as he drove past, the six inch white letters on a green background, watching as they slid past his vision and fell from sight.

"Franklinton," he whispered aloud, his hands directing the car toward his destination through muscle memory. Some fraction of the aggravation he felt at Cleary fell away, or was at least moved to the side, as he let the single word play across his thoughts.

There was something there. It was tenuous, ethereal even, just beyond his grasp, but his mind refused to let it go.

"Franklinton," he repeated. "Not The Bottoms. Why the hell are we looking at a string of murders and assaults miles from the worst part of the city?"

Envisioning the misshapen grid of the 8th Precinct jurisdiction, Reed knew the entire region was technically named Franklinton, though the vast majority of it was spliced off into The Bottoms subsection. That was where most of the crime – robberies, assaults, vandalism, even murders – usually took place. In his six months with the new department, four days prior was the first time he had ever taken a call in the surrounding neighborhoods.

From what he could tell, they were almost all alike, cookie cutter streets with residential dwellings. They were on the lower end of the socioeconomic scale for sure, the kinds of homes that would never be seen in the northern suburbs, but they certainly weren't government housing projects. They were inhabited by people like Ira Soto, folks who were making the best of a bad situation.

People who rarely, if ever, ran afoul of the law.

"Somebody's trying to tell us something," Reed said, again glancing into the rearview mirror, seeing the twin spires of Billie's black ears. "The crime scenes might be clean, but..."

Pausing to allow a car to turn out of the precinct parking lot, Reed leaned across the passenger seat. He extended his upper body over the expanse of the car and reached into the pocket on the inside of the passenger door, going by feel until he found what he was looking for and drew it up beside him. Once he had it, he turned into the station, going straight for the back of the parking lot.

There he jammed the gear shift into park, leaving the engine running.

The map was one he'd gotten from a local gas station when he first moved over. Despite working just north of Franklinton for more than a decade, he and Riley had both made a point to stay far away from the area as much as possible. They had their own cases to work. They did not need to be seeking out even worse cases to the south.

The first month in this precinct Reed had left the map on the passenger seat beside him, checking the street names for every call that came in. With time, the place become as familiar as his old beat had been, the map getting folded up and stowed away.

It was the first time Reed had it out in the better part of five months, the creases and corners a little frayed, though otherwise still in pretty good shape. He unfurled it to full size, allowing the breadth of it to extend across most of the car, the air from the vents causing it to sway in front of him. He left it there just long enough to get a clear look at what he needed before folding it in half and then the remainder in half again, focusing his attention on the western quarter of the precinct.

Billie's cool nose passed against his right triceps, her face emerging beside him. Raising his arm at the shoulder, Reed rubbed against her neck twice before opening the middle console and extracting a pen.

"Okay," he said, thinking out loud. "This is where Henry Ruggles lived."

Reed traced along Water Street, finding the corresponding intersection and circling it. A bold line of blue ink appeared as Reed moved on to the dog park where Ruggles's body had been found. "And this is where he was dumped."

The two locations were no more than an inch apart, the second site north-northwest of the first. For a moment Reed stared down at them, his gaze passing over the web of streets, at the labyrinth of parks and schools and public works all listed on the map, hoping for something to jump out at him.

Nothing did.

"It's not enough," Reed said, looking down at the two indiscriminate points. Even working with just a fraction of the overall jurisdiction, there was still too much space for a pair of locations to reveal anything. "Unless..."

Moving two inches north of the dog park, Reed found the address for Esther Rosen. He circled it as well, his heart rate picking up a tiny bit, a clear pattern starting to emerge. In short order, he pushed his gaze further north still, the site for Ira Soto completing the quartet.

What had been too few was now too much to ignore.

Chapter Thirty-Eight

"What time are Greene and Gilchrist on tonight?"

The question was directed to Lou at the dispatch desk, the first stop Reed made upon entering the precinct. His sudden appearance, a solid black wolf look-alike by his side, startled the man so bad Reed thought he was on the verge of a heart attack. He raised a hand to his chest and gasped.

It took a full minute for the man to catch his breath, for his heart rate to slow down so he could speak, for the sideways glances from the opposite side of the room to cease coming their way.

"6:00," Lou said. "They're working a double tonight, covering for some guys who are going out of town for the weekend."

Glancing up at the plain black and white clock on the wall, Reed nodded. Their arrival was still a few hours off. He needed to know if they had found anything at Ruggles's home, if their canvas had revealed the slightest bit of useful information, but he still had plenty to keep him busy until then.

"Thanks," Reed said, slapping the desk twice as he departed.

The look on Lou's face relayed Reed could feel free not to stop by again anytime soon.

Reed led Billie back in the opposite direction. He could tell they were garnering attention, his gaze not once wavering as he cut straight through the desks and jerked his chair back.

He dropped down into it without ceremony, pushing his stomach up against the edge of the desk and lifting his phone. Just as fast he dropped the receiver on the desk and dialed a number, reading it from the list of contacts in his cell-phone, before picking it up and pressing it to his ear.

He counted off three rings before it was answered, the first response nothing but heavy breaths on the other side.

"Bishop," a voice finally said, annoyance, agitation, plain.

"Bishop, Reed Mattox," Reed opened, pausing to allow the man on the other side to register who was calling and hopefully drop some of the angst. Right now they were still in mid-shift and he could picture him riding shotgun, covering his phone and mouthing Reed's name to Iaconelli behind the wheel.

"Hey, Detective, what can I do for you?" Bishop said, a faux joviality barely surfacing.

Reed let it go without offense, knowing he would react the same way to a call from either one of them. "That assault case you guys got handed, anything come of it?"

A moment passed, nothing audible over the phone but the noise of a car in motion. Reed considered adding more to the inquiry, filling in some of the blanks, letting them know why he was asking, but ultimately decided not to. He knew the pause had nothing to do with the details of the case, everything stemming from the silent discussion they were having about how much to share.

"First thing," Bishop said, "it wasn't an assault. She died less than an hour after arrival, bumping it to murder."

Reed cradled the phone between his shoulder and ear, scribbling down the information. Grimes had mentioned a fourth murder during the TV interview, but Reed had been so wrapped up in his own two cases, he had failed to equate that with the assault Bishop and Iaconelli had handled.

"Woman's name was Sandy Jurgensen," Bishop said. "Home address is listed as Hilliard, meaning she's outside our jurisdiction."

"But she was brought to Franklinton Memorial?" Reed asked, trying to picture the exact location.

"Yeah," Bishop said. "She was from the south end of town, lived beyond the outer belt, maybe five miles from the hospital."

Keeping the phone wedged tight, Reed rose and pulled the map from his back pocket. He peeled back the quarter he'd been working from and unfolded it to include more of the surrounding area. Rising to his feet, he leaned forward and used one finger to guide his search.

Not until a fat bead dripped from the end of his nose and landed inside the circle of Esther Rosen's house did he even realize he was sweating.

"Still," he said, "There must be two or three other health facilities closer than that."

"We know," Bishop said, a sigh plain in the two-word response. "Been a hell of a lot easier if the killer had taken her to one of those, or if she had lived in Franklinton. As is, the whole damn thing has turned into a jurisdictional pissing match."

Reed continued to let his gaze move over the area Bishop had mentioned, seeing it fall well outside the outline of the 8th domain on his map. "I bet."

"Actually, you have no idea," Bishop replied. "Why? You got something?"

Reed remained silent. He took up a pen and marked the Franklin Memorial Hospital, the new black orb falling directly in the center of the crescent formed by the four blue circles.

Pressing both palms flat on the desk on either side of the map, Reed stared straight down at the page, letting his vision grow blurry until only the five circles remained, a pattern so obvious it was almost infuriating.

"I'll be son of a..." Reed muttered, blinking himself back into focus. As he did so the various lines and topographical features became sharper, the map returning to its previous state.

"Why?" Bishop repeated. "You got something?"

Rising to full height, Reed opened his mouth to speak, only to close it again. His mind raced, trying to put together everything he'd learned in the last few days, attempting to force some coherence before he plunged forward again.

"Mattox!" Bishop snapped on the end of the line, jerking Reed from his thoughts. He flinched slightly before grabbing the receiver with his hand and pressing it to his mouth.

"How long are you guys on tonight?" Reed asked, ignoring Bishop's question.

"6:00, why?" Bishop asked, his annoyance rising with each passing moment.

"Meet me here at 5:30," Reed said, smashing the phone down before the man had a chance to respond. He held the receiver down a split second, just long enough to cut the connection, before taking it up a second time. Any longer and he knew Bishop would call right back, trying to get more information, most likely not being real subtle about his feelings on the matter.

The second number he dialed from memory, hoping with everything he had that the person on the other end would answer.

To his surprise, she did.

"Reed Mattox here. I need a favor."

Chapter Thirty-Nine

The call was a bit premature, but Reed knew that if he were going to set something up, he had to put things in motion now, even if it meant skipping a few administrative details. If anything turned up in the meantime to prove his theory wrong, it would be easier to cancel than try to get started later at a moment's notice.

Plus, in 12 years of police work, Reed had learned it was easier to say sorry than ask for permission.

The person on the other end of the line was Dr. Solomon, Reed just catching her during the tail end of a patient write- up. Another five minutes and she would have been back in the lab, inaccessible for the duration of her current autopsy.

It was apparent from the tone of her voice that she had been expecting him to call, her own suppositions working much faster than his. Unhampered by multiple cases and outside considerations, she had been able to strip things away and view just what was before her. While that was a luxury Reed could not afford, it was one that in this instance was looking more and more like the correct path.

It took less than five minutes for Reed to outline what he was considering. Halfway through she picked up on it, the two of them going back and forth, filling in bits and pieces, thinking out loud. By the time they were done, Reed didn't even need to ask for the favor, Solomon already knowing what came next and agreeing to set things up.

The moment they were finished, Reed went into the DMV databank and pulled the licenses for Esther Rosen, Ira Soto, and Sandy Jurgensen. He didn't bother with Henry Ruggles, already aware of how he fit in, his license unable to add any new information.

Each of the three licenses appeared in a separate window on his computer, Reed minimizing their dimensions so they overlapped. Lined up in row, the reality of the situation appeared so simple, so clear, so obvious now that he knew what to look for. And yet it would have been so easy to miss it if Solomon had never examined Ruggles, he might still be wandering around, hoping for something to jump out at him.

The images for all three were now folded up in Reed's back pocket as he parked in front of a two-story structure in the Short North, less than two blocks from Nationwide Arena. Nearby, the Olentangy River moved by in a lazy crawl, the lack of rain causing the waterway to have grown stagnant, the smell of garbage just barely present on the wind. On the opposite side of it skyscrapers rose upward, their misshapen outlines looking like fingers striving for something just out of reach.

The late afternoon sun reflected off their glassy exteriors, casting an unnaturally bright hue over everything.

Turning his back to the blinding glare, Reed hooked the short lead to Billie's collar and led her inside. As they walked, he fished out his badge and hung it around his neck, in no mood to be stopped by someone reminding him that he was entering a hygienic facility and that animals were off limits.

They were both detectives, and they were finally making headway on a very important case.

Reed almost dared someone to raise an objection.

The building was two stories tall, made from dark brick, with large windows flanking a massive front door. Thick wooden blinds were tilted down, keeping both the sun and any curious onlookers from peeking in.

The style of the building resembled a home, the parking spaces outside the only indication of the business housed within. There was no sign on the door, no official insignia visible. Twice Reed had to check the wrought iron numbers screwed into the brick, following Solomon's directions, trusting she would get him where he needed to be.

Passing through the front door, the character of the building changed instantly. No longer was any dark brick visible, replaced instead by white walls and blonde wood floors. Despite the blinds being down, plenty of natural light filtered in, making the place seem much brighter than anticipated.

Just inside the door was a reception counter behind a glass window, manned by a young woman that appeared to be a student of some kind. As Reed entered she glanced up from her reading, her gaze shifting from the badge to Billie before finally settling on Reed.

"Good afternoon," she said, adding a smile as an afterthought.

"Hi, Detective Reed Mattox here to see Dr. Erin Levin."

One eyebrow rose as the receptionist lifted the phone beside her. "Sure, just let me tell her you're here. You can have a seat. Won't take a second."

Casting a glance over to the dozen or so empty hardback chairs clustered nearby, and at the smattering of magazines on the table in the center of them, Reed elected to stand. He took two steps away from the counter so as not to appear imposing, and rested his shoulder against the wall.

She had said it wouldn't take a second. In truth it was more like a minute, though still much faster than Reed anticipated.

One moment, Reed was working the blend of information in his head into a rough outline, trying to figure out the best way to fit everything together, to present his findings as questions. The next, Dr. Erin Levin appeared in the hallway, striding straight toward him, her hand outstretched.

"Detective Mattox," she said, stepping right up to him and gripping his hand, hers slightly wet from what was probably the 100th washing of the day.

"Dr. Levin," Reed said, releasing the grip and motioning to Billie. "My partner, Billie."

A smile formed as the doctor looked down at Billie for a moment. She clasped her hands in front of her and leaned forward an inch at the waist, Reed knowing she wanted to reach down and pet her before stopping just short and pulling back.

He liked her already.

She was a tall woman, only a few inches shorter than he, though quite slender. She had straight brown hair that disappeared somewhere behind her shoulders and an open face that was just starting to show lines around the eyes and mouth. A long white coat enveloped most of her body, extending to just past her knees.

"Come on back to my office. I'll be happy to tell you anything I can."

The two-part harmony of Reed's running shoes squeaking and Billie's toenails hitting the hardwood followed Levin down the hallway, her own square heels adding a third rhythm to the impromptu symphony. It continued past a trio of offices, two standing dark and empty, the third with the door pulled shut. On the wall between each one was a Norman Rockwell style painting depicting young children doing their best impression of medical professionals.

They finally stopped at the end of the hall, Levin standing to one side of an office door and motioning for Reed to enter. "Please, have a seat."

Her tone suggested it was the exact thing she said to patients dozens of times each day.

"Down," Reed said, Billie pressing herself flat to the floor beside the lone visitor chair in the room. He waited for Levin to circle around her desk and take a seat before doing the same, leaning back in the padded cloth chair and resting his elbows on either armrest, his fingers laced before him.

The office was functional, a space meant for performing academic and administrative duties. The center of the room featured a hardwood desk made of oak, or perhaps cherry. On it was a laptop and three even stacks of paper, not a single knickknack or personal item of any kind. Behind the desk was an executive chair for the doctor, and a single bookcase was situated on the side wall. More artwork like those in the hall hung on two of the walls, and a large window was behind her desk, the blinds drawn tight.

"I understand you and Patty work together in Franklinton," Levin opened.

It was the first time Reed had ever heard Solomon referred to as Patty, or even considered the possibility that she would be. "We do. She's been quite an asset since moving to the new outpost. I'm glad to have her. She said you two went to medical school together?"

"That's right," Levin said, nodding, her hair brushing against the tops of her shoulders. "Right up the road at Ohio State. Go Buckeyes."

The phrase, the team, everything about the Buckeyes, often brought a cringe to Reed's face, though in this instance he fought to keep it down. Born and raised in Oklahoma City, his tastes ran much further west, a fact he had to often keep in check while working in Columbus.

One way to ensure earning the enmity of coworkers, witnesses, and pretty much anybody in the greater Columbus area, was to dare speak ill of the Buckeyes.

"And she tells me you are a heptologist?" Reed asked, saying the last word slowly, letting it be known he wasn't exactly sure on the pronunciation.

"Hepatologist," Levin corrected, smiling. "Close though, better than most."

Reed matched the smile, using the moment to collect his bearings. "I'm not sure how much Dr. Solomon told you, so let me just start at the beginning. I'll admit before I say a word that it's a working theory, and once I'm done you can fill in any blanks I have or shoot the whole thing down in flames. That work?"

"Good for me," Levin replied.

"Okay," Reed said, running his hands down the front of his thighs. "Four days ago we had a 911 call from someone stating that a woman was having a heart attack. When officers arrived a few minutes later, they found her already dead, though it was determined after the fact that efforts had been made to resuscitate her. The caller was never identified."

He paused, making sure she was with him, before continuing. "The next night we got another 911 call from somebody claiming that a woman was committing suicide. Responding officers found the second victim sealed into her car with duct tape, a hose connected to her exhaust. Once again, she was already dead, though no attempt at CPR had been made this time. And again, the caller was never identified."

"Hmm," Levin said, a crease appearing between her eyebrows as she listened. "And how was the first victim killed?"

"Sorry," Reed said, realizing he had skipped over that part. "Suffocation."

A small grunt in acknowledgement was the only response, the line growing a bit deeper as her eyebrows drew in closer. If she was surprised at the subject matter, or had any objections to it, she did nothing to show it.

"Two days ago," Reed said, "a woman was beaten badly and dropped off at the Franklinton Memorial Hospital. Less than an hour later, she died."

The look of concern on Levin's face increased, one elbow going to the arm of her chair, her fist coming up under her chin.

"And finally yesterday," Reed said, "a body was found in a dog park in Franklinton. Painfully skinny and covered in bruises, our first inclination was to think drugs, though the autopsy revealed he was actually experiencing end-stage liver disease due to hemochromatosis."

Reed waited a split second to see if the doctor would correct his pronunciation. Instead, she shifted slightly in her seat, crossing her right leg over her left.

"Okay," Reed said, again passing his palms over the front of his jeans, realizing he was sweating despite the air conditioning in the room. "Sorry, I know that was a lot, but I wanted to get it all out there so you could see what brought me here."

One corner of Levin's mouth turned up, her hand still propped beneath her chin. "That's quite alright. Patty kind of prepped me ahead of time that this might be a difficult conversation. I'll commend you though, you summarized it pretty well."

Another half-smile was the best Reed could manage in response. He was fast approaching the moment of truth, the part where he was told if his theory held water or if he had to call Iaconelli and Bishop and inform them it was a false alarm.

"Earlier today I was looking at the Ruggles case," Reed said, "and I plotted out his home, where we believe he was killed, or at the very least taken, and the park where his body was found. With just the two, there wasn't much to work with, but on a hunch I plotted out the sites for Esther Rosen and Ira Soto's homes as well."

Shifting onto his hip, Reed extracted the folded up map from his back pocket and placed it on the table in front of him. The creases were already beginning to loosen from the continued use, a few new wrinkles appearing on the pages. Smoothing them out the best he could, Reed folded back just the pertinent portions and turned it to face Levin.

"As you can see, the more points I plotted, the more a pattern emerged."

He didn't bother pointing out the different sites circled in blue or the final destination in black, allowing the doctor to infer for herself.

"So, everybody was taken within a certain radius of Franklinton Memorial Hospital," Levin said, glancing from the map up to Reed. "Why?"

Reed left the map in place and returned to his seat. "Here's the part that I need your help on. Again, the key words here are *working theory*.

"The one victim in all of this that just didn't seem to fit was Ruggles. The other three were all women. I haven't looked into the Jurgensen case much, but I know Rosen and Soto both lived alone, were attacked at their home well into the night, both middle-aged, both healthy."

The same concerned look remained on Levin's face, though she gave no indication that she was picking up where he was leading.

"So why the deviation?" he asked. "Why suddenly go after a man who had just days to live? It didn't make sense to me until I set his case aside for a moment and pulled the driver's licenses of all three women."

He removed the second clump of papers from his back pocket, the sheets folded into quarters. As a group he pressed them out flat before separating them and placing them side by side on top of the map.

Leaning closer, Levin rested her elbows on the edge of the table. One at a time she glanced at each of the photos, making it through all three before Reed saw a bit of recognition click and her gaze pass back over them in sequence.

"They were all organ donors," she whispered.

Reed nodded. "That's what I believe. I think that's why the killer tried to resuscitate Esther Rosen and why he picked a much slower cause of death for Ira Soto. When that didn't work, he beat Sandy Jurgensen and left her on the doorstep of the hospital."

All color drained from the doctor's face as she raised a hand, covering her mouth. Her eyes widened, and she stared from him to the pictures on her desk.

"My God," she whispered. "But, that doesn't explain Henry Ruggles. Why kill him too? He wasn't a donor, he was..."

A second realization hit Levin, her eyes sliding shut.

Reed didn't bother finishing her sentence. They both knew what she was trying to say.

The killer was eliminating competition. Sandy Jurgensen was the only one of the three who had survived long enough for her organs to be harvested. Best guess was that whoever the killer was had not received the liver that they needed and had gone after Henry Ruggles, presumably somebody higher on the list.

If not for the inclusion of Ruggles, Reed would not have even known what organ the killer was targeting.

"What this tells me," Reed said, "is that the killer still has a need for a liver. That means either more donors or more people on the waiting list are going to die. I freely admit I don't know a lot about this stuff, so anything you can give me would be much appreciated."

There was no response of any kind from Levin as she pondered the information.

Finally, when she spoke, her features were paler than Reed remembered, her lips drawn into a tight line. "First thing, your killer is acting on behalf of someone. Anybody with a case of liver failure this advanced doesn't have the strength or the stamina to be doing any of the things you're describing."

"Okay," Reed said, nodding.

"Your theory does make sense," Levin said, "in a very rudimentary way." She paused and held a hand up, her palm facing him, her fingers splayed outward, "No offense."

Reed shook off the apology.

"But it sounds like the killer has a very rudimentary understanding of the way this all works as well," she said.

"How so?" Reed asked.

"Well, for one thing," Levin said, "the process isn't strictly geographic. It's obvious that the killer believes it is, which is why you found the pattern, but it's actually much more involved than that."

Reed leaned in, resting his elbows on his knees. He wasn't sure how much of what he was hearing would be pertinent, but knew it was better to be armed with too much information than not enough. In an hour, he was going to be standing before his captain and two ranking detectives, probably a few other individuals as well. The more complete a picture he could give them, the more it gave credence to his theory.

"The waiting list is national," Levin said. "It's run by an organization called the United Network for Organ Sharing, which in a roundabout way is under the control of the federal government. It maintains an automated ranking of individuals and updates it at least daily.

"Geographic proximity factors in to the decision as to who gets an organ. They certainly won't be able to fly someone in from Hawaii for a liver in Massachusetts, but it isn't the most prominent factor by far."

"Why not?" Reed asked. "And if it isn't, what is?"

The previous looks of repulsion, of abject horror, had receded from Levin's face. She was now back in her element, not forced to face the kind of things Reed dealt with on a daily basis. Instead, she was in her familiar cocoon of medical knowledge. With each question she grew more assured, the confidence she displayed upon first meeting becoming more evident.

"To answer the first question," Levin said, "an organ is only viable for so long once it is out of the body. For a kidney, you might have upwards of a half hour, but for a liver you're looking at closer to 10 minutes. Twelve if you're lucky."

"And since most donors pass suddenly..." Reed prompted.

"Right," Levin said. "What's interesting about the way your, um, perpetrator, chose to do things is he was actually causing brain death, not actual death. Asphyxia, especially from carbon monoxide poisoning, would make a person unresponsive, but they could be kept alive for days or longer if necessary."

"Giving the hospital time to bring in someone higher on the list from further away," Reed said.

"But in the case of sudden passing," Levin said, "the hospital has to go with whoever can get there in time."

Both fell silent for a moment, Reed processing what he'd just heard. The doctor's previous assessment that the killer was operating under a very rudimentary understanding of things was quite clear, displaying either a level of naivety or desperation that was quite unsettling.

"So what is the most important thing in the determination?" Reed asked again.

"The list is done using what's called a MELD score," Levin said, "Model for Endstage Liver Disease. Blood tests are taken and a computer calculates a score from 6 to 40. The higher the number, the more urgent the need."

Adding this to the misshapen tangle of information he already had, Reed's gaze drifted to the side. It fell on a painting of a little boy playing doctor, using a stethoscope to check the heart rate of an enormous dog. He left it there until his vision blurred, trying to force everything he was hearing to make sense, trying to put himself in the killer's position.

"This list, where would one get it?"

"Simply put," Levin said, "they wouldn't. Like I said, it's run by a government agency, accessible only by facilities with transplant capabilities, like Franklinton Memorial."

"Mmm," Reed said, the sound coming out more like a grunt. "And, ballpark, how big are we talking here? 500 persons awaiting a donor? 1,000?"

"Nationwide?" Levin asked. "Closer to 20,000."

"Damn!" Reed spat, saying the word before he even realized it. He felt blood color his cheeks as he looked back at her, raising a hand in apology.

This time it was she that waved it off without comment.

"20,000 people and somebody thinks they can control the outcome right here in Franklinton?" Reed asked, making no effort to mask his surprise.

Levin's eyes grew a bit larger as she nodded in agreement. "Exactly. A rudimentary understanding, at best."

"No kidding," Reed muttered. "Too bad the damn killer couldn't just give his liver. Save us all a lot of time and headache."

"Well, they probably tried," Levin said. "The liver is remarkably durable, by far the hardiest of any organ in the body. A portion of the liver can be removed from a live donor and implanted into someone, after which it will regenerate itself in both parties."

"So why go through all this?" Reed asked. "Why not just go under the knife, give a chunk, and be done with it?"

"The liver is tough," Levin said, "but it's not indestructible. There are still compatibility issues that must be cleared and there is always the chance of rejection."

"So, like you said," Reed said, "they probably did try, it just didn't work."

Chapter Forty

Time was not The Good Son's friend. He could feel it pinching inward on him from all angles. Every hour his mother sat on the couch was one spent wasting away. Each day her conditioned worsened, her weight plummeted, her skin grew a little more yellow. At her last consultation, the doctor said her liver had basically stopped functioning and was down to its final days, though from the looks of things, she didn't even have that long.

The thought of losing her, now, after all he had done, was too much to bear. It caused The Good Son's chest to constrict, his breathing to become short.

Despite everything she had inflicted upon him - the beatings, the hunger, the cold – he still couldn't bring himself to consider a world without her in it. It was his fault she was in the predicament she was in. He had been unable to save his father, but this he could do. This situation was salvageable. He'd already proven that. Now, all he had to do was get it right one more time and everything would be okay.

Before that, though, he had something else to do.

Never before had he seen the police so blatantly go on television and proclaim their failure, asking for the assistance of the public-at-large. It was a bold move, one that reiterated the magnitude of what he was doing, of the necessary lengths he must go to in order to see things through.

Nothing was changed though. It was a new hurdle, but he still had tasks to complete, a charge to oversee. He now had to be more careful, but he could not slow down.

There just wasn't the time for it.

The reality of the situation struck The Good Son as he pulled up in front of the overgrown two-story house. Just six blocks from the home of Henry Ruggles, less than two miles from his own house, there was very little resemblance to either. Situated on the edge of The Bottoms, the house looked like most every other The Good Son had seen in the area, like at any moment a health inspector would arrive and condemn the place.

At one point the building had been constructed of wooden siding and painted white, a lean-to front porch stretched across the front. Over the years, the paint had flaked away, leaving only misshapen streaks behind. Large splotches of mold and mildew dotted the wood, enormous chunks having crumbled away, the combination of termites and weather having done their worst.

A single elm tree stood in the front yard, easily the only salvageable item on the property. Its branches hung out in a wide canopy, serving as an umbrella, blocking out the late afternoon sun. Below it the yard was nothing but a dirt patch, the occasional thistle or milkweed sticking up at odd intervals.

Seated behind the wheel, The Good Son took it all in. Again, the feeling of doubt, of uncertainty, seeped in around the edges of his resolve. No part of him wanted to leave the car, much less walk to the front door and knock. The sun was out and he was in plain sight. He had no prior chance to scout, no way of knowing for certain who or what else was inside the house beyond his reason for being there.

Closing his eyes, he drew in a deep breath, trying to steel his resolve. The obstacles between him and completion did not matter. All that was important was reaching his objective.

The driver side door let out a wicked squeal, a spur of adrenaline shooting through The Good Son. His first reaction, ingrained from the last week, was to crouch low, watching for anybody nearby. Just as fast the response faded, his legs extending back to full height.

Forcing an uneasy smile, The Good Son walked around the front of the car. He hopped the short curb and cut a path through the lawn, puffs of dust rising around his ankles with each step. Halfway across the expanse, his path intersected with the concrete sidewalk.

Up close, the house looked even rougher than from the road. Gouges were visible in the wood, giant slivers that had been torn away collecting on the ground. Mixed with flakes of paint, they were scattered on the floor of the porch like dead leaves in the fall.

The smell of garbage and decay found The Good Son's nose, tightening his stomach even further.

Finding the address had not been easy. It had taken a considerable bit of digging, both through his mother's records and through Henry Ruggles's. Even at that, he had only the faint hope that he was in the right place, no signs of life anywhere to confirm or deny it.

The wood of the front porch bowed beneath his weight as he stepped onto it, emitting a low creaking sound. With each step more of the same became audible, only adding to the unease, the trepidation roiling through him.

A few more steps. That's all he needed, a few more steps, and he would be there. He could step inside and finish what he needed to.

A ragged door hung at an angle across the front opening, the screen covering it torn in several places, one entire corner hanging down. Reaching through the gaping hole, The Good Son knocked against the solid structure behind it, hearing the sound echo through the house. He paused, letting the sound die away, before knocking again and taking a quarter-step back.

There he remained until finally the old building creaked with movement. He forced himself to remain rigid as every nerve ending in his body hummed, the sound growing closer, the door slowly easing back on its hinges.

Chapter Forty-One

Five men were seated around the table as Reed walked in. Each of them turned as Reed and Billie entered, their faces ranging from curious to hostile. Reed barely noticed any of them, knowing that whatever expression they wore now would soon be shifting once they heard what he had to say.

Tucked away on the third floor, the space was called a conference room, though the half dozen men and Billie more than filled it.

"Thank you all for being here," Reed said, swinging the door shut behind him.

There was no response from the table. To his left were Officers Greene and Gilchrist, both already dressed in their black uniforms. Their faces bore neutral expressions despite being called in an hour early, their hands folded in front of them.

On the opposite side were Iaconelli and Bishop, both showing the effects of a long day. Heavy sweat rings underscored Iaconelli's armpits, his face even redder than usual, more pronounced by the shirt he wore of the same color. His hair was soaked and plastered back against his head, and he was sneering as always. Beside him Bishop looked like he might keel backward at any moment, his skin still void of any color, his long arms folded in front of him.

Captain Grimes sat at the head of the table. He had been the last person Reed called with the request to meet, not especially happy about it and insisting the meeting should be no more than half an hour. At the longest.

"I know we've all got places we'd rather be," Reed said, ignoring the chair and standing, "so I'll get right to it."

He turned his attention to the left and said, "Officers, were either of you able to pull anything from Henry Ruggles's home or the canvas of his neighborhood?"

Gilchrist glanced to Greene before looking down at his hands, deferring to the senior man. Greene leaned forward, resting his forearms on the edge of the table.

"Ruggles's house came back clean. No signs of forced entry, no signs of a struggle. We told the crime scene crew to be on standby, but there was no reason to call them in. All indicators seemed to be that he was taken somewhere else, if not the park itself."

Reed nodded. There were few reasons he could think of as to why Ruggles's body would be left out in the park, the primary one being that it was a location of convenience. The killer probably knew that Ruggles's appearance would lead responding officers to believe it was drug related, hoping to focus attention in that direction.

The only other reason that remotely fit was if somebody had seen the killer enter Ruggles's house, requiring them also be seen leaving together.

"As to the second part," Greene said, "given the early hour, nobody on the block saw anything. One lady thinks she might have seen a silver car pull in around 6:00, but she couldn't be certain. Just happened to see headlights and glance outside while she was making breakfast."

Reed grunted. It only confirmed that the park was an easy place to get rid of the body. There was no need to get Ruggles to the hospital fast, so it didn't matter where he was left, just that he was already dead when he got there.

"Okay," Reed said. "Thank you guys for doing that. I got pulled in a couple different directions today, but appreciate you coming in early to debrief."

"Yeah, so what about us?" Iaconelli asked, making it clear that he did not appreciate being there, despite technically still being on the clock.

"Sandy Jurgensen," Reed responded, not rising to the bait, floating the name out in hopes of immediately putting Iaconelli on his heels.

It didn't have quite as much effect as intended, but it was enough to stop Iaconelli before he could object further. "Yeah? You call up your old buddies at the 19th and get some inside scoop?"

Reed paused. When Bishop mentioned earlier that things were locked in a jurisdictional quagmire, he hadn't even considered calling on anybody from his old unit. Just as Franklinton was barely a slice of the 8th, no more than a couple of neighborhoods of Hilliard extended into the 19th.

"No, actually, I worked backward from Esther Rosen and Ira Soto." He made a quick pass around the room, seeing no signs of recognition from anybody. "The *Night Stalker* cases."

Bishop and Gilchrist both nodded at the name. Greene and Grimes remained motionless. Iaconelli assumed his usual position, his hands resting on his stomach, a glare on his face.

Starting with the map, Reed laid out everything for the men just as he had for Dr. Levin. He outlined the various locations where each of the victims had been killed, beginning with Rosen and ending with Ruggles.

Once the obvious geographic pattern emerged, he placed Jurgensen at the center of it, just inside the circle outlining Franklin Memorial Hospital.

There he waited for any questions or comments, and when none came, he went on with his working theory. He showed each of them the driver's license copies for Rosen, Soto, and Jurgensen, followed up with a few of the pictures from the autopsy of Ruggles.

After he had the interest, however begrudging, of every man in the room, he raced through what Dr. Levin had shared with him. They all listened in silence as he left out most of the technical jargon, the scoring charts and blood samples and such, instead seizing on the facts that there was a list and that his working theory was feasible.

Somewhat misguided, maybe a bit choppy, but feasible.

Just like every single crime scene they'd found so far.

From start to finish the explanation took 13 minutes, in that time Reed being the only one to speak. Gilchrist nodded enthusiastically throughout much of it. Greene and Bishop both made sufficient eye contact to let him know they were following. Even Iaconelli dropped his hard-ass demeanor halfway through, listening as Reed made his case point by point.

At the far end of the room Grimes sat with his gaze aimed at the opposite wall, his arms folded, a frown in place. To some it might have appeared he was brooding, bordering on an explosion, but Reed had seen the pose often enough to know it merely meant he was processing.

Once his theory was completely outlined, Reed released his death grip on the back of the chair and pulled it out a few inches. He left the map and various papers strewn before him and lowered himself into the seat, slouching back against it.

"Obviously there are holes," he said, "and still a lot left to do, but I truly think this is where we are."

The statement was meant to open up the floor, to let it be known that they were moving from presentation to discussion, though nobody said a word. The men to either side stared at him briefly before averting their eyes, Gilchrist beginning to fidget as the slightest hint of awkwardness appeared.

"Assuming this is all true," Grimes said, his voice thick, as if he hadn't spoken in quite some time, snapping the attention of each man in the room in his direction, "what's next?"

Reed placed a hand on either arm of the chair and raised himself up a few inches.

"Start with the holes," Grimes instructed.

"Okay," Reed said, "right now, first thing has to be identifying our suspect and protecting the other liver transplant candidates in the area."

"That all?" Iaconelli asked, a touch of the earlier bitterness present.

Reed ignored it. "It is very clear that someone is trying to manipulate the donor system. I tend to agree with Dr. Levin, that there is no way someone experiencing end-stage liver failure could possibly do this, meaning we're probably looking at someone with a close personal connection to a particular candidate."

"I thought you said the list was protected?" Bishop interjected.

"It is," Reed said, "but I think I have a way around that. It'll be my first priority once we break here."

"And if you don't?" Iaconelli asked.

"Henry Ruggles's ex-wife mentioned a support group. We'll start there, get as many names as we can and work our way out. There might be 20,000 potential candidates awaiting donors, but how many of those can be down to their last days? Especially living right here in the greater Columbus area?"

He glanced around the room, waiting for another remark from Iaconelli that never came.

"After that," he said, "we work through them. Run their names, their families, start whittling things down."

It was rough, and would require a great deal of luck, but it was the best they had to work with. Eight hours ago there were four open murders without a single credible lead. Now, at least, they had a heading, something to be moving toward.

Again, the room fell silent. There were a few exchanged glances, a couple of looks to the paper still spread on the table, but nobody said a word.

Reed decided against adding anything further. He had stated his case. It was now up to the captain to decide what to do with it. Like him, every other man in the room knew it, one at a time looking to the head of the table for direction.

Oblivious to the stares, Grimes continued to focus his gaze on the back wall. He raised a hand to his chin and rubbed vigorously, his late-day whiskers scratching against his fingers.

"Ike, you and Bishop start with the ex-wife," Grimes said. "Get a list of names, whatever she has, and start working through them."

True to form, Iaconelli glanced up at the clock on the wall and scowled, Bishop simply nodding beside him.

"Greene, Gilchrist, you guys be on standby. Once these two get a list, they'll split it with you. I'll have someone cover your patrol tonight."

Both men nodded in unison.

"How do we handle it?" Greene asked. "Bring them into protective custody? Just tell them to be alert?"

Grimes paused a moment, his mouth half open, pondering the question. "For the time being, just tell them to remain indoors, to keep things locked up tight. Our guy hasn't used a gun or knife yet, so they should be okay. If we do get our hands on the list and are able to narrow things down, we may bring them in later."

A short grunt was Greene's only response, Gilchrist removing his notepad from a chest pocket and scribbling notes.

"And you're going after the list?" Grimes said.

"I am," Reed said. "I'm also going to have my guy take a look into the financials of our three female victims. The only way he could have possibly known they were all organ donors was to have seen their driver's licenses, which probably means he works in some kind of service industry job where he has to check ID's."

"That opens up a hell of a lot of possibilities," Bishop said, glancing over to him.

"True," Reed said. "I'm hoping something in their spending history will show a commonality. Might help speed up the identification."

Eight feet away Grimes nodded. He looked at Reed, his arms still folded, and asked, "This contact of yours, he wouldn't be the same one who helped us out a few months ago would he?"

Chapter Forty-Two

The number of things Riley taught Reed in their time together was too many to count. She was two years younger, but somehow had managed to cram more life experience into her days than most people who lived two or three times as long. Rarely did a day go by that Reed wasn't reminded of one of her lessons, never more so than when he was approaching the bucolic house in Worthington.

"If I teach you nothing else in our time together," she would say, "let it be this. Never, *ever*, show up at this house empty handed. The man inside provides a very specific set of skills which requires a very specific type of payment. This might be the only place on earth where cash isn't going to get it done."

It was the first time Reed had been back to the house in three months, since the incident Grimes had alluded to in the conference room. In the time since, he had made a point to call twice, if for no other reason than to not only show up when a favor was needed.

Derrick Chamberlain and Riley were classmates together at Ohio State who somehow had managed to meet, tolerate one another, become friends, and remain that way for nearly a decade after graduation. To see them together was to witness a true Mutt-and-Jeff pairing, one a detective with an increasingly cynical view of the world, independent to a fault, the other a man stuck in a state of arrested development, content to live in his grandmother's basement, playing video games and insisting everyone call him Deek.

As far as Reed could tell, the man worked in cyber security of some sort, keeping odd hours and getting compensated handsomely for it. Riley had mentioned more than once that he could buy the entire street if he wanted, choosing instead to indulge in every game system ever invented and consume enough Red Bull and candy to feed a small village.

Despite the sun fast streaking toward the horizon, Reed brought Billie along with him. The summer evening was still too hot to risk leaving her behind, especially without knowing how long this task would take. He held her short lead in one hand and the payment for Deek in the other, a canvas gym bag used to get it inside. Around his neck hung his badge, the sun winking off the polished brass.

The doorbell to the home, a one story ranch painted yellow with blue shutters, chimed a short three note tune as Reed pressed it and stepped back, Billie by his side. The sound had barely died away as footsteps approached, the movement sounding like slippers sliding across tile.

"Good evening, can I help you?" a woman well into her 70s asked, peering out at him. Already, she had retired to pajamas for the evening, a pair of fuzzy slippers on her feet. Tight curls encased her head and thick glasses rested on the end of her nose, making her eyes appear to be the size of golf balls.

It was at least the 20th time the two had met, though she acted as if she'd never seen Reed before in her life.

"Good evening, Mrs. Chamberlain," Reed said, extending the badge an inch or two toward her. "Is Deek home?"

In years past, Riley would have handled all early salutations, the two falling into friendly banter within seconds. Less than a minute after arriving, Mrs. Chamberlein would usher them in and try to force food at them, laughing the entire time.

Those days were now gone. She peered at Reed with a momentary look of distrust before her gaze found the badge, and then Billie. "Yes, of course, Officer. Deek's in his office working. You go right on down."

Reed thanked her and stepped inside, Billie staying close. He managed to keep his face clear of any reaction to her use of the word *office* as he passed through the foyer and opened a side door to the basement, carrying the bag containing Deek's payment.

He descended a set of wooden stairs, pushing himself to the outer edge where there was only bare wood, allowing Billie to take the middle, her paws using the carpet there for extra stability. With each step the structure groaned under their combined weight, the sound of music growing louder as they went.

How they had not managed to hear it from the first floor, or the front step, or even as they drove up, Reed wasn't certain, the volume and the associated bass reverberating through the space.

"Hey!" he called as he reached the bottom, glancing around the room. He could see no movement of any kind beyond a psychedelic screensaver on the 80" television to his left, the vibrant colors moving in time with the music.

"Hey!" he yelled again, raising his voice and extending the word a couple of extra syllables.

Once more, his was voice drowned out by the persistent thumping of the music.

He leaned down to Billie and commanded, "Speak!"

Four vicious barks rang out, each one louder than the previous. After the second one the music cut away, the silence jarring as Billie completed her outburst and resumed her position beside Reed.

"Good girl," Reed said, patting her on the neck.

"What the hell?!" a voice exclaimed, a head appearing on the opposite side of the room a moment later.

A bank of computer monitors obscured everything about the voice's owner from the beck down, but that was all Reed needed to confirm it was Deek.

"Oh, you," Deek said, a look of mild surprise on his face, though not nearly as pronounced as the first time Reed had shown up unannounced months before.

"Me," Reed replied.

"And you brought your, um..."

"Partner," Reed said, shooting Deek a look that let it be known no further comment was required.

"Right," Deek said. In slow, stilted steps he came out from around the computer screens.

At 6' tall, he stood a bit shorter than Reed, and weighed at least 50 pounds less. A plain black t-shirt and gym shorts hung from his frame, and a plume of blonde hair jutting from his head. "So, to what do I owe the pleasure of a visit this evening?"

Reed raised his eyebrows, sensing the sarcasm, not quite believing the stop was a pleasure for either party. The simple fact was, the man vacillated between being annoying and a full-on pain in the ass, though there were few better in the cyber world, and none Reed knew personally.

Reaching to his side, Reed unzipped the bag and wrapped his hand around the neck of a bottle of Johnny Walker Blue, sliding it free. "I need a favor."

Like Pavlov's dog, Deek's mouth dropped open, the man almost salivating as he stared. "No, a favor is when somebody shows up wanting something for nothing. What you've got there is a down payment on any damn thing you need."

"Just like that?"

"Considering you're wearing your badge, that makes this an official request, which means it isn't anything that can land both our asses in jail, so yeah...just like that."

Reed couldn't help but smile. As strange as the logic was, it did make sense.

"Down," Reed commanded, leaving Billie by the staircase. He dropped the empty bag to the floor and walked halfway across the room, the bottle held at arm's length.

To his right, the basement had been converted into a living space with a king size water bed and kitchenette. Neon signs for various brands of alcohol illuminated the area, casting a harsh glow over everything. On the left, a single leather recliner rested in front of the enormous TV, a tangle of video game controls on the floor between the two.

Between the two was Deek's workstation, the backs of a half-dozen monitors facing the stairs. From where Reed stood he could not see a single screen, was not sure he even wanted to.

"Two tasks," Reed said. "One pretty simple, the other I'm not so sure."

Five feet away Deek crossed his arms over his chest, the stance managing to make him appear even skinnier. "Shoot."

"You heard anything about the murders in Franklinton this week?" Reed asked.

For a moment Deek's eyebrows came together, appearing to make a genuine attempt to answer. "No. To be honest, I'm not even sure what day it is right now. Been pretty buried with work."

A handful of retorts ran through Reed's mind, but he let them slide, knowing better than to offend someone whose help he needed.

"Well, there have been four of them," Reed said. "Three of them were women living in the area. I need you to run their financials and see if they have anything in common. All three women were organ donors, and we think the killer had access to their driver's licenses. Best bet is it was someone who worked a cash register or a front door checking ID's."

"Huh," Deek said, dropping his hands to his side and shrugging. "Okay, easy enough. What's the second request?"

"I need you to hack into a federal government database and get me a list of people awaiting liver transplants in the greater Columbus area."

Chapter Forty-Three

The first task took Deek a grand total of eight minutes. Normally, pulling someone's credit card reports and financial statements would have taken longer, but using Reed's position as a detective allowed them to bypass a lot of red tape – as long as no one found out.

Under the guise of forensic accounting, they pulled everything for the previous four weeks on all three female victims, Deek placing them side by side on a trio of adjacent monitors. He then ran a quick algorithm, explaining everything to Reed as he worked in a language that barely resembled English, before highlighting three businesses.

Over the time leading up to the death of Esther Rosen, all three women had shopped at a Wal-Mart, a BP gas station, and a lawn and garden supply store known as Big Q.

With the sun already beginning to dip below the horizon, Reed left Deek to work on the other request. Against his better judgment, he left the bottle of Johnny Walker behind, trusting that his temporary consultant would have the willpower to withstand breaking the seal until the second objective was accomplished.

After that, Reed knew all bets were off.

Together he and Billie cut a path straight across the front yard and climbed into the car, ignoring the fact that the interior temperature was just a degree or two cooler than the sun as they took off.

Two of the three common businesses, Reed felt fairly safe in disregarding for now, at least placing them at the bottom of the list. He had purchased enough gas in his life to know that most people paid at the pump by credit card. There was no need for them to enter the store, much less show anybody ID.

As for Wal-Mart, Reed stopped in occasionally for things on his way home in the morning. One of the reasons he preferred the store to the K-Mart down the road was they had self-service checkouts, allowing him to avoid any human contact on the back end of an overnight shift. And on the rare occasion he paid a cashier, he was never asked for ID.

That left only Big Q, a place Reed vaguely remembered seeing some print advertisements for, but had never actually seen in person, much less been inside. Aiming his way south from Deek's, he punched the location into his GPS and listened as the directions were spit back at him, the store on the outer edge of Franklinton, just barely within the jurisdiction of the 8th.

And just a short drive from all four victims.

Propping his elbow up on the middle console, Reed used a hand to shield his face from the setting sun to his right. He pinched his gaze against the glare of it and kept his speed 10 miles above the limit, his mouth pulled tight as he plotted his next steps.

Right now Deek was digging for the organ transplant list. Iaconelli and Bishop were en route to speak with Bethanee Cleary, a task Reed was all too happy to hand off and would no doubt hear about later. Somewhere nearby, Greene and Gilchrist were awaiting instruction. Grimes was up-to-date on everything, seemingly willing to offer any further support that was needed.

Encroaching media and a chief hell bent on closing every case the minute it was filed had a way of doing that.

For the time being, everything Reed could control was covered. Knowing that did nothing to calm his nerves, didn't deter the need to catch whoever was doing this, but at least it allowed him to narrow his focus.

Go to Big Q. Find out if anybody there might be his guy.

If so, investigate him. If not, hope that Deek had made enough progress to begin moving on somebody else.

The grating voice of the GPS directed Reed to a building that stretched almost a block in length. From the outside it looked like a warehouse that had been repurposed, most of the structure made from concrete block painted grey. Flowers of every color were stretched along the building garden center, just to the side of the wide front entrance. On either end of the building a pair of roll top doors stood open, ready for customers to load up larger purchases.

Pulling into the lot, Reed made a quick scan of the parking lot, seeing a pair of silver vehicles, one an SUV, another a pickup truck.

Nothing resembling the sedan the witnesses had described.

Leaving the front windows rolled down, Reed climbed out, jerking his damp t-shirt away from his chest and lower back. The movement brought a puff of air against his skin, the temporary relief much welcomed as he opened the back and clipped on Billie's short lead. The badge swung from his neck as he led her to the front door, aware that they were drawing a few stares. He made a point of meeting every one, watching for any suspicious behavior, holding the eye contact long enough to make people uncomfortable, waiting for someone to get jumpy.

Each one became a bit fidgety before hurrying on their way, but nobody did anything that seemed out of the ordinary for a citizen being stared down by a cop and his wolf sidekick.

The front doors of the store parted automatically, a breeze passing over them as they stepped through, the building cooled by fans circling overhead. Reed paused just inside the door, letting his vision adjust to the lower level of light.

Just as the exterior had indicated, the place was a lawn and garden store similar to Lowe's or Home Depot. The aisles were extra wide and exceptionally tall, steel steps on rollers placed at intervals throughout to help reach the highest items. White boards announced various sales in thick black marker.

Arriving unannounced, Reed walked straight to the closest cash register, a middle aged woman who barely came to his chest behind it. She glanced up at him, her unease showing, before a forced smile crossed her face.

"Good evening, sir," she said. "How may I help you?"

Reed didn't bother lifting the badge from his chest. It was already eye level with her, clearly visible. "Hi, is the manager available, please?"

The smile wavered just a moment, the woman reaching for a red telephone mounted on a pole beside her. "Sure," she said, lifting the mouthpiece. "Mr. Beauregard to register three please, Mr. Beauregard to register three."

The distorted sound of her voice spilled from overhead speakers, echoing throughout the store before fading away. Quickly, she replaced the receiver and took a step back from it, another pained smile crossing her face.

"Thank you," Reed said, releasing the poor woman from her misery and stepping away from the counter. He moved until there was nearly 10 feet between them before stopping and hooking his thumbs into the rear pockets of his jeans.

He heard the manager long before he saw him, a pinched, angry voice descending from one of the aisles. It seemed to materialize from nowhere, drawing the attention of both Reed and the woman behind the counter.

"Dammit, Cindy," he said, extra bravado inserted for effect, "what have I told you about using the PA system for non-emergencies?"

A moment later, the owner of the voice emerged from two aisles over. A short, slovenly man, he was only nominally taller than the woman he called Cindy, a thin smattering of bottle-black hair smashed flat to his scalp. A rotund middle section hung down over wrinkled khakis, his gait more side-to-side than straight ahead, something Riley would have referred to as a duck walk.

Behind the counter Cindy stood rigid. She raised her right hand and pointed a single finger over toward Reed, saying nothing.

The man took three steps forward, ready to berate her further, before turning to see Reed and Billie waiting for him. On sight, the venom he carried just a moment before evaporated, his pace slowing as he redirected himself. Six inches at a time he walked closer, his jaw working up and down in silence.

"Detective Reed Mattox," Reed said, taking a step closer, "my partner, Billie."

The man nodded, glancing down to Billie before looking up at Reed. "Uh, Dan Beauregard. How can I help you, Detective?"

He cast a quick look around as he asked the question, on the lookout for any stray customers who might be lingering nearby to watch the interaction.

Normally, Reed would take the man aside, asking if he had an office where they could speak in private, saving anybody the indignity of meeting with a detective out in the open. Tonight though, running short on time and having already seen the way the man treated his employee, Reed didn't feel the inclination.

He had a job to do, and protecting feelings wasn't a part of that.

"Two questions," Reed said, holding up the index and middle finger on his left hand, the proverbial peace sign. "First, are you the manager here?"

Beauregard's voice misfired twice before he finally spoke. "Yes, I am."

"Do you folks require customers to show ID when making a credit card purchase?"

Chapter Forty-Four

The nap was a rare occurrence, something The Good Son hadn't done in years. The combination of nerves pulled taut and the nocturnal schedule he'd kept lately had finally caught up to him, his body succumbing to complete exhaustion. When he awoke, he was face down on his bed, his cheek smashed into his pillow, his skin feeling sweaty and sticky.

"Damn," he muttered, running a hand back over his forehead and wiping it against the bed beside him. He looked toward the window, seeing no light through the blinds, the world outside dark.

A bolt of electricity shot through him as he checked the digital clock glowing red beside the bed.

"Shit!" he spat, rolling onto his feet and stumbling down the hallway, his body careening from one side to the other, fighting for balance.

This was not something he could do right now. They were on a schedule. He could not afford to make mistakes like this, no matter how tired he was.

"Mama," he said, crossing straight into the living room and turning on the lamp beside the couch. His heart pounded as he knelt down, placing one hand on her shoulder and shaking gently. "Mama. Mama, it's time to get up. You have to take your medicine."

There was no response from the shriveled form as The Good Son slid a hand beneath her ribs and the other under her knees, lifting her and shifting her toward him. He rotated her almost a full 180 degrees, before lowering her back into place.

Her doctors had warned of this. With each passing hour, the need for a new organ was growing more urgent, the meds alone no longer enough to keep her functioning. She should be in a home, being watched around the clock, but her adamant refusal and their dwindling funds made that impossible.

Instead, the responsibility was his, just one of many he had inherited.

His heart pounding, The Good Son rose and ran into the kitchen, his heavy steps shaking the living room. He went straight for the medicine bottles there, stopping by the sink just long enough to run two inches of water into a cup.

Balancing everything against his chest, he deposited it all on the coffee table, sinking to his knees beside her.

"Mama, drink this," he whispered.

There was no response as he raised her body upright and positioned it back against the sofa, her eyes fluttering open to slits before closing again. She made no effort to help or hinder him as he tilted her head back and poured just a sip of water down her throat, her body not even registering that it had entered until she coughed a moment later.

The wet spasm forced some life back into her as she hacked three times, most of the water coming back out. Only then did her eyes open wide enough for her to look at him, remaining silent.

"Here," The Good Son said as he lifted the cup again to her lips, using his opposite hand to tilt back her chin and pour in just a few drops.

The doctor referred to the method as lubrication, opening the passage up a little bit before attempting to get the pills down. Only once she was able to consume some water would she have any hope of getting the small white pills down, the medicine vital to keep her body processing what little it could.

"Okay," The Good Son said, the word clipped, his voice taut as he moved for the first bottle. With practiced hands, he popped the top and fished out a tiny white pill, holding it to her lips and following it with a bit more of the water.

Throughout, she merely stared at him, the occasional flicker behind her eyes the only sign of life.

"Just keep fighting, Mama," he whispered, moving directly for the second vial. "Almost. We're almost there."

The nap was a mistake, but the current situation was also indicative of where they were. Time was up. If something didn't happen in the next day, in the coming hours, she would not make it. There was no point going back to the doctor, no excuse to let them continue drawing blood, poking and prodding the poor woman and running their endless tests.

Until there was a healthy liver, moving her didn't make any sense. It took too much out of them both, cost money they didn't have.

The Good Son watched as the third and then the fourth pill went down. He saw her eyes become more responsive with each one, every sip of water waking her a bit more, though she still remained silent. She simply sat and fixed her gaze on him, the same sad, longing expression she always wore during moments like this.

It seemed to be the only time the hatred that had taken root in her ever subsided, moving away long enough for The Good Son to see some glimpse of the mother he once knew.

Staring back at her, sensing exactly what she was trying to say, The Good Son made a decision. The only other person who could possibly be ahead of her on the list was gone. That meant the next organ to come available was earmarked for her. It had to be. Even if he had to carry her and the new donor in together, regardless of what it meant for him, he had to get his mother that liver.

"Hang in there," he whispered, reaching out and patting her on the shoulder. He held the pose a moment before leaning down, pulling her frail form against his bare chest, and hugging her.

He hated himself for what he was about to do, but just like the others he had killed, there was no way around it.

If that meant Paul Neil Tudor's time was up, then so be it.

Chapter Forty-Five

Reed had no reason to believe the flashers were necessary, but he couldn't shake the feeling that time was running out just the same. They had been fortunate to avoid another casualty the night before, but that guaranteed nothing moving forward. He opted against using the siren just yet, letting the flashing front headlights clear a path as he drove back to the precinct.

On the seat beside him was a printout that Dan Beauregard, the store manager, had provided him, the sheet weighed down by Reed's badge. The corners of it flapped slightly as wind pushed through the car, cooling the interior only nominally.

In total there were 31 names listed, 20 of them male and 11 female. Beyond the list, Beauregard had been little help whatsoever, explaining that they still had an older style machine for card transactions and that they did require ID checks on all credit purchases.

That part aside, he explained that virtually all 31 employees had access to the registers, every new hire starting as a cashier before moving out into various departments.

More than once Reed had tried to drill down a little further, asking the man if he knew of anybody with a direct connection to a sick relative or if anybody had shown signs of skittish, unusual behavior in the past week. After much fumbling and stammering, he had come back with nothing, Reed getting the distinct impression that Beauregard was the type of manager who looked down on his employees. He wouldn't risk the indignity of actually fraternizing or getting to know a single one of them, no doubt having earned their unending ire in the process.

His next stop was back to the precinct to run the names he'd been given. If there was only one or two he could call Jackie and ask her, but with this many he needed to be able to see the data for himself. Right now he was still operating on the premise that he knew what he was looking for, but that didn't mean there wasn't much more waiting to be uncovered.

He couldn't leave that to her. Really couldn't sacrifice the time it would take dealing with her unending nosiness.

The shrill sound of Reed's cell phone erupted from the cup holder on the middle console, ripping Reed away from his train of thought. Using the controls on the door, he raised both front windows and lifted the phone, Bishop's name appearing on the screen.

"Mattox."

"You could have mentioned we were walking into a damn hornet's nest," Bishop said. There was no greeting of any kind, just straight to the comment that showed considerable irritation.

Reed nodded, remembering his own encounter with Bethanee Cleary all too well. "Yeah, she's a peach, isn't she?"

"A real live Mother Teresa," Bishop agreed.

The two detectives could spend the next half hour bemoaning Cleary and every other witness they'd encountered like her over the years. That was the sort of thing to be done over a beer at some point, though, not on the phone in the middle of an active search.

Redirecting the conversation before it got too far off track, Reed said, "Was she able to help at all?"

"Eventually. She was sure to let us know that we were intruding, even threatened to have her new boyfriend – she kept referring to him as that, as if it would make a difference – kick our ass for interrupting their Friday night."

Picturing Iaconelli and Bishop standing side-by-side, the human depiction of the number 10, one tall and thin, the other short and round, elicited a laugh from Reed. Imagining anybody threatening to kick their asses was almost too much.

Almost.

"After Ike threatened to haul her ass in for obstruction she finally disappeared inside, came back with a handful of mail she'd received for Ruggles since the split. Every last piece of it had been opened, though she claimed it all arrived that way."

"All of it," Reed said. "Right."

"Yeah," Bishop said. "If we hadn't wanted to get our asses out of there, we might have pointed out what she'd done was a federal offense, but we let it slide. But maybe when all this is over…"

Reed shared the sentiment, waiting for Bishop to get to the part he needed. In front of him, a pair of SUV's drifted to the side of the road, letting him move right past, the flashers doing their job.

In the distance ahead he could see the precinct come into view, the flagpole out front lit up by a spotlight.

"One piece of particular interest was from the support group," Bishop said, "an announcement of a memorial for a former member who had passed. No name or anything on it, but there's a return address on the front.

"We called Greene and Gilchrist and told them to head over. We're on our way down there now."

In one quick movement, Reed jerked the wheel across two lanes, pushing the sedan into the front lot of the precinct. He pulled directly into the first visitor stall and killed the engine, grabbing the keys and his phone at the same time.

"Good," Reed said. "I'm at the precinct now. I'm going to give Grimes a quick recap of everything and then run the employee list I just got from Big Q."

If Bishop wondered at all what Big Q was or why Reed had pulled the employee list, he didn't voice it.

"I'll be in touch as soon as I know anything."

"We'll do the same," Bishop responded.

Chapter Forty-Six

When pulling into the lot, Reed hadn't noticed the van parked three spaces from him. Parked alongside it, though, he could see the letters KCMH and the logo for the local Channel 4 news affiliate. Alongside them was the face of Yasmin Leveritt, a different suit jacket, but the same plastic smile stretched across her face.

"What the hell?" Reed asked, clipping Billie's lead and waiting for her to scramble down. He let the question linger in the air, the printouts rolled up in his hand as they cut across the front lawn and through the entrance.

The air inside was almost the same as that outside, the effect of nearly every employee having left in the preceding hour.

Together he and Billie went straight for Grimes's office, finding the door open and the lights on, but nobody inside.

"Must already be upstairs," Reed said, raising his pace to a jog, Billie falling in beside him as they passed back through the doors and up the staircase. Reed took them two at a time, still no match for Billie as they reached the second floor, jogged around to the other side, and moved on to the third.

As they went Reed caught a flash of Jackie's hair in his periphery, making no effort to stop or even acknowledge her as he went.

There would be time for that later.

On the top floor, Reed and Billie went straight for the same room the interview had taken place in a night before. There was no sign of movement outside as they came closer, though shadows played across the floor and voices could be heard.

By the time Reed arrived it appeared that a second interview was just about to take place. The same cameraman was in position, his long body stooped low, getting both people in the shot.

Leveritt was in her previous spot, her head turning to Reed as he appeared unexpectedly.

Across from her Grimes followed the cue, shifting in his seat to see Reed and Billie standing there. "Pardon me a minute," he said, rising from his seat. He left without waiting for a response, pulling the door shut behind him.

"What's going on?" Reed asked, glancing from Grimes to the closed door.

"Chief Brandt," Grimes said, making it clear he was not pleased with anything that was transpiring.

"*She* sent them down here?" Reed asked, his eyes bulging.

"Says that after last night, she wants to put people at ease. She's afraid they might get the wrong impression."

The explanation brought a deep frown to Reed's mouth as he thought of her sitting downtown, more concerned with running damage control than apprehending an active killer.

"And what impression is that?" Reed asked. "That people should be mindful of a serial killer loose in Franklinton?"

Grimes opened his mouth to respond, raising both hands in surrender, before dropping them with a heavy sigh. "She told me to get on TV and tell people we're making progress. That their help was instrumental, and we've developed solid leads."

The frown on Reed's face only grew more pronounced. "So she told you to get on the air and tell people to stop calling."

"Pretty much."

"Jesus Christ."

"Pretty much."

Reed paused, trying to force down the anger he felt for the entire bureaucracy in the department. He thought of Brandt, and her lapdog Dade, before shaking his head to expel the images.

"Alright," he said. "I'm just here to update you, use the information if you want. The only three places that showed up in the financial history of all our victims were Wal-Mart, BP, and Big Q."

The previous look of disgust faded from Grimes's features. He raised a hand to his chin, listening intently as Reed continued.

"The first two I bounced for obvious reasons. I just went out to Big Q and confirmed they do still check ID's by hand." He waved the rolled up paper at Grimes and said, "I've got their employee list here. Going down right now to start digging."

Grimes nodded. "Good."

"Also, Bishop said they got an address on the support group. No names, might be nothing. Greene and Gilchrist are en route now, the detectives will meet them there."

Once more Grimes nodded. He said nothing, his gaze glossing over as he stood, deep in thought.

"We good?" Reed asked.

"We're good," Grimes responded. He looked back at the door behind him and said, "Hear me out on this. You're making good headway. This thing is starting to crack open. If I go in there right now and say that to the cameras, though, like Brandt wants me to..."

A moment passed, Reed processing the statement before picking up on the insinuation. "Could scare our killer off, send him underground."

"Right," Grimes said. "I'm certainly not trying to dangle anybody out there as bait, but I don't want to trip you up either."

Reed hadn't considered it, the second interview coming on him so suddenly there hadn't been time to really think about the possible outcomes, though the captain was correct. Now more than ever, he needed the killer to be moving about as usual, unaware that they were finally starting to circle closer.

"Have the phones turned up anything useful yet?" Reed asked, already knowing the answer.

"Not a thing," Grimes said, both knowing the move was made more as a warning to citizens than a plea for actual help.

"She'll chew your ass for it," Reed said.

"Probably," Grimes said, "but remember what happened last time? We catch the damn killer, in the end there isn't a lot she can say."

Chapter Forty-Seven

"Hey, Sugar, what's going on?"

Reed stopped at the landing on the second floor, his back to Jackie, and let his eyes drift shut. He pinched his face tight, gritting his teeth, cursing himself for being so foolish.

Every office in the world, without fail, had a designated gossip, the person who lived for being the first to discover some juicy tidbit of information and disseminate it to all other coworkers, often inserting themselves somehow into the story.

Jackie was that person in the 8th Precinct. Most of the time that was fine, everybody humoring her with the occasional morsel, or at the very least a feigned apology when they could not afford to tell her anything.

Tonight, Reed didn't have the time or the energy for either.

Rotating on the ball of his foot, Reed took a single step closer.

"Chaos," Reed said, summarizing things with just one word. "About 10 different threads suddenly emerged at once, so we've got everybody running a different direction trying to get a handle on them."

"Oh," Jackie said, her lips protruding in a slight pout. "Does that mean you don't have time to fill me in right quick?"

No part of Reed wanted to say another word. He had things to do, things with a very finite timeframe. Under the best of circumstances, he tried to limit his time at the dispatch desk to only that which was necessary, and even then it was well down his list of favorite things to do.

To his eternal luck though, he didn't have to say that.

The phone on his hip sprang to life, the chirping of the ringtone echoing throughout the space, Jackie's face falling as Reed pulled the phone free and glanced down at the screen.

DEREK GREENE.

"Hey, I'm really sorry..." he said, wagging it once in her direction. Across the room she waved in acceptance, her attention already returning to the magazine spread on the desk before her.

"Mattox," Reed said, answering the phone. He remained at the top of the stairwell, unsure whether to bolt back to the computers or run down the stairs for the car.

As far as he knew, Greene was on his way to look into the support group. There weren't many reasons why he would already be calling, none of them especially good.

"Hey," Greene said, his tone telling Reed everything he needed to know, pushing him down the stairs. "We just arrived at the address Bishop gave us. Nobody answered the door but most of the lights in the place were on, so we came inside."

Reed's stomach seized tight as he passed through the lobby and hit the front door, never once breaking stride. The humidity of the outer world wrapped around him the instant he stepped out.

"Dead body?" Reed asked, already knowing the answer.

"Yup," Greene said. "Male, late 40s, looks to be in nominally better shape than Henry Ruggles."

Again, Reed ignored the front walk in favor of the grass. Despite the humidity, it was brittle to the touch, crackling beneath his feet. "Got an ID?"

"Not yet," Greene said. "The place is rough, but doesn't look like it's been worked over. Should have something pretty soon here."

"I'll call Earl, and be there by the time you do."

Chapter Forty-Eight

There existed no doubt in Reed's mind that this was another in what was becoming an unending string of connected murders. Just the same though, if there was even the smallest chance that the killer ever stood before a judge, Reed had to make sure that every last crime committed was accounted for.

He also needed to make sure that his canine partner was best positioned to do what she did best. There was no way for Reed to know for sure that her skills would be called on, but the way things were going, it seemed like a safe assumption.

Pulling out of the precinct, Reed kept the flashers running. The neighborhood was already pretty quiet, only a couple of pairs of brake lights flaring and drifting to the side of the road. Again, he ran without the siren, not seeing the need for it, knowing it would only draw attention at a time when that was the last thing he wanted.

By the time he arrived, Iaconelli and Bishop were already there, their car parked on the street behind Greene and Gilchrist's cruiser.

The interior of the house was lit up like a Christmas tree, silhouettes moving behind shades.

His first inclination was to burst out of the car and rush the house,

Billie by his side, intent to help sift through every scrap of paper until they had something to work with.

A roster of support group members. A set of phone numbers. Even a photograph with everybody present.

He fought the urge, though. As much as he wanted to, there were already capable people handling that. He needed to stay outside, wait for Earl and his team to show up, to handle things properly.

This case was about to make its second round through the airwaves. The third would be when they solved it. There didn't need to be a forth later on talking about how badly they mishandled things.

Reed sat behind the wheel, the windows up and the air on, waiting until a pair of headlights appeared in the rearview. Sitting up high and square, he recognized the crime scene unit van, waiting until they pulled in behind him before exiting.

Stepping from the driver's side, Earl was dressed as usual in bib overalls, beads of sweat gleaming along his bald head. Behind him a pair of techs moved immediately to the back and began to unload supplies.

"Would have been here earlier," Earl said. "But it took me a few minutes to find this."

He stopped a couple of steps from Reed and extended his hand, a clear plastic evidence bag in it holding a stone the size of a soda can, a smear of dried blood on it.

"Thanks for bringing it," Reed said. He knew the request had been an odd one, something he had thought of on the fly and asked of Earl when he called in the body. He reached out and accepted the bag, holding it by the sealed top.

"You sure about this?" Earl asked. "You know once that's opened it won't be admissible anymore."

"Doesn't matter," Reed said, gripping either side and pulling it apart like a bag of potato chips, the adhesive seal along the top ripping open. "This rock was used for a canine homicide, which is hardly our biggest concern right now. It might not have held a fingerprint, but it will damn sure hold a scent."

Reed peeled back the sides as he opened the rear door and held the bag in front of Billie. "Smell."

Just as she had outside Ira Soto's home, Billie moved straight to it. She kept her nose just millimeters away from the stone, careful not to touch anything, silent as she drew in the signature scent of whoever had held it last.

Reed knew there was no way Billie had forgotten the smell. She worked with scents the way humans worked with their eyes, her memories linked inexorably to certain aromas. The only occasional problem came because of her extreme abilities, which made it difficult for her in places where multiple smells had been left.

Give her one specific scent source, though, and tell her to find it, there was none better on earth.

It took Billie only seconds to reacquaint herself with the smell, still standing in the back of the car, before she let Reed know she had the signature down.

"Search." The word came out hard and fast, a clear command. The sound of it still hung in the air as she darted from the back seat, a black bolt of fur that shot past Reed onto the street and went to work.

Reed didn't bother to attach her to a lead, giving her the freedom to move as she needed to. Instead, he circled around to the edge of the car, watching as she held her nose just inches above the ground, working in a sweeping pattern in search of that one particular smell.

"Damn, look at her go," Earl whispered, Reed having completely forgotten the man was still standing there.

"Just wait until she picks it up," Reed said, leaving the big man standing in the street and walking a few steps across the dirt patch that served as the front yard.

Eight feet to Reed's left, Billie caught the scent, picking it up running in a diagonal line for the front door. In an instant her body went rigid and the sweeping pattern she was moving in stopped, replaced with a path straight toward the house. Feeling his pulse pick up, Reed fell in line behind her, watching her go to the front door.

There she stopped, her body poised, clearly wanting to pursue further.

Stepping up behind her, Reed clipped on the short lead, only vaguely aware of Earl and his team following behind. Gripping the lead in his right hand, Reed pulled open the front door with his left.

Instantly, Billie tugged straight ahead, yanking Reed through the kitchen. He barely had the time to notice the yellowed linoleum floor or the stove and refrigerator, all remnants from the 70s, before moving straight into the living room.

"Heel!" Reed snapped as they entered the space, Billie pulling up short the moment it left his lips. She dropped her backside to the floor and looked up at him, her ears lowered. "Good girl."

On the floor in front of them was a male in his mid-to-late 40s, just as Greene had said on the phone. He was lying flat on his back, his arms extended outward in a starfish pattern, his eyes staring straight up at the ceiling. He wore a pair of khaki shorts and a Cincinnati Bengals t-shirt, the exposed skin of his arms and legs mottled with bruises. Between the ugly green and blue spots the skin was the color of straw, the result of both jaundice and the extra bright lights illuminating him.

Like Ruggles, there was no readily visible cause of death, though Reed figured it wouldn't take much to discover a broken neck once again.

The body was positioned flat in the middle of a threadbare rug. Along one wall was a faded green couch and on either end a pair of collapsible dinner stands that served as end tables. Opposite them were a short television stand and a flat screen TV, far and away the nicest thing in the house.

"What did she find?" Bishop asked, appearing in a doorway on the opposite end of the room, a stack of papers in his hands.

"It's our guy," Reed said. "We gave her the scent from one of the previous murders, she caught it within seconds and followed it straight in here."

Bishop nodded, Reed able to hear someone behind him continuing to rummage, the additional sound of footsteps moving about on the floor above.

"We get a name yet?" Reed asked.

"Frederick Handley," Bishop said, holding an envelope out in front of him, the top edge of it torn open. "Appears he lived alone, was renting on a week-to-week basis."

Neither one needed to comment on the motive attached to that, able to see Handley's condition for themselves.

"Anybody else?" Reed asked.

"No," Bishop said. "No sign of a list of other members in the support group either. We've got a laptop, but it's going to be a while before forensics can send someone down here to start digging through it."

"Shit," Reed whispered, running a hand over his face. He wiped the sweat against the leg of his pants, glancing down to Billie and the body of Frederick Handley on the floor beside them.

In any other career, the scene would be nothing short of perverse, two men having a discussion with a fresh corpse lying just inches away from them, neither even glancing at it.

Given the situation, and their job at the moment, neither Reed nor Bishop gave it a second thought. They had both grown far too accustomed to dead bodies over the years.

Seizing on the last thing Bishop said, Reed stared down at the floor for a couple of seconds, thinking. They needed a roster, names and addresses, somewhere for them to go next. If not to find the killer, then at the very least to ensure that more scenes like this one weren't popping up throughout the area.

The problem was, nobody did things on paper anymore. In this day and age, everything was digital. If there was a list, it wouldn't be written, it would be somewhere Handley could use it efficiently at a moment's notice.

"The laptop," Reed said, "does it have internet?"

Bishop turned in the doorway, staring back in the opposite direction. "Hey, Ike, does that laptop have internet?"

The sound of papers being tossed about stopped. "Christ," Iaconelli muttered, his footfalls heavy. "We've got a power cord and a white cord coming out the back of it. Does that mean we've got internet?"

Reed didn't bother to respond. Instead, he went straight for his cell phone, dialing from the recent call log and leaving it on speaker for all to hear.

Chapter Forty-Nine

Paul Neil Tudor.

Three days ago, The Good Son had never even heard the name. He had no idea the man existed, no reason to at that. One glance at him in the Big Q that afternoon proved he was from a different social class. Everything about him, from the car he drove to the way his hair was cut, even the way he carried himself, made it plain for all to see.

That no longer mattered. What did was the opportunity the man presented. Perhaps even more important, he had also mentioned having a wife. Assuming she was around the same age, she would be a prime target as well. If he was a donor, it stood to reason she would be also.

Two potential livers would guarantee success. It had to. There was simply no time for anything else.

At 9:30, The Good Son parked two blocks down from their house. He was old enough to know how the world worked, had seen enough to know where he did and did not fit. Never had he begrudged someone who had more than him anymore than he hoped others looked down on him for having less.

The Tudors had clearly awoken under a better star than The Good Son. That was fine. That was not why he was slumped behind the wheel of the car, watching, waiting.

Parked behind an enormous pickup nudged tight against the curb, The Good Son reclined the driver's seat down as far as it would go. From there he could just barely see over the steering wheel, like a drowning man holding his nose an inch above water.

With each passing moment, the temperature inside the car climbed. Despite the late hour, the heat still lingered, seeming to radiate up from the asphalt. Combined with the humidity that hung like a film in the air, the temperature inside the car held at close to triple digits.

At such a reclined angle, The Good Son was helpless to stop the sweat that streamed down his forehead. It traveled over his cheeks and onto his neck. It burned his eyes and tasted salty on his lips, his t-shirt soaked through.

After twice circling the block, The Good Son had settled on his position because it afforded him the best combination of seeing the Tudor's house and remaining in the shadows. As much as he wanted to crack open the windows, to run a towel over his face, to gulp from the bottle of water beside him, he couldn't.

That kind of movement would only draw attention.

He had not seen anybody else out on the street, but he couldn't take the chance. Not now. Not with the end so close.

The Good Son sat and stared at the light burning bright in the upstairs window two blocks away, focusing on the single yellow glow until it became a blur, his mind thinking back to everything that had landed him here.

Not once had his mother ever let him forget that her condition was his fault. He'd known it for some time even before she started using it as a weapon against him, the kind of thing he overheard once in a conversation long ago, his mother on the phone, him supposed to be asleep in bed.

She was suffering from end stage liver failure brought on by two and a half decades fighting hepatitis C.

Most people heard the word hepatitis and immediately associated it with some form of venereal disease, mistaking it for type A. They didn't realize that types B and C were even more deadly, more pervasive the world over, claiming hundreds of thousands of lives every year. It was often contracted congenitally, through no fault of the patient.

In the case of his mother, it was caused by a birth complication bringing him into the world.

Since the moment he had found out years before, The Good Son had begun steeling himself for moments like this. Perhaps not sitting out in the dark, waiting to commit yet another unspeakable act, but times when his mother would be very sick. Always in the back of his mind he had held out hope that a cure would be developed, that it would be affordable, that a perfect donor match would arise, but deep down he knew how unlikely that was.

Hope. The kind of thing that often teased people in places like Franklinton, but never seemed to actually materialize.

Months before, when it became obvious that sitting and hoping was futile, The Good Son had begun to condition himself to what must be done. He spent hours by his mother's side, forcing himself to watch her deteriorate, knowing it would be those images that sustained him.

Parked on the street, staring at the light two blocks away, The Good Son thought of his mother curled up on the couch. He thought of how unresponsive she was, how her feeble body was barely able to take even a sip of water under her own control.

The image brought on a shudder, a momentary chill despite the suffocating heat inside the car. It caused his throat to tighten and his heart to palpitate, knowing just how close he could be to losing her.

Just as fast, the feeling passed. It was replaced with steely resolve, his features hardening. His vision became clear again, focusing on the upstairs light down the street.

The Tudors were in there. They would provide everything needed to heal his mother, to ensure she stayed with him for a long time to come.

He would do what needed to be done. He had to.

There wasn't time to even consider failing again.

Chapter Fifty

The search of the house had been called off. The rest of the place was just as Spartan as the living room, Frederick Handley having winnowed down his entire existence to nothing more than bare subsistence. The sole place in the entire home with much real wealth at all was the bathroom, enough pharmaceuticals to outfit the rest of the house in top-of-the-line goods.

Matching Reed's initial assumption, precious little of any value was actually put down anywhere on paper. There was the usual assortment of bills a person accumulates – water, sewage, electric – along with a 6" stack of medical bills.

The only thing each one had in common was the red stamp announcing that the bill was past due.

Nothing resembling a support group roster was found.

All five men were crowded around the laptop. Reed was the only one to have touched it, first lifting it up to recite a series of numbers and letters on the bottom. It took him three tries to get the right combination that Deek was looking for, eventually figuring out the serial number and the IP address. Once those were in place, he opened the top and hit the power button, standing back as the computer took on a life of its own.

Placed on the table beside it was Reed's phone, set to speaker, though Deek remained silent as he worked.

The only sounds came from Earl and his team as they wrapped up in the living room.

Reed's attention was focused on the small white arrow on the screen, Deek having remote access from his basement miles away. In quick order, he was past the standard log-in screen, moving right into the files, a long list of titles stretched along the right side of the monitor.

"Anything in particular?" Deek asked, the voice sounding detached and somewhat robotic, drawing the group in closer.

"Can you blow these up any?" Iaconelli asked. "I don't have my glasses on."

A caustic remark flitted through Reed's mind at the request, disappearing just as fast. In front of him, the window was enlarged to full screen, the titles growing two sizes larger.

"That work?" Deek asked.

"Yeah, we're good," Reed said. He rested his hands on his knees, bent forward at the waist, and ran over the list of titles, all arranged in descending alphabetical order.

Prayer request. Memorial template. Fundraiser – Luncheon.

"At the bottom," Greene said, Reed shifting his attention down to the last entry in the window.

Active Membership.

"Active membership," Reed said, resisting the urge to reach out and begin maneuvering things, watching as Deek did it for him.

The file was an Excel spreadsheet, a list of eight names in a column. Spread out to the side beside each one were mailing addresses and telephone numbers, even a few email addresses.

"Jackpot," Iaconelli whispered.

"And two of these we can cross off," Reed said, extending a hand toward the screen. "Henry Ruggles and Frederick Handley are both already gone."

"So that leaves six people to be warned," Bishop said.

"Or six people who might be our suspect," Reed said. He stared at the list momentarily, then pushed himself to full height, bumping into

Gilchrist behind him as he did so, the young officer leaning in close to see the screen.

With the laptop no longer serving as the hub of everyone's attention, all five took a step back, standing in a loose cluster, Billie still on the floor by Reed's feet.

Nobody said a word, a few exchanging glances, as Reed digested what he'd just learned. They now had six names, presumably one of which was working with an accomplice to target the others. Somehow, they needed to figure out who that one was and warn the others without setting off any warning signals.

"Officer Gilchrist," Reed said, "can you run out to my car and grab the papers folded up on the passenger seat?"

Casting a quick glance to Greene, Gilchrist nodded and disappeared through the doorway, excusing himself past the techs in the living room.

A moment later, they heard the front door swing shut as he headed outside.

"Big Q employee list," Reed said as way of explanation to the others. "Didn't think I'd need it when we got here."

Greene and Bishop both nodded. On the opposite side of the circle, Iaconelli stood and wiped sweat from his forehead.

"Okay," Reed said, thinking out loud, "we now have a roster of everybody in the support group. So far two members have been eliminated."

"So we presume that the killer will continue targeting them?" Bishop asked.

Reed didn't answer right away. He took a step forward and glanced through the open doorway into the living room, at the body lying prone on the floor. Around him, Earl and his crew were busy setting things up, a series of lights on tripods clustered nearby.

"Earl, can we get some illumination on the victim for just a second, please?"

On cue the two closest lights came on, two large saucers that threw an unnaturally bright hue over the scene, exposing every last bit of the depravity on Handley's skin.

"Okay, that's good!" Reed called. He waited until the lights flipped back off, the room seeming much darker. "Thank you, sir."

One single sound came back that sounded kind of like, "Yup," but Reed couldn't be sure.

"Alright," Reed said, glancing back to the group, his gaze settling on Bishop, "the answer to your question, I think, is maybe. They're all certainly at risk and need to be warned, if not protected."

"But what if he's already taken out who he needs to?" Greene said.

"That's why you had Earl flip the lights," Bishop said.

"Yeah," Reed said. "I wanted to see what kind of shape he was in, if he was anywhere near as bad as Ruggles."

"Was he?" Iaconelli asked.

"On the outside?" Reed replied. "Maybe even worse."

"If you give me a name, I might be able to help."

For the first time in several minutes the phone on the desk had come to life, Reed having completely forgotten that Deek was still on the line. By the looks on the faces of the other men, they had as well.

"Say again, Deek?"

"That list you asked me to look into," Deek said, "from the government database. It took some doing, but I got it."

The list. With so much going on in the last hour, it had slipped Reed's mind.

"Were we right? Were Ruggles and Handley the highest?"

"Doesn't really work that way, least not that I can see," Deek said. "There isn't a numerical ranking, just something called a MELD score and a categorical listing. Both were ranked a 40 on the score, listed as Category 1."

The information fit exactly with what Dr. Levin had told Reed. Both men were maxed out using all the usual blood work parameters, were at the most critical stage for needing to receive a new organ.

"So there's no actual list?" Reed asked. "No number one, number two?"

"There probably is," Deek said, "but to take a look at that means crossing some serious boundaries. Patient records, confidentiality, all that jazz. What I'm into now is more of a database. I can see how they score and what their category is; anything beyond that I'm going to need a signed Get-Out-Of-Jail-Free card from a prosecutor."

They were standing within feet of their fourth victim, knowing full well that at least one more was likely on the way. They didn't have time to be dealing with bureaucracy.

As much as he wanted to tell Deek to forge ahead, to find the rank order, to do whatever he must, he knew he couldn't. Deek was a civilian. He was doing him a favor for the down payment of a bottle of booze. What he needed couldn't be protected, even by cooperating with the police.

There was no way he could endanger Deek. Even the thought of it would be enough to pull Riley back from the beyond to throttle him.

"Okay, Deek, can you pull the records for each of the six on the list? I know we can't get a clear heading, but maybe we can cross somebody out."

"Roger that," Deek said, the line falling silent.

Again Reed glanced at each of the men before looking down to Billie. She was still seated on her haunches, both ears upright. She stared at him, coiled energy practically rolling off of her body.

Reed knew the feeling.

"Gilchrist!" Reed shouted, stepping forward and looking out through the house. He ignored Earl and his men working in the foreground, staring at the door on the far end of the kitchen, before the screen swung back and the young officer stepped in, panting badly.

Sweat streamed down his face as he thrust the two pages out before him, droplets staining them in a couple of places. Reed laid them side by side on the table in front of the laptop, his gaze moving between the sheets and the list pulled up on screen.

Bishop was the first to appear beside him, his own head shifting up and down as he compared the two. All air seemed to suck out of the room as everyone leaned in tight, watching, waiting.

Halfway down the sheet, Reed found what he was looking for. His heart lurched in his chest as the name jumped out at him, looking between the paper and the list on the screen twice to be certain.

"Deek, can you look up Amber Morgan for me? What are her MELD and category scores?"

The only response was the clatter of a keyboard, Deek searching for the information.

"Same as the first two," he finally said. "Both are completely maxed out. That woman does not have long."

Chapter Fifty-One

Free of the stuffy interior of Frederick Handley's house, the air outside bordered on cool. It picked at the perspiration soaking Reed's back, dropping his core temperature a few degrees, though the high humidity kept any hope of evaporation at bay.

Grouped into a loose circle on the front lawn, Reed stood with Billie by his knee. To either side were Officers Greene and Gilchrist, Detectives Iaconelli and Bishop, everybody intently listening to the voice coming through Reed's speaker phone.

"Okay," Captain Grimes said, his voice much thicker than Deek's had been. Just from the tone it was obvious his nerves were stretched tight, Reed guessing it stemmed from his earlier encounter with Leveritt, but knowing better than to ask.

"Amber Morgan, 53-years-old, lives on 21st Street," Grimes said. The address matched with the list Handley had on his computer. "Completely clean sheet. No priors, no citations, not even a damn parking ticket. Wow."

The phone was balanced in the palm of Reed's hand as he listened. Around him he could see the others either staring straight at it or avoiding eye contact, Gilchrist shuffling from side to side, shifting his weight back and forth.

The decision to bypass Jackie at the dispatch desk and go straight to Grimes was one Reed made unilaterally, despite knowing he would probably catch flack for it. He could tell Jackie was practically salivating earlier, looking for any morsel of insider info.

The idea of being bypassed now would not only bruise her ego, it would hurt her feelings in a way that would take weeks to repair.

Reed knew there was no chance Grimes would step away until things were wrapped up, at least for the night. He also knew the man had no ego in situations like this, would not think twice about curt inquiries or quick hang-ups.

"How about Kyle Morgan?" Reed asked, reciting the name on the list of Big Q employees Beauregard had given him.

"Um," Grimes said, holding the sound out as he sought what Reed was asking for, sounding like a giant insect buzzing across the front lawn. "Kyle Anthony Morgan, 25-years-old. Two speeding tickets, neither too outrageous. Otherwise, he's clean."

Unable to hide it, Reed's face scrunched up in confusion. He looked at the others around the circle, trying to force things into place.

The kinds of crimes they were seeing did not simply appear out of nowhere. Nobody ever jumped from being clean to committing multiple murders. There was almost always, especially for someone so young, a history of escalation. Theft. Assault. Animal cruelty. Something that would indicate future behavior.

"This has to be our guy, right?" Bishop asked, voicing what Reed was already thinking. "I mean, young, capable, a direct tie to someone very high on the list."

"Geography fits," Reed agreed. He paused, running through the list of everything Bishop had just mentioned, going over all that had transpired in recent days.

"What about a car?" Reed asked. "What does Kyle Morgan drive?"

More heavy pounding could be heard, followed by, "A 1999 Chevy Silverado."

"Shit," Reed muttered.

Everything pointed toward Morgan being their guy, but things refused to fit into place the way they were supposed to. Right now all they had was supposition, albeit strong, but that wouldn't be enough to move on.

"What about the mother?" Reed asked, staring back down at the phone.

Another moment passed. "Looks like there is a 1995 Chrysler LeBaron registered in her name."

"What color?" Reed asked, feeling his pulse rise.

"Um," Grimes repeated, again drawing it out. "Silver. Why?"

"Finally," Reed said, looking up at the others in the group. He could see questions on both Iaconelli and Bishop's faces and said, "Witnesses at both Esther Rosen's and Ira Soto's reported thinking they saw a silver car parked nearby."

"This has to be our guy," Iaconelli said, slapping his hands together before him and rubbing them twice.

Reed nodded, the same thought in mind, the slightest bit of nervous excitement arising with it.

"How you want to play it?" Bishop asked.

His pulse continuing to move at a frenetic pace, Reed remained silent for several seconds. Right now he had a strong lead suspect, and some people who needed protection. He also had the possibility that Morgan would bypass the others on the list altogether and target a new donor.

Piece by piece, he fit everything together in his mind.

"Captain, can you put out a BOLO for both of the Morgan's cars? If he's out hunting for another organ donor, I want him found and stopped immediately."

"You got it," Grimes replied.

"Greene, can you and Gilchrist take the list we got from Handley's computer and begin alerting the other members of the support group?"

"Yes, sir," Greene said.

"McMichaels and Jacobs should be on by now too. You can split the list with them and anybody else who might be available."

This time the only response was a nod, both officers wheeling and heading toward their car. Reed watched as they jogged away, the shadows soon swallowing up their black uniforms. Once they were gone, he looked at Bishop and Iaconelli beside him, reached down and ran his hand along the scruff of Billie's neck.

"And the four of us go pay the Morgans a visit?"

Chapter Fifty-Two

Sweat dripped off the end of The Good Son's nose. It started up high on his head, running through his hair, trickling down over his forehead. Some of streams passed along the outside of his face, making their way down his jaw line while others went straight for his eyebrows. Every so often one split them evenly, traversing the ridge of his nose, and dropped straight down off the tip.

The Good Son paid it no mind. He stood with his back pressed against the rear of the house, the brick warm to the touch, just as it had been at Ira Soto's. Unlike that night though, there was no small dog that needed to be let out to make things easy for him.

Less than five minutes had passed since the light in the upstairs window went out, the cue The Good Son had been waiting for. He had no idea what time it was, his best guess putting it somewhere close to 11:00 as he had eased the driver's side door open and stepped out. Every instinct had told him to crouch, to dart behind the truck in front of him, to run as fast as he could.

Just like at Frederick Handley's that afternoon though, he had to make himself look natural. In the off chance there was someone watching, he had to look like he belonged there. He had to ensure they saw, processed, and dismissed him all in a matter of seconds.

Nothing more than a young man out for an evening jog.

Exiting the car, The Good Son turned in the opposite direction of the house. Taking advantage of the sweat already coating his body, soaking his t-shirt through, he walked to the corner before turning left, his gait rising into an even lope.

By the time he made the next corner his skin had passed from moist to sopping wet, sweat leaking from every pore. His breath became short in his chest, a combination of nerves and exertion. Still he kept up an even pace, moving forward through the night, passing house after house. Nearly all of them appeared to already be shut down for the night, a couple of televisions in the darkened front rooms the only signs of life.

For three blocks The Good Son kept his pace even. Years of living in the area had instilled in him a keen understanding of the gridded street system, all of them running in 100 yard squares. At the end of the third block he hooked another left, fighting the burning in his lungs as he came back to the street he had started on.

Slowing to a walk, The Good Son made a show of extending his hands high over his head, hoping that anybody who happened to be nearby would accept the charade, continuing to believe he was nothing more than a late runner. His steps uniform, his pace measured, he walked forward to the Tudor home and made a final turn up the darkened driveway.

The front of the house was completely shadowed as he approached. No security lights lined the front walk, no overhead beam showed down from above the garage.

As The Good Son grew closer, he realized the home was much larger than it appeared from the car. Gray brick with black trim, it rose two stories, stretched nearly the entire width of their lot. The driveway sloped upward to a two-car garage.

Not once did The Good Son slow his pace as he walked up the driveway, glancing over his shoulder before sliding off to the side. His steps quick and light, he passed along the side of the garage and into the backyard, nudging his way around the corner.

Dropping to his knees, The Good Son crawled across most of the rear yard of the house, using a waist-high hedge for cover. The grass beneath his palms was soft and supple, the result of untold amounts of watering.

Twenty yards across he came to a stop, a patio of matching brick extended out from the rear of the home. The Good Son could see a barbecue grill and a hot tub with assorted lawn furniture arranged around them. Interspersed between were large potted plants, everything shrouded in shadows as he rose to his feet and inched his way to the wall.

Three minutes had passed since he'd assumed his position against the brick. In that time, his only movement was the sweat that continued to drip from his nose.

It was time. If he was going to finish things, to make sure his mother was taken care of, this had to be the moment. There was no way to know what waited inside, but that didn't matter now.

All that mattered was his mother across town, her tired body giving out, too frail to continue fending for itself.

Now was the time to do right by her.

Using his hips, The Good Son pushed himself a few inches away from the wall. He crept two steps to his left and extended a fist out from the door, holding it there briefly, feeling his entire body quiver with anticipation.

Allowing his eyes to slide shut, he slammed his hand back against the glass of the door once, twice, three times, listening as the sound of it echoed through the cavernous house.

Chapter Fifty-Three

Reed still didn't bother with the siren. He let the flashers clear the way for him, the few cars that were out peeling off to the side. Iaconelli and Bishop ran right on his tail, their front headlamps dancing from side to side in his rearview mirror.

In a place as geographically dense as Franklinton, sirens could be all the warning someone like Kyle Morgan would need. The wail would pierce the night for blocks before the detectives arrived, giving him a several minute head start if he chose to run.

Reed felt reasonably certain that if he tried to move on foot, Billie could track him down with ease. The bigger concern would be if he happened to jump into a car, weaving his way through the gridded streets of the area. The freeway was just a few miles away and could present all kinds of problems, ranging from a high-speed chase to having to call for much wider assistance across the region.

The mere thought of that, and the field day Eleanor Brandt would have with the 8th over it, was more than Reed wanted to consider at the moment.

Instead, he focused on where they were going, on the address his dashboard GPS was leading him to.

Over the preceding six months Reed had driven past the place probably 20 times while making various rounds, though the location itself didn't stand out at all in his mind. He knew most of the streets on the edge of Franklinton were pretty much identical, near replicas of the places Rosen and Soto were both found. The home would be single story, brick, aged, built in the '60s for a single family. It would have a small, square plot of land wedged in tight between two like it or one and an adjacent cross street.

The speedometer rose and fell like an Indy car as he sped where he could and slowed down when he had to.

Five days had passed since this all started, though it felt like much, much longer. In that time he had slept precious little, his body clock turned upside down, his mind refusing to slow long enough for him to rest. The heat was intent on trying to sap what remaining energy reserves he had, leaving him feeling like he was fighting a constant losing battle against dehydration.

At the moment, though, Reed felt none of that. A wave of adrenaline had surged within him, propelling him forward. The knowledge that things were coming together, that they could be within minutes of finding a conclusion to so much chaos, refused to let him slow down. When things were over, he and Billie would both take the weekend. They would eat and drink and sleep, not leaving the house until replenished.

Not quite yet though.

The neighborhood was exactly as Reed had anticipated. Low-slung brick homes lined both sides of the street, cars from the mid-'90s with pockets of rust parked in most of the driveways. A couple of the yards were badly in need of attention, though by and large the place was a duplicate of many just like it in central Ohio.

Anticipation crept steadily upward as Reed stared out, ignoring the GPS in favor of matching numbers on mailboxes. He drew in a sharp breath and held it as their destination came into view.

He slid past the driveway to the far corner of the yard and put the car in park. Behind him he could see Iaconelli pull up blocking the driveway, both corners of the property now covered.

The front lawn stretched about 20 yards in length, the grass brown but rutted, as if it had been cut recently. The front of the home was brick, a large window to one side indicating the living room with two smaller ones on the opposite side for bedrooms. A single door stood in the center of it, a black light pole a few feet away rising from the middle of a flower bed.

A two car garage was attached to the far end, though no vehicles were visible outside the home.

Opting to work without a leash, Reed let Billie out of the backseat and met Iaconelli and Bishop between the two cars. Both of their faces were painted with sweat as well, the moisture shiny, catching any bit of light.

"You guys go to the front door," Reed said. "I'll stay out here with Billie in case he tries to run for it."

Both men nodded, knowing exactly what he meant. They both turned for the front door and walked straight across the front lawn, each drawing his service weapon as they approached.

Doing the same, Reed drifted back toward their car, positioning himself at the corner of the driveway. Billie stayed close by his side as he did so, her body coiled, head low, ready to explode in any direction on the sound of his voice.

Stopping just outside the front door, Bishop turned and glanced at Reed. Holding one thumb up, Reed nodded, extending his Glock out before him.

From his current vantage point, Reed could see the entire front and side of the property. If Morgan tried to go through the garage he was in a position to stop him and if he crossed out the back and to the right, he would set Billie loose. That left only the possibility of going out the back and disappearing in the opposite direction.

The thought of positioning himself around back and leaving the detectives to cover the front occurred to him just a moment too late, leaving him hoping that their current configuration would be sufficient.

The sound of Iaconelli pounding on the front door echoed through the quiet neighborhood. Three times in succession he slammed the side of his fist against the wood before pausing and adding three more.

"Amber Morgan, CPD," he announced. "We need you to open the door right now."

Reed cocked an ear to the side, listening for the sound of a back door opening or a window being wrenched upward.

Three more slams against the door yielded nothing, the house void of life.

"Shit," Iaconelli said. He turned toward Reed and said, "Do we even have PC right now?"

Probable cause. The standard by which an officer could reasonably enter a home and hope to have anything found inside be admissible in court.

Lowering his weapon before him, Reed remained silent. At this point they had a mountain of evidence pointing at Kyle Morgan, most of which could admittedly be argued as circumstantial by any trial attorney worth his salt.

If they entered now, whatever they found could get booted, putting their whole case in jeopardy.

"Give me one minute," Reed said, holstering his weapon and jogging toward his car. He didn't have to tell Billie to follow, the sound of her toes on the asphalt audible behind him.

Going straight to the front passenger door, Reed ripped it open and reached into the floor well, drawing out the evidence bag from Ira Soto's once more. Again he peeled back the adhesive flap to expose the rock used to kill her dog and extended it to Billie.

The scent was still fresh in her nose after scouring Handley's home. It took her only a second before she stepped back, ready.

"Search."

Billie shot forward three quick paces onto the lawn, stopping just as abruptly. Her body was rigid as she moved back and forth, not in her traditional sweeping gesture, but in a more pointed, agitated stance.

"What's wrong?" Iaconelli asked.

"She can't find anything?" Bishop called.

Reed remained silent for a while, watching Billie work. Rarely before had he seen her movements so stilted, pulling side to side across the lawn, the gesture unmistakable.

"No," Reed said, "quite the opposite. His scent is so damn strong she's having trouble getting a clear lead."

He slid his gun from his hip and began to backpedal toward his corner spot in the driveway again. "Breach the door. This is our guy."

Chapter Fifty-Four

The front door was no match for the right leg of Pete Iaconelli. His unique dimensions, and the full force of 250 pounds, surged straight through the wood. The frame of it splintered on contact, the sound hanging in the air, drawing Reed's every nerve taut as he watched the door swing inward and both detectives disappear through it.

Without even realizing it, Reed crept forward. His Glock extended out in his right hand, his left cupped under it for support, he inched up the driveway. Noticing the shift in his physiology, the growl coming from Billie grew more pronounced. She nudged her way out in front of him, both keeping a watch for anybody attempting to flee the house.

In the wake of the front door breach, no other sounds could be heard. Nobody bolted from the home. The neighborhood remained silent.

"Clear," Bishop called, standing in the doorway. "You better come see this, though."

Just as fast he was gone, his pale face almost ethereal in the way it appeared and vanished within seconds.

Remaining in his crouch, Reed stared past the garage. Every part of him wanted a shadow to dart out into the night, to provide a visible target, to allow him to end everything right then.

There was nothing, though. Not even the slightest hint of a breeze pushing limbs back and forth. No movement of any kind.

"Come," Reed whispered, a tiny twinge of disappointment as he holstered his weapon and jogged for the front door.

The first smell to assault his nostrils as he arrived was sawdust, tiny particles of the door still hanging in the air. Two steps into the room it changed over to stench, the combined scents of body odor and stale air and bad food and sickness all washing over him. The concoction was so strong it almost caused his stomach to turn, his throat clenching, forcing him to twist his head and cough into his sleeve.

The source of the smell was sprawled on the couch.

A woman - Amber Morgan, Reed guessed - was stretched out on the couch, her appearance every bit as bad as Henry Ruggles's and Frederick Handley's had been. Extended out flat, she didn't manage to reach either end of the sofa, her body giving the impression of a sponge that had been left out in the summer sun for days. All muscle mass and fat had vanished, leaving only wrinkled skin, the outer shell much too large for the inner body. Splotches of various colors dotted her.

She made no effort to look at Reed as he entered, her light blue eyes staring up at the ceiling.

"Is she?" Reed asked, glancing to Iaconelli and Bishop. Both stood on the opposite side of the coffee table running parallel to the couch, their arms folded over their chest.

"Yeah," Iaconelli said.

"Any sign of Kyle?"

"No," Bishop said, giving his head a quick shake. "House is empty."

"What about the garage?" Reed asked.

The two men glanced at each other, neither saying anything.

"We'll check it out," Reed said. "Go ahead and call this in."

Both men dropped their arms to their sides and shifted a few steps, allowing Reed and Billie to slide by.

Using the exterior of the house as a rough guide, Reed stepped through an open doorway from the living room into a small kitchen. Like the rest of the house, it had a décor that was at least two decades outdated, everything beginning to yellow with age and abuse.

There were two doors in the room, one facing the rear of the house, another facing the side. Starting on the back end, Reed walked over and checked the lock, finding the chain still slid shut.

If Kyle Morgan had been on hand when they arrived, there was no way he had escaped through it.

Reaching to his hip, Reed tapped at the butt of his weapon as he turned to the second door and peeled back the dingy lace curtain covering the window. The fabric weighed nothing as it slid to the side, revealing a two car garage.

Extending a hand, Reed flipped up a trio of light switches on the wall beside the door. In unison, an overhead light in the kitchen sprang on along with a single bare bulb in the garage. Both cast down the same pale yellow light, illuminating everything around Reed.

Seeing nothing move, he opened the door a foot. "Clear."

Billie was through before he even took a step, shooting into the garage. She sprinted around the Chevy Silverado pickup truck parked in the middle of the space, disappearing from view for a split second before coming around.

She finished right back in front of Reed, letting him know the place was empty.

"Good girl," Reed whispered, lowering his weapon as he stepped into the garage.

Besides the truck, the place housed some yard tools and an upright freezer that hummed persistently in the corner. A pair of grass-stained sneakers sat on the floor by the door.

Swapping out the gun for his phone, Reed went to his recent call log and hit the latest entry. He kept it on speakerphone and held it out in front of him as he did a revolution of the truck.

Just as the captain had said, it was getting a little older, though still in pretty good shape. The blue paint had a few minor dents and nicks in it, but not yet any signs of rust. The bed had been sprayed with a black rubber liner and it looked to have been washed recently.

"I was just picking up the phone to call you," Grimes said as an opening, his voice its usual gruff pitch.

"Just talk to Bishop?" Reed asked, reaching out and opening the driver's door of the truck. It gave way with an awful screech of metal on metal, the hinge in dire need of lubrication.

"No," Grimes said, the agitation in his tone growing louder, "and what the hell was that?"

"Kyle Morgan's truck door," Reed said, leaning forward into the cab.

In the middle console was an empty plastic water bottle and a handful of change. A cheap pine air freshener hung from the rearview mirror.

Otherwise, the truck was just as nondescript as the garage it was parked in.

"You're at the house now?" Grimes asked.

"Yes," Reed said. "Iaconelli and Bishop are inside with the body of Amber Morgan. There is no sign of Kyle Morgan."

"I know," Grimes said. "We just a got hit on his mother's car."

The news pushed renewed urgency through Reed as he jerked himself back out of the truck and strode back toward the kitchen, slapping a hand against his thigh for Billie to follow.

"Where?" he asked, moving into the living room and motioning for Iaconelli and Bishop to both pay attention.

"Twelve blocks north of you," Grimes said.

Reed ran the numbers in his mind, superimposing them on the 8th's land map. "That's the 19th's turf," Reed said. "Call and tell them we're on our way."

Chapter Fifty-Five

The Good Son had expected more of a fight. Paul Neil Tudor was older certainly, but he looked like a sturdy fellow standing on the opposite side of the checkout line that afternoon. The kind of guy who woke up early and worked hard every day. Came home to a large house and a classy wife.

He should have known better, though. Like most things that filled The Good Son's life, the notion was outdated. Nice homes and beautiful women no longer went to the men who worked long and hard. They went to small, nebbish types that had never thrown a punch in their life, like the man sprawled out on the kitchen floor.

Accountants, bankers, men who got manicures and called people like him whenever they needed manual labor done.

When the man's shadow first appeared at the back door, The Good Son had steeled himself for a brawl. He had filled his mind with images of his sick, bedridden mother, letting them provide him with renewed purpose.

Collateral damage was something he had worked hard to avoid. He had gone out of his way to choose Esther Rosen and Ira Soto because they lived alone. Even the slaying of Soto's dog had filled him with remorse, hating the idea of killing any more than necessary to fulfill his singular purpose of saving his mother.

The time for such concessions was past, though. Waiting outside the door, The Good Son even considered looking around for the closest weapon, debating whether he should pick up a rock or try to pry a brick free from the edge of the patio. His fists clenched and his blood surged, waiting for the door to open.

It never did. After a bit the shadow disappeared, the man content that whatever had been knocking was gone.

The move, one of not being taken seriously, of being blown off, brought a new emotion to the The Good Son. Gone were thoughts of his mother, replaced by images of Beauregard at work, people who looked down at him. They didn't realize that he had chosen the path he was on, bypassing his last year at college to care for his mother.

And he would not let them stand in his way.

Extending his hand outward, The Good Son knocked again. This time he used the side of his fist, slamming it into the wooden frame of the glass door, hitting it so hard the entire structure rattled in its casing. The sound carried out into the night, a dog in the distance picking up on it and barking in return.

The Good Son did not care. He knew with each passing moment that the odds of him escaping again were low, but that didn't matter. If prison was what it took for his mother to survive, so be it.

Keeping himself pressed against the wall, he waited, listening as footsteps again grew closer, a shadow appearing. This time, though, it was accompanied by the sound of the lock mechanism turning.

"Hello?" Tudor asked as the door cracked open.

The Good Son shot forward, slamming into the door. The edge of it swung back hard against the man on the other side, knocking him to the ground, his body splayed across the floor.

Scrambling on all fours, The Good Son crawled the length of him and snapped a hard right cross. It connected at the corner of Tudor's mouth, mashing lips against teeth, bloody spittle oozing out over his chin. Drawing his arm back like a piston, The Good Son took aim and fired again, a direct shot to the temple. The man's eyes rolled back as a single tendril of blood appeared in the soft tissue, streaking down and disappearing into his thinning brown hair.

His body fell limp, no sound escaping at all.

Specks of blood dotted the back of The Good Son's hand as he rose and stepped around him, the home matching everything he had envisioned to the letter, the floors made from pale oak with white carpeting. Expensive furniture and appliances filled the space, artwork and portraits of the happy couple hung from the walls. The scene only managed to raise his ire.

Walking through the dining room, The Good Son found the massive staircase rising to the second floor bedrooms.

Up. That was where he needed to go. There he would find Mrs. Tudor.

Together the couple would ensure that this time, without fail, The Good Son provided the cure his mother needed.

Chapter Fifty-Six

The glow of red-and-blue flashers could be seen from a block away. Any hope Reed had that the officers on site might have the good sense to lay back and not alert Kyle Morgan that they were on to him was dashed the moment he saw them. He kept his mouth pressed tight to keep a string of expletives from spilling out, ignoring the GPS and using the lights to guide him in.

The car was parked halfway down the block. The neighborhood here had taken a noticeable step up, the divide between Franklinton and Hilliard obvious as more than just an arbitrary line on a map. Instead of faded brick ramblers, the homes here appeared to be custom-built with lots of wood and glass, professionally manicured lawns and expensive cars parked in the driveways.

Using all of that as a backdrop, it wasn't hard to pick the '95 LeBaron out as Reed approached. Even without the pair of blue-and-whites parked alongside it pinning it to the curb, the car was more than a decade older than anything nearby. The back fender was bent badly, and a plume of rust had mushroomed over the rear door.

Leaving his sedan back a few yards, Reed slid to a stop and jerked the keys from the ignition. He let Billie out the back, pausing just long enough for Iaconelli and Bishop to climb from the car behind him.

Four officers were clustered around the LeBaron, their profiles illuminated by the flashing lights. Three of the men openly stared at the approaching detectives while a fourth held a Maglite up to the window, peering into the car.

"I think you can kill the lights now," Iaconelli said. "You've let him know we're here. Good job."

The fourth clicked off his flashlight and raised his head, sneering. He glanced to his fellow officers and said, "I don't recall asking for any assistance from the 8th, do you?"

Two of the officers shook their head from side to side, the last of the group remaining motionless, watching. Reed pegged him for the rookie, not yet tainted by the politics of precinct rivalry.

"Has there been any sign of Morgan yet?" Reed asked, ignoring the man's comment, hoping to move past any unnecessary posturing.

Right now time was seeping by, time that the next victim didn't have.

"You mean besides the car we found here?" the self-appointed leader of the group asked. "Not yet, but don't worry, when our guys get here they'll be sure to track him down for you."

There were two ways Reed could play it. He could reason with the man. He could tell him to call Grimes, or his own captain, and get the necessary clearance to stop being a prick and let him do his job. Try to appeal to a sense of greater good, of law enforcement brotherhood.

Or he could just say to hell with these guys.

Reed drew his right hand up into a ball so fast the two closest officers both flinched. He held it at shoulder height, extended out from the side of his body, and left it there.

The non-verbal command had the same effect it always did, morphing Billie from an imposing partner to a savage animal. A vicious growl began low in her diaphragm, rolling out in unquestioned anger. Her shoulders rolled forward as her lips peeled back over two rows of razor sharp teeth.

"Listen, guys," Reed said, "we don't have time for this shit right now. This is our guy, and we're going after him. You have a problem with that, things are going to get real ugly."

The lines sounded cheesy and canned even to his own ears, but that wasn't the point. The entire situation was ridiculous. He just needed to get past it and on his way to finding Kyle Morgan.

The men all stood rigid, staring at Billie, nobody saying a word.

"That's what I thought," Reed said. He lowered his fist in a slow outward motion, the move having the effect of an off switch, the hostility bleeding out of Billie. "Now if you'll excuse us."

He took another step forward and said, "Track."

Billie shot forward at the sound of the command, her nose just inches from the ground. Her sudden movement caused the officers to peel back, all four of them recoiling from the movement.

Paying them no heed, Reed walked right through where they had been standing, watching Billie search the area, grabbing the scent within seconds. Still fresh in her nose, she snatched it up outside the driver's side door and took off at a trot, Reed breaking into a jog to keep up with her.

In his wake, he could hear the heavy footfalls of Iaconelli and Bishop trying to catch up.

The path took a long and meandering route, circling a couple of blocks around. There was no attempt at evasive maneuvering or trying to hide his tracks, the trail remaining right in the middle of the sidewalk. It circled away from the car for half a block before turning west a block and then coming back south.

The sounds of Iaconelli and Bishop grew a little further back as the jog continued on, block after block passing beneath Reed's shoes. Sweat poured from his body, drenching the front of his shirt, matting his hair to his head. In front of him he could hear Billie panting, see her tongue hanging out, as she pushed forward, never once breaking stride.

At the end of the third block Billie made a left. A hundred yards further she made another, completing the circle. A couple blocks away Reed could see the lights of the cruisers still flashing, made out the silhouettes of the four men milling about.

Not until Billie made an unexpected left onto private property did Reed jerk his attention from them. He followed her a few steps up the driveway before whispering, "Heel," putting as much bass in the command as his lowered tone would allow.

The word stopped Billie where she stood, causing her to turn and stare back at him. Her tail wagged as she seemed to look on in confusion, trying to determine why she was called to a halt.

"Just one second," Reed said, running his gaze over the front of the house, looking for any signs of movement. He drew his weapon and stayed there, waiting until Iaconelli and Bishop appeared around the corner. They came to a stop at the end of the drive, sweating and sputtering, leaning forward and pressing their hands to their knees.

"What's going on?" Bishop asked between deep pulls of oxygen. Beside him Iaconelli looked like he might collapse, his face a deep shade of red bordering on purple.

"Trail just turned," Reed said. "My guess is, he sat in the car casing the place, waited for the lights to go out, made a loop around the block."

Bishop nodded, neither man saying anything.

"Track," Reed said, bypassing further conversation. A jolt of renewed energy passed through Billie, her form crouching back into position and rocketing forward.

As a group, all four stepped off the driveway and into the yard, the ground soft underfoot. Unlike most every other blade of grass in central Ohio it was green and supple, Morgan's footprints plain before them.

Reed increased his pace, drawing even with Billie as they made the corner and moved past a waist high hedge along the back of the house onto a square brick patio. At the back of it was a single step rising to meet a back door, which was standing open.

"Heel," Reed said, his voice raised just slightly. Beside him Billie came to a stop, staying no more than a few inches away as Reed turned to Iaconelli and Bishop. He motioned to the back door, got a nod of recognition from each, and stepped forward.

Chapter Fifty-Seven

The man lying on the kitchen floor was just beginning to wake. He moaned softly as Reed knelt by his side, his lips busted and puffy. The left side of his face was bleeding, the area around his eye already starting to swell.

"Sir," Reed said, holding a hand to the man's shoulder, trying to force him still. He kept his voice low, nothing more than an urgent whisper. "Sir, is there anybody else in the house?"

Billie's muzzle was just inches past his shoulder, her hot breath on his skin. Standing at the man's feet, both staring down at him, were Iaconelli and Bishop, each with their weapons drawn.

"This is a waste," Iaconelli breathed. "The guy's still out of it. Let Billie track our guy."

Reaching out, Reed gripped the man by the chin. He turned his face toward him and leaned in closer, just inches separating the two. "Are you the only one home?"

The man's eyelids fluttered as he tried to focus on Reed. "Wife...upstairs..."

Reed didn't bother to wait for more. He released the man's head and pounded straight through the dining room toward the stairs. For the first time all night he didn't care how much noise he made, his singular focus on getting to the stairs and keeping Kyle Morgan from doing any more harm.

"Hold!" Reed yelled, sending Billie hurtling forward in front of him. She made it to the front foyer two full seconds before he did, her feet sliding across the polished floor for just a moment before gaining purchase and shooting straight up the stairs.

Heart pounding, his own breaths coming in quick gasps, Reed hit the corner and headed up the stairs as well, taking them three at a time. The sound of Billie barking, signaling to him that she had cornered their target, caused him to churn his legs even faster.

Just as important to him as saving whoever was at the top of the stairs was making sure he was there to protect his partner. He had lost Riley because he was across the country at a football game instead of by her side when things went sideways.

Never, ever, again would he allow that to happen.

Adrenaline pulsing through his body, Reed made the top of the stairs and turned to his right, Billie's barking leading the way. With his weapon stretched out parallel to the ground, he inched his way through a doorway into a bedroom, seeing Billie's black body moving back and forth on the carpet in front of him.

"Kyle Morgan," Reed said, hearing Iaconelli and Bishop arrive behind him, stepping forward so all three could enter. "Columbus Police Department."

The room was enormous, much larger that it appeared from the street. Plush white carpeting stretched across the floor, a massive four-poster, king-size bed the centerpiece of the room. His and hers dressers with mirrors, a sitting area for reading and a spa-like master bath completed the space.

All of these details Reed processed and dismissed in a seconds. Instead, his attention was drawn to the area between the bed and the far wall.

Standing erect in the corner, his shoulders wedged in tight, was a man who Reed presumed to be Kyle Morgan. He had never seen the young man, but he was in his mid-20s, he was in good shape, and he carried a strong resemblance to Amber Morgan. He was taller than Reed expected, at least two inches taller than he was, his arms tanned and muscled. They glistened with sweat in the light of the room.

In front of him stood a woman who Reed guessed to be the lady of the house. Dressed only in a silk shift, one strap of it torn, she was pulled back in tight against Morgan's chest, his hand cupped over her mouth. A tendril of blood ran down from one of her nostrils, her eyes wide with terror.

"Kyle Morgan," Reed said, nudging closer. He kept his gun extended as he went, almost yelling to be heard over Billie's barking.

"Get that damn dog away from me!" Morgan yelled. "And you stay back too! I'll kill her, you know I will."

Just like with the officer outside, Reed knew there were two ways he could play it. He could try to negotiate with him, even put his own gun away, try to talk him out of doing something stupid. The woman's life was the most important thing, and he had to act in a way that would best ensure her safety.

At the same time, negotiating might not necessarily do that. The acts that Morgan had committed were of such depravity, there might be no reasoning with him. He saw everything through the lens of what he wanted most. He had to believe that was no longer attainable if Reed had any hope of succeeding.

"Your mother is gone," Reed said.

Blood flushed Morgan's face deep crimson as he clenched the woman tighter. His upper lip curled back in a snarl as he stared at Reed, incredulous. "Don't you say that. Don't you *dare* say that!"

"She is," Reed said, wanting to take a step closer but knowing better. "Heel."

In front of him Billie stopped pacing, falling silent. In the wake of her barking the room suddenly felt much larger, all attention on Morgan.

Reed knew the effect would unnerve him. "I'm sorry. We just came from your house, over on 21st Street, with your Silverado in the garage."

The last details were thrown in just to show Morgan that he was serious, that he had in fact been there just moments before. They seemed to find their mark, Morgan's face remaining red but the snarl receding a bit, his gaze flicking between the three men.

"It's true," Bishop said. "We were there too. I'm sorry."

"Sorry," Iaconelli murmured, just barely audible.

A flicker of anguish passed over Morgan's face before he composed himself, drawing his mouth into a tight line. He looked up at them, dubious, and gave the woman a quick shake. Beneath his hand she tried to scream, the sound just barely passing through his fingers.

"No. No, I don't believe you. My mother is at home, all she needs is a liver, and she'll be fine."

"So, what?" Reed said. "You're going to kill this woman too? In front of four detectives? You think there's any chance, even if your mother was alive, that we'd let her get anywhere near that liver?"

"Or that she'd even want it, knowing what you've been doing?" Bishop added.

An obvious crack formed in Morgan's façade. His mouth quivered as he tried to formulate a response, fighting to determine if anything at all he was being told was true.

This was the moment Reed needed to seize. He had to keep Morgan thinking, guessing, far away from rage or wanting to hurt this woman.

"I get it, I do," Reed said, nudging just an inch closer.

"Stop moving!" Morgan screamed, spittle flying from his mouth. It landed on the woman's shoulder, her body trembling, fresh tears streaming from her eyes. "And you don't understand a damn thing! None of you! It was my fault, all of it!"

He gave the woman a shake, lunging an inch forward. "She wouldn't be sick if it wasn't for me. She reminded me of it every day of my life! I have to fix it, have to!"

"But you can't," Reed said. "She's gone. It's over."

In that moment, Reed saw realization finally set in. He watched as Morgan passed through the first few stages of grief within seconds, going from denial to anger in short order. His arms clenched as he drew the woman back toward himself.

There was no room to get off a shot. The woman was too close to him. Even at such a short range, the risk of hitting her just too great.

There was only one option.

"Attack!"

Billie leapt from the floor to the bed in one bound, from the mattress onto Kyle Morgan in another. Reed's command still echoed through the room as she slammed into Morgan's shoulder, knocking both people to the side. All three slammed into the wall and rolled to the floor in a heap, Reed dropping his gun and rushing forward. With both hands, he grabbed the woman and pulled her free, handing her off to Iaconelli behind him.

By the time he got back to the opposite side of the bed, Billie had Morgan pinned to the floor, teeth gnashing. He lay flat on his stomach with his hands covering his head, wicked gouges torn into the exposed flesh of his arms. Blood dripped from the wounds, spotting the white carpet, painting Billie's muzzle as she balanced herself on his shoulder blades.

One time after another she growled into his ear, two even rows of teeth bared.

"Heel," Reed said, coming from the side so she could see him in her periphery before laying a hand on her back. He kept it there as the tension ebbed away, her taut muscles relaxing as she stepped back. "Good girl."

Moving in to replace her, Reed dropped his knee into the middle of Morgan's back. Removing a pair of handcuffs from the back of his belt, he jerked Morgan's wrists down to his waist and cinched them just a little tighter than necessary.

Morgan didn't say one word.

Instead, he wept like a baby.

Chapter Fifty-Eight

The first sliver of sun was just breaking over the treetops, another hot and sticky day on tap. The golden light spilled across the front lawn of the precinct, moving steadily toward the loose gaggle of men standing outside, transforming the world from night into day.

"Thank you, guys. Seriously," Reed said, going around the circle and shaking hands one by one. Clearly the night had been just as long and exhausting for the officers, three of the four having shed their black uniform shirts, standing only in thin cotton t-shirts or ribbed tank tops, all of them soaked through with sweat.

"No worries, any time," Jacobs said, returning the shake and stepping back a few feet.

"Like we said before, at any point you have some overtime to throw our way, we greatly appreciate it," McMichaels added, also shaking Reed's hand.

A smile spread across Reed's face as he raised a hand in farewell to the partners drifting back toward the parking lot. "I'll remember that. Thanks again, guys."

Both men raised their hands in return, taking a few more steps before turning toward the lot.

"Overtime," Gilchrist said, drawing Reed's attention back to the remaining two officers. "I wondered why they seemed so excited when I called and told them we needed a hand with the other members of the support group."

"Yup," Reed said. "You know how tight things have been this summer. McMichaels has his eye on a fishing boat, word is Jacobs might have a new lady friend."

Both men snorted at the explanation, smiles soon following.

"Well, I know you guys need to get home and get some rest," Reed said, stepping toward Gilchrist and extending a hand. "Thanks for everything these last couple days. I know canvassing and babysitting duties can be a real chore, but they definitely helped us bring this one in."

Gilchrist nodded, his palm sweaty as he shook Reed's hand. "Is it true Morgan bawled as you handcuffed him?"

Reed flicked a gaze to Greene, an expression on the senior officer's face that seemed to read, "Kids."

The look, the demeanor, the slow shake of Greene's head almost brought a smile to Reed's face as he looked back at Gilchrist.

"Man just found out he lost his mom. That's tough."

Blood colored Gilchrist's cheeks as he released the grip, breaking eye contact. "Yeah, that's true. Hadn't considered that."

Whether it was true or not, Reed couldn't be certain. While Morgan had just lost his mother, a woman he loved enough to kill for, he had also just had the full fury of Billie unleashed on him.

Once before in training Reed had been hit by her charging full speed, the impact akin to a linebacker teeing off on a defenseless quarterback. He had been wearing protective gear at the time and still ached for days afterwards.

Given the way she had hit Morgan, and the damage she'd inflicted on his arms, it was a pretty safe bet to say the tears were at least 50% her doing.

"Detective," Greene said, stepping forward and shaking his hand, the only one of the four still in full uniform. "You did good work this week. Be glad to help out whenever you need it."

"Thank you," Reed said. "You as well."

Like McMichaels and Jacobs before them, Greene and Gilchrist drifted off toward the parking lot. Reed stood on the front steps of the precinct station, the warm sun on his face, his skin already beginning to feel moist, and watched them go. Only once all four were in their vehicles and driving away did he turn for the front door, holding it wide for Billie to pass inside before him.

Minutes before 7:00 on a Saturday, the precinct was deserted. A couple of desk lamps had been left burning for the night, though otherwise there was no sign of life on the first floor. The glow of morning sunlight passed through the front windows, illuminating desktops, throwing long shadows across the floor as Reed led Billie past the frosted glass door toward Grimes's office.

It was the second time this week they arrived to hear voices drifting from the office, the same three men waiting inside. On this occasion Reed bypassed the chair in the hall, knocking once on the door before entering, Billie by his side.

The two visitor's chairs were already occupied by Iaconelli and Bishop, both turning to look as he entered. Neither one made any attempt to move, or even stand, merely watching as he strode to the table along the wall next to Grimes's desk. He leaned back against it, letting his backside rest against the tabletop, and folded his arms across his chest.

Without being told, Billie lay down flat at his feet.

The men around the room all looked about the way Reed felt, each working on the backend of a day-long shift. Bishop's eyes appeared even more hollow than usual, his face especially angular. Beside him Iaconelli had a hand towel around his neck and a bottle of Gatorade in his hand, his shirt damp with sweat.

Of everyone, Grimes was the only one who appeared remotely ready for a new day. He was dressed in a fresh uniform, brass gleaming, creases sharp, the effect only nominally taking away from the heavy bags that hung under his eyes.

Every last person in the room needed breakfast and a nap, Reed and Billie included.

"Detective," Grimes said in greeting. "These gentlemen were just telling me about an unorthodox method you used for getting past a little turf issue last night."

A Cheshire cat smile slowly crawled up Reed's face. He glanced at Bishop and Iaconelli, both with similar expressions, and said, "If those guys had their way, we'd all still be standing around that car right now."

Grimes raised his eyebrows in concession, though his face conveyed none of the mirth of the others. "You realize of course..."

"Yeah, I know," Reed said, cutting him off with a raised hand. Right now there was too much attention on the bust for anybody to fuss over some bruised egos, but at some point in the future the topic would be addressed.

Grimes would probably catch flack, as would Reed. Maybe even an official reprimand.

At the moment, he wasn't especially concerned with it.

"What's the occasion?" Reed asked, nodding at Grimes.

For a moment Grimes said nothing, merely staring back at Reed, letting it be known that the previous discussion would be addressed again later, before letting it go. "Yasmin Leveritt. I have my third and final interview with her shortly."

He rolled his eyes and added, "Has to be done in time for the morning news."

Reed matched the eye-roll with one of his own. Working with the media was always a tricky proposition, something they had both known from the beginning. Involving them had worked in that it provided enough pressure to get things moving, but it now also came with the expectation of unfettered access on the back end.

"How are the Tudors?" Bishop asked.

After making the arrest, he and Iaconelli had delivered Morgan to jail for processing. Reed had been left behind to clean up the scene, an arrangement he was more than okay with.

Given that Billie occupied his entire backseat, transport of any kind would have been an ugly affair.

"As you'd expect," Reed said. "The husband suffered a pretty bad concussion and his wife is shook up as hell, so right now they're in a state of shock."

They had all seen similar situations over the years, knowing the way most victims of domestic crimes took things. They began in shock, followed closely by a loss of security and extreme fear. They would respond by fortifying the place, only to later turn angry when they felt like they were bunkered in, hidden from the world. At some point far in the future they would emerge, maybe not quite as okay as they were before, but pretty close.

"I guess the husband stopped by Big Q just yesterday," Reed said. "It was around lunchtime and Morgan waited on him. Paid with a credit card."

"He's lucky Morgan hit the people in the support group before getting to him," Bishop said. "If not, we might have never figured things out."

Reed nodded. "Eventually we would have caught the Big Q connection, but otherwise they were all over the map. I mean, who thinks to check on a victim's organ donor status?"

Nobody said anything. The obvious response was that they all would in the future, but that was only through the benefit of hindsight.

"He say anything at all?" Reed asked, looking over to Iaconelli and Bishop.

"Naw," Iaconelli said, shaking his head, his jowls bunching beneath his jawline. "Whimpered the whole time, but didn't say anything."

"Did you hear him there in the bedroom?" Bishop asked. "Any idea what he meant about it being his fault?"

"Actually," Grimes said, pulling everyone's attention back his direction, "I can answer that one. Last night as I was sitting here playing air traffic controller for everything, I made some calls and had someone at Franklinton Memorial look into Amber Morgan's file.

"Apparently she contracted Hepatitis C shortly after Kyle's birth. The records seemed to indicate there were some complications and she'd needed a blood transfusion."

"And somebody's blood was infected," Reed finished.

"It would appear that way," Grimes said. "They obviously tested her before birth and she was clean. Two years later, she came back for some routine blood work and the disease was present, but not in Kyle."

"Damn," Bishop muttered.

"And later on, when he tried to donate a portion of his liver to her," Grimes added, "it was determined the two were incompatible."

A low, shrill whistle passed over Reed's lips.

"That's one hell of a guilt complex to inflict on a kid," Iaconelli added. "End up having him pick off a half dozen people."

Reed nodded. Both men were right. It was a hell of a jump for Amber Morgan to blame him and for her son to go to such lengths, but he had seen worse things done for lesser reasons.

One of the few lessons he had learned with any certainty in his time as a detective was it didn't matter if the motive made sense, it only mattered if the perpetrator believed it enough to act on it.

Before anybody could comment further, a knock sounded at the door. Unexpected and extra loud in the quiet building, it jerked everybody's attention over to find Lou, his uniform shirt seeming larger than usual, threatening to slide right down off his shoulders.

In his hands were a couple of sheets of paper, on his face a look that said he would rather be anywhere else in the world.

"Um, good morning," he said, his jaw working twice as fast as the number of words coming out. "I'm sorry to bother you all, but we just got a call from the Lazy 8's Motel. Looks like somebody broke in last night, officers on the scene have asked for a detective."

Both Bishop and Iaconelli turned back to face front. Bishop simply stared while Iaconelli rocked his head back, a low groan rolling out.

Lou paused and stared down at the papers, his hands almost shaking. "I'm very sorry guys, but you're up in the rotation."

Every iota of Reed's being wanted to go home. He wanted to stop somewhere along the way and grab a bag of nasty, greasy food, share it with his partner, and then climb into bed for the foreseeable future.

He also hated like hell the idea of walking out of the office owing Iaconelli and Bishop a favor, the events of the last two days eroding some of the still lingering animosity or not.

"Give it here, Lou," Reed said, extending a hand. "We owe them this one."

Epilogue

The sprinkler was something Reed had found in the bottom of a box in the old barn in the corner of the property, one of just a handful of items he had been able to salvage from the dilapidated structure. He had kept it in his garage for more than two months, completely forgetting it was there before stumbling across it the night before while searching for a flashlight. From there it was a simple matter of connecting it to the end of the garden hose coiled along the side of his house and dragging it into the middle of the backyard.

It had taken Billie a good five minutes to figure out what to make of the fan of water passing back and forth in even sweeps, standing on the edge of the deck, her head twisted to the side in puzzlement. Only after Reed peeled his shirt off and made a couple passes through did Billie get the gist of things, soon joining him in the water.

Thirty minutes later, long after he retired from the venture, she was still at it. Her tongue drooped from the side of her mouth as she bounded back and forth, stopping every so often to shake herself off before diving back in for more.

Sprawled across the cloth lawn chair on his deck, Reed watched with a sense of bemusement. His left elbow was propped up on the arm of the chair, a bottle of water in hand, the tips of his hair still damp. His wet footprints had already long since faded, his shorts now dry, but the jaunt through the water had been enough to keep the afternoon heat at bay, his skin free of sweat, drinking in the sunshine.

Sitting and watching his partner enjoy a moment of summer frivolity, Reed couldn't help but think back. In his mind he could almost see Riley out there with Billie, the two of them bouncing back and forth, both flinging water from their hair.

The thought brought a smile to his face as he watched Billie, eventually setting his bottle down and reaching over to the small table beside him. From it he picked up his cell phone and thumbed through the directory, finding the number he was looking for and hitting send.

It rang just twice before being picked up, the voice on other end so loud and enthusiastic he had to pull the phone back an inch from his head.

"Hey, Mama. How are you?"

Turn the page for a sneak peek of *The Kid*, book 3 in the Reed & Billie series.

Then keep reading for a second sneak peek of *Ham*, a standalone thriller!

Sneak Peek #1

THE KID, REED & BILLIE BOOK 3

The brakes were brand new, touchier than The Kid anticipated. Depressing the pedal caused the oversized SUV to lurch to a stop in a series of jolts, a far cry from the smooth deceleration he was expecting. With each spasm his upper body jerked forward a few inches before slamming back again, a small puff of air releasing through his nostrils, an audible expelling of the emotion balled within.

Under different circumstances, his angst would have been aimed at the shoddy handling of the vehicle he was now seated in. It was an expensive ride, one far too pricey to be experiencing such shortcomings.

Tonight, though, whatever mechanical failures there may have been did not even register with him. It was the first time he had ever been behind the wheel of it, the exorbitant asking price one that he had not had to pay.

Within an hour or two it would be cast away, nothing more than a prop, a tool needed for the completion of his task.

Instead, his emotion was a contorted mass of competing feelings, each just as strong as the others, all demanding to be realized and acknowledged. Anger, hatred, vengeance, even a bit of sorrow, all wrapped into a tight package and hermetically sealed in his nether regions, threatening to burst out at any moment, at the very least to consume him from within.

The SUV finally came to a full stop with a mighty squeal of rubber against rubber, the hulking mainframe of the car rocking forward a few inches before settling back onto its chassis. The moment it came to a rest The Kid jammed the gearshift into park, needing both of his hands free for what lay ahead.

Sweat beaded across his brow as he sat in the driver's seat, thick sunglasses on despite the late hour. Their purpose was explicitly for this moment, meant to protect his vision as he stared into the rearview mirror, a pair of fluorescent flashers passing from one headlight to the other in the automobile pulled off the road behind him.

In equal three second pulses they passed from end to end, making a quick revolution around all four corners of the square lamps before jumping to the opposite side. Above them a pair of silhouettes could be seen seated in the front seat. On the right was a short, squat man, his bulk dominating much of the space. Beside him sat a man so tall the top of his head was hidden from view, as if jammed into the hood of the car.

The Kid felt his pulse tick upward, staring back at them.

It was the right car. It had to be.

Sliding his right hand over to the passenger seat, The Kid extended his grip over the gnarled grip of a .9mm Beretta. Keeping his movement hidden from view, he pulled it over onto his lap and passed it into his left hand before reaching across and taking up the second of the matching pair.

Keeping his fingers outside the trigger guards, The Kid squeezed the handles on both tightly, the muzzles for each pointed in opposite directions as they rested across his thighs. Veins stood out on the back of his hands as he stared down at them, feeling the reassurance of cool resolve flood through him.

It was time.

The second part of his plan was finally here.

A light breeze passed through the interior of the SUV as The Kid sat and waited. He watched as the two men behind him seemed to be in conversation, their heads rotating toward each other and back again behind him. No doubt they were running the plates on his car and making sure there was nothing outstanding before approaching, making him wait in a way that only cops could.

It wasn't like they ever considered that the people they were pulling over had lives they needed to get back to or that their evening wasn't already ruined enough.

As each moment ticked by The Kid felt his animosity grow, the feeling only serving to reaffirm his actions.

Outside, an 18-wheeler sped past, laying on the air horn twice in succession as it went. With the windows rolled down, the sound reverberated through the interior of the car, rattling through The Kid's head, his pulse jumping just slightly.

Fighting the urge to raise his middle finger to the trucker getting a good laugh at his expense, The Kid remained completely stationary, only his eyes moving as he alternated glances between the car in his rearview mirror and the guns on his lap.

A full eight minutes after coming to a stop, he watched as both doors on the car behind him swung open. A bevy of misshapen shadows were visible as a man climbed from each side of the car, both adjusting their pants before slamming the doors shut and stepping toward him.

Once more The Kid felt his pulse rise. His breath caught in his throat as he slid his index fingers beneath the trigger guards, counting the seconds in his head as his targets walked closer.

It was time.

For Big.

Download *The Kid* and continue reading now!

Sneak Peek #2

THE HAM

Prologue

The ground absorbs any sound made by my footfalls. Walking heel-to-toe, I make sure each foot is placed down carefully, the thick bed of pine needles insulating the earth and masking my movements.

Moving in a serpentine pattern, I trace a path through the thin underbrush of the forest, this place one of the few in the world I have ever called home.

And right now, this man is here violating that. Not just with his mere presence but with everything he represents. Everybody he is associated with, every intention he has in mind.

With every thought, every realization, every moment, I am in his presence I can sense my animosity growing higher. I can feel as it raises my pulse, increases my body temperature, even tightens the grip on the rock in my hand.

To shoot this man would be easiest. To simply sight in on the back of his skull and ease back the trigger, knowing from this distance there is no possible way I can miss.

But the easiest path right now won't necessarily be the easiest moving forward.

And it would damned sure be far, far kinder than this man deserves.

Chapter One

The last sliver of orange has just slid beneath the western horizon as the ring announcer steps through the ropes. It sends a thousand shards of shimmering light across the surface of the Pacific Ocean with its last gasps, the sudden absence plunging the world into a state of exaggerated darkness.

And just as they always do, the strands of bare bulbs strung high above the ring kick on a moment later, casting a straw-colored pallor over everything below.

The aging ring is built on pressure-treated 4x4's buried directly into the sand, spots of blood and assorted detritus dotting the canvas mat. The twin aluminum risers are on either end, both loaded with drunken revelers, their skins painted shades ranging from tomato red to dark tan. Beers in both hands, tobacco juice or sunflower seeds hang from their lips and the assorted forms of facial hair stuck to their chins.

Per usual, the overwhelming majority of onlookers are men, the few women that are mixed in serving clearly as accompaniment, still dressed in bikini tops from the day or already in leather anticipating the night ahead.

No in-between.

On the east and west ends of the ring are scads of wooden folding chairs, what were once even rows already a twisted jumble. Housing most of the regulars, they're grouped into random clusters, seats turned so they can see some combination of the sunset, the ring, or each other.

Considering that every last one of them had to pay to get in, I'm not sure anybody rightly gives a damn what they look at.

Least of all, me.

Despite the open-air venue, the recent sunset, the faint breeze pushing in from the sea, there is a palpable charge in the air. That familiar buzz that I've known for decades now, the unshakable feeling that seems to reach deep inside, igniting the parts of me I spend most of the week keeping tamped down.

For the last hour, the crowd has sat and watched the undercard for the night. Beginning with less than half of what is now on hand, the combination of buckets of beer and the cheap cover charge has managed to pull in enough to fill the bleachers, easily the largest crowd we've drawn in a while.

It also doesn't hurt that the first several bouts turned into little more than backyard brawls. Bloody affairs with over-muscled men that had once been high school athletes and can't let it go, so they come out here to the sand every weekend. Smaller guys that work the fields nearby, carrying resentment for damn near everything in their lives, entering the ring with something to prove.

And of course, a healthy sprinkling of fools that have watched a few too many MMA bouts on television and figured it didn't look that hard. Little more than chum for the crowd, they have done their part, sacrificial lambs for the maddened rabble.

With each passing bout, I sat in the back and felt the energy rising. Starting low, it worked steadily upward, cresting into a veritable hunger, bordering on lust, the feeling so strong I can feel it pushing in from every angle.

Goose pimples cover my exposed forearms and calves as I assume my stance in the corner, waiting as the ring announcer steps through the ropes. A cordless microphone in hand, he doesn't pretend to be some sort of Michael Buffer knockoff, showing up in the traditional attire of a tuxedo and polished wing tips.

Opting for little more than board shorts and a tank top, the tail of his unbuttoned Aloha shirt flaps to either side. No more than a couple of hours from the surf, his long hair is sun bleached and pulled back, a crooked grin on his face.

All in all, a look that holds no pretense, neither confirming nor denying the fact that he's a Los Angeles trust-fund baby down here hiding from his family and the real world and all the responsibility both brings with them.

Not that I give a shit. This isn't the place anybody ends up unless they're hiding from something.

Myself included.

"Ladies and gentlemen," he says, his sandals slapping against his heels as he saunters to the center of the ring. A quick squawk of feedback through the cheap mic echoes through the speakers, vocal displeasure sounding out from the audience.

Pretending not to notice, he pushes on. "Let's hear another round of applause for our last combatants, Charlie Reed and Eric Montrose!"

Calling the last two guys combatants is something like calling the Grand Canyon a ditch. Both big and beefy, the bout quickly devolved into a couple of gorillas trying to see who could withstand more haymakers.

It was like watching three rounds of the last forty seconds of every Rocky Balboa fight.

The crowd had loved it.

The reception to his request is weak at best, what clapping there is accompanied by a healthy smattering of boos. Already the crowd has moved on from the last spectacle, ready for the next in line. A small shower of peanut shells and paper napkins rain down, the items dotting the outer edges of the ring, some even landing within a few inches of my feet.

Not that the announcer seems to notice. Even with the top of my head buried into the corner pad, my gaze aimed straight down at the ground, I can imagine the look on his face. One corner of his mouth is rising higher, his grin growing ever more lopsided.

He lives for this shit, inciting the masses, feeling like he's some sort of ringmaster in his own personal circus.

All bought and paid for with his daddy's money.

Not that he — or any of us — have any delusions about where we are and what we're doing. The last guys beating the hell out of each other just means there are a few more stains on the mat going forward. Pelting the ring with garbage doesn't mean we're going to slow things down to sweep up. It's just that much more crap for me to now roll around in.

This isn't Las Vegas, or New York City, or even Rio. The people that have shown up to watch know that. Those of us that step inside the ring damned sure know it.

And here we are in spite of it.

Or, some might even argue, because of it.

"All right," the announcer says, a bit of his surfer accent sliding out, making him sound like McConaughey in *Dazed and Confused*. Rotating at the waist, he looks to either side before saying, "and with that, I'll get us straight to what we all came here to see tonight."

"*Ham!*" a stray voice calls out. "*Ham!*"

My eyes slide shut. This is the worst part. That damn chant that some drunken idiot always gets started.

"*Ham!*"

Ignoring him, the announcer calls, "For tonight's main event, we have one of the most anticipated bouts in Shakey Jake's history."

His voice cracks as he walks around the ring, pretending that he's trying to whip them up a bit more, though there's no need. The collective energy has continued to rise, the lack of walls or a roof having no negative effect on the tension brimming in the air.

No, this is about him siphoning off a little piece of things for himself, reminding everybody here who is responsible for all this.

Because it has been a whopping fifteen minutes since he last pointed it out.

"Two women, different in every way," he continues. "One Latina, the other white. One from South America, the other North. One making her Tijuana debut here tonight, the other putting her crown and perfect record on the line!"

The hype achieves some modest bit of effect, enough to at least push a swell of cheers and applause from the crowd.

Again, I hear the same inebriated bastard attempt to get a chant going, calling, "*Ham! Ham!*"

Once more, the announcer ignores him. My time will come. Right now, he's still milking his moment.

"In the blue corner," he continues, his voice rising and ebbing, "a woman coming to us straight from the underground club circuit of Colombia. Standing six foot two and weighing one hundred and sixty pounds, with a 38-2 record, the Bogota Brawler herself, Victoria Rosales!"

I don't bother moving from my spot in the corner, already knowing exactly what the woman looks like, her actual physical description enhanced the standard twenty percent by announcer hyperbole.

On a good day — in boots — she might go six feet even. Weigh maybe a pound or two above a buck forty. Striated muscle lines her arms and shoulders but her midsection is a bit softer, free of definition, with small bulges visible above her trunks.

Not that all of that is easy to see, most of it obscured by dark ink etched into much of her skin. Beginning around her ear, it wraps down one side of her neck before spreading over her back and, eventually, making it all the way to her calves.

With basic coloring and blurry lines, it's the sort of thing referred to in the States as *prison ink*, though I don't have enough knowledge of the girl or parlors in Colombia to know if she got hers inside or if that's just how tattoos look down there.

Not that it much matters, my lifetime interaction with her is about to come to an abrupt end in about ten minutes.

Perfunctory cheers ring out as a bit more debris lands in the ring. Right now, I imagine she has a fist or two raised into the air, making a small circle, the announcer remaining silent, extending the moment as long as he can.

Same cocksure smile on his face.

The first few times I was down here, I played the part. I stayed upright in the corner, responding to all the cues, doing what was expected.

That was long ago, well before I came to see that it went the same way every time, that the kid was more interested in playing out his own little fantasy than actually doing justice to the venue or the fighters.

Now, I just stay in my corner, wrists draped over the ropes, top of my head pressed into the pad, waiting it out.

"And her opponent," he eventually pushes out, "a woman that you all already know. Making her way down from just over the border and standing before you tonight with a perfect twenty-eight-and-oh record, your champion — Haaaaam!"

Download *Ham* and continue reading now!

Thank You

This letter comes to you with a double dose of gratitude. First, thank you so much for taking the time to read my work. I know I say it at the end of every novel, and that is because the appreciation is genuine for every reader each and every time you take a chance on something I've written.

Second, thank you so much for the enormous outpouring of comments and requests for a follow up to *The Boat Man*. As a longtime dog owner myself, I've always wanted to feature a canine as a major character, finally developing Billie as a direct result of that. Apparently many of you feel as strongly as I do about your animal friends, as the outpouring of support has been overwhelming and is the single greatest reason for this novel existing.

Once again, if you would be so inclined, I would love to hear your thoughts on this novel. I have heard everything that has been stated so far, having brought in a new editor to my team, a longtime reader and former English professor, and am currently working to begin shadowing the K-9 Unit with the Honolulu Police Department in hopes of providing as authentic a reading experience as possible.

Thank You

As always, as a token of appreciation for your reading and reviews, please enjoy a free download of my novel *21 Hours*, available HERE.

Best,
  Dustin Stevens

Welcome Gift

Join my newsletter list, and receive a copy of 21 Hours—my original bestseller and still one of my personal favorites—as a welcome gift!

dustinstevens.com/free-book

About the Author

Dustin Stevens is the author of more than 50 novels, the vast majority having become #1 Amazon bestsellers, including the Reed & Billie and Hawk Tate series. *The Boat Man*, the first release in the best-selling Reed & Billie series, was named the 2016 Indie Award winner for E-Book fiction. The freestanding work *The Debt* was named an Independent Author Network action/adventure novel of the year for 2017 and *The Exchange* was recognized for independent E-Book fiction in 2018.

He also writes thrillers and assorted other stories under the pseudonym T.R. Kohler.

A member of the Mystery Writers of America and Thriller Writers International, he resides in Honolulu, Hawaii.

Let's Keep in Touch:
Website: dustinstevens.com
Facebook: dustinstevens.com/fcbk
Twitter: dustinstevens.com/tw
Instagram: dustinstevens.com/DSinsta

Dustin's Books

Works Written by Dustin Stevens:

Reed & Billie Novels:
The Boat Man ✓
The Good Son ✓
The Kid ✓
The Partnership ✓
Justice ✓
The Scorekeeper ✓
The Bear ✓

Hawk Tate Novels:
Cold Fire
Cover Fire
Fire and Ice
Hellfire
Home Fire
Wild Fire

Zoo Crew Novels:

305

The Zoo Crew
Dead Peasants
Tracer
The Glue Guy
Moonblink
The Shuffle
(Coming 2020)

Ham Novels:
HAM
EVEN

My Mira Saga
Spare Change
Office Visit
Fair Trade
Ships Passing
Warning Shot
Battle Cry
(Coming 2020)

Standalone Thrillers:
Four
Ohana
Liberation Day
Twelve
21 Hours
Catastrophic
Scars and Stars
Motive
Going Viral
The Debt
One Last Day
The Subway
The Exchange

Shoot to Wound
Peeping Thoms
The Ring
Decisions
(Coming 2020)

Standalone Dramas:
Just A Game
Be My Eyes
Quarterback

Children's Books w/ Maddie Stevens:
Danny the Daydreamer…Goes to the Grammy's
Danny the Daydreamer…Visits the Old West
Danny the Daydreamer…Goes to the Moon
(Coming Soon)

Works Written by T.R. Kohler:
The Hunter

Made in the USA
Columbia, SC
02 April 2020